Explosive Crossroads

A LUKE DODGE ADVENTURE NOVEL

BOOK TWO

C.F. Goldblatt

Trident Publishing
315 Meigs Rd. Ste A 289
Santa Barbara, Ca 93109

This book is a work of fiction. Any references to historical events, real people or real places are used fictitiously. Other names, characters, places and events are products of the author's imagination, and any resemblance to actual events, places or persons, living or dead, is entirely coincidental.

Explosive Crossroads

C.F. Goldblatt

C.F. Goldblatt

Foreword

Foreword… this part should be called the backward, as that is the direction I am looking at the completion of *Explosive Crossroads*. As I sit here, it is just three days before my triumphant return to the U.S. with my wife Nicky in tow. It has been nearly five years since my German born wife said the wrong few syllables at the Sumas border crossing in Washington State. She and I were punished, (without trial) with a permanent, lifetime ban from entry to the U.S. From one day to the next our lives were torn apart, then, just as quickly reconstructed by the hands of fate and destiny.

On a whim, we relocated to the Republic of Panamá for what we thought would be a six-month vacation to sort matters through. Five years on, and a lifetime of experiences richer we have won our battle and we are homeward bound. Ironically my flight lands in Los Angeles at 11:59 on the 4th of July.

My time in Panamá has enriched my wife and I, strengthened us and most of all allowed me to understand, perhaps for the first time what it means to be an American. Often, what we consider to be our national identity is just something somebody told us it should be. We rarely test the bonds of patriotism and determine for ourselves, how we truly feel about the land from which we come.

With few exceptions, the people places and things in this book are real and true. I have had the wonderful experience of fishing and spearfishing in remote places on the Colombian border with the Emberá and Kuna Indians. Many reefs I fished and dived are so remote they have yet to be named. I have seen such underwater magic in Panamá that it can only be rivaled by my most vivid childhood dreams. All the amazing fishing and spearfishing described in the following pages are true and were experienced first-hand.

I want to thank Panamá and her people for sharing with me her untouched emerald rain forests, mysterious offshore islands, her bountiful seas and living Indian cultures.

---C.F. Goldblatt
Republic of Panamá

For Panamá, Tina, George and those who continue the fight
to keep the oceans open for fishing and spearfishing.

Long live a free ocean!

Explosive Crossroads

Chapter One

PANAMÁ, AH, PANAMÁ, mused Luke Dodge as he donned his free-dive gear.

"I love it here."

Sitting on a rock in his 3-mm camo green wetsuit, he slipped a bootie on his left foot and then one on his right, slung his custom-made 60-inch mahogany and zebra wood spear gun on his back, wrapped the tow line and its small dangling buoy around his shoulder, clicked the 12-pound weight belt into place at his waist, and checked his snorkel and black silicon mask.

He recited the prayer he always said before diving: "I pray for respect of all living creatures and should I die, please take care of those I love."

Holding his three-foot Italian dive fins in one hand, Luke scaled the forbidden break wall at the edge of the Panamá Canal. Two hundred feet above him, in the warm orange glow of late afternoon, arched the famed Puente de las Américas, the

Bridge of the Americas. With its completion in 1962, the one-mile metal span became the only permanent link between North and South America since workers severed the land bridge to create the Panamá Canal, which opened in 1914 to connect the earth's two greatest oceans.

Luke flipped silently over the short concrete wall, stepped into his fins and slid into the water, cocking an ear to some agitated Spanish being spoken on the other side of the hedgerow.

"¡El buzo de gringo, búsquele, captúrele pronto!"

They were looking for him. Charged with the mission of keeping the valuable waterway open and free from terrorist attacks, the Panamanian Canal guards were well-equipped, took their job seriously and did not fool around. Luke had heard stories of their single-minded efficiency.

Breaking a basic safety rule, Luke skipped his usual warm-up dives and breath- holding exercises. Just as the guards came into view, half of them holding U.S. made M-16 assault rifles and the others brandishing Russian-made AK-47s; Luke took a deep breath and disappeared into the green brackish water.

Four minutes later he surfaced. The guards had moved on.

Now, Luke could get on with hunting his quarry, the elusive Panamá robalo.

The strange-looking robalo, known as snook in the U.S., has a sloped head, a beak-shaped, toothless mouth and a sturdy frame with a horizontal black pin stripe running tail to head. The robalo's white body terminates with a distinctive heart-shaped tail. The best robalo hunting grounds are in this highly restricted area of Panamá; which also is home to some of the largest freshwater crocodiles in the world, sometimes approaching 25 feet, end to end. The crocodiles hunt deer, pigs, even monkeys. The crocks frequent these brackish waters for the same reason Luke did, for the tasty fat-filled flesh of the Panamá robalo.

The area under the bridge is truly the crossroads of the world -- a big "X" where all corners of the world meet.

The man-made bridge connects the continents and the man-made Canal connects the Atlantic and the Pacific oceans. The bridge is at the mouth of the Pacific side of the Panamá Canal, an area known as the Miraflores Locks. Each day the 94-year old set of locks allows scores of 700-foot ships to transit the 51 miles from the Atlantic to the Pacific and vice versa in less than eight hours. The alternative is a deadly two-week 8,000-mile journey around Cape Horn. The Canal fees per cargo ship can be as much as $200,000.00, but the savings in time and money justifies the expense.

Americans are the number one clients of the Canal, followed closely by the Chinese and the Middle East oil consortiums.

As each set of ships clears the locks, millions of gallons of fresh water pour into the Bay of Panamá on the Pacific side. This constant flow of fresh water is what brings the robalo, the crocs and Luke here. The only problem was that after September 11, 2001, security at the mouth of the Canal had been increased ten-fold.

During World War II both the Germans and the Japanese had concocted plans to plug up the Canal by sinking a ship in the locks. The remains of a Japanese midget submarine lay on a sand pit not far from Luke, rusting testimony to the plans of Imperial Japan. Carrying out the plan then would have decreased dramatically the Allies' ability to wage war. Doing so today would greatly hamper global trade, causing shortages of every kind and driving the cost of consumer goods out of reach for many people – just the kind of upheaval that terrorists specialize in.

Luke suspected that he had been spotted scaling the break wall and/or the surrounding fence - and that the 20 special-forces guards would be back. Rather than cutting his losses and abandoning the dive, Luke pressed on. He glided upstream past a gnarled mangrove patch until he was a baseball diamond away from the gates that discharged the massive cargo vessels into the sea. It was here that Luke would begin his dive session.

He took a moment, cleared his mind and began to breath up. He took 10 full inhales, which he held for a second or two before pursing his lips and a slowly emptying his lungs. On his last breath; he gulped air a dozen times to top off, then slowly glided down to the rocky bottom 40 feet below. The murky green water, together with the eerie echoing of the cars crossing the long suspension bridge overhead and the deep thundering bunker-fueled mains of the nearby passing cargo vessels made the whole enterprise a little spooky.

Dusk had arrived and it would be dark soon. This was hands down the best time to hunt robalo. Unfortunately, the crocodiles knew this as well. In the dark, the special forces charged with maintaining Canal security might be in a less understanding, shoot-first mood, as well.

Using his big fins to propel him around the murky depths and finding nothing of interest, Luke kicked to the surface. He rested on the surface for several minutes, allowing his oxygen-depleted body to recharge. Luke kept one eye on the massive 100- year-old, 90-foot tall steel doors which locked in the vessels waiting to clear the two-tiered lock system. On the other side of the doors could be any type of vessel from 700-foot oil tankers to small private sailing vessels, to the world's largest and often gaudiest mega yachts.

In this case it was the latter; a motor yacht, the *Gulf One,* from Dubai sat inside the lock gates. Her 145-foot-long by 42-foot-wide gleaming white, Dutch built hull was supported by millions of gallons of brackish water waiting to be spilled into the Pacific. She was as loaded as they come, replete with double heliports, each sporting sleek looking six-seater French built choppers, three smaller fishing launches, a dozen jet skis and any number of other rich people toys. The decks on all three levels were made of solid Honduran mahogany and the interior was laden with tacky trim and fixtures plated with 18-karat gold.

Three men dressed in traditional Saudi Arabian garb rushed about on the aft poop deck. The fatter of the three, a man named Saeed wiped sweat from his brow as he fumbled through a tool chest, apparently making minute adjustments to some type of apparatus.

"Patty cake, patty cake, baker's men, bake a cake just as fast as you can." A tall thin man who had eyes as black and lifeless as a Great White shark and a long jet-black beard sang as he played patty cake with two boys and a girl all under ten-years-old. "And some day you will be the greatest, smartest people I know. You are all blessed children of Allah." The man said as he hugged the three children. "Now I have to go."

"Wait, wait Father, when do I get to drive the boat?" The youngest boy asked. "Just as soon as I finish with some important business."

"What type of business?" The young boy probed.

"Oh, you are so clever, I have to go make the world a better place, make a better future for you and all of Allah's children."

"Come back soon, Father!" the boy cried.

The Father hurried up onto deck, snapping at Saeed. "What are you doing, idiot? The gates are about to open, if we miss this time the plan is finished."

Chubby Saeed replied with fear in his voice, "I am sorry, Father, but I cannot get the timer to activate."

"Let me see that." Saeed handed the tool chest to the Father who quickly went to work on the device."

"There, it is set." The father then pushed the activation button on the crude yet effective detonation device which was made from a waterproofed cell phone.

"Now, we just have to wait and make a very special phone call." The Father jotted down the numbers to dial that would activate the device, *64977927.*

Luke watched as the gates opened. The loud fog horn blared three times signaling the *Gulf One* to proceed.

You are a long way from home, Luke thought.

Luke sat floating on his back like a sea otter eating an abalone, admiring the ultra- modern design of the super yacht from his vantage point, 20 meters away. Luke could see the men working at a frantic pace on the lower, after poop deck. He noticed their traditional Saudi dress and black headbands and watched as the men, using a small crane, hoisted three cargo nets- each containing several barrels- and dumped them over the side into the water. The barrels sank just yards from the Canal entrance gates.

"Damn polluters," Luke's murmured in anger. "What are they thinking?"

Luke continued diving. After two hours in the water he came across what he was looking for. Next to some old rubber tires a robalo hovered motionless, almost in a catatonic state. The fish looked to be close to 50-pounds. Luke glided toward it, marveling at the fish's beautiful shape and her ability to hover without so much as moving a fin.

By now it was almost completely dark and Luke was short on time. He took aim and gently pulled the trigger. Luke tried for a spine-breaking, paralyzing stone shot but hit the fish high in the gut, causing it to go ballistic. In no mood to attract a hungry croc, Luke put on the brakes. Risking pulling the shaft out, he refused to let the big fish take any line, and he swam full speed to the surface. The fish's strength was an even match for Luke. The two were deadlocked. Luke began to lose ground as the big robalo pulled him down in his first powerful run, typical of white meat fish, and quickly lost steam.

Luke held on long enough for the robalo to tire, and horsed her to the surface. He wasted no time in stabbing the fish in the head, but swam hastily back to the bank. After a quick look around for the Canal guards, Luke slung the robalo over his shoulder, grunted under the weight and began to clamber and crawl up the break wall.

After a grueling 20-minute, Mount Everest-style rock climb, Luke made it to high ground. He could see his car on the other side of the fence. As he neared the fence, he somehow triggered an alarm and sirens blazed, search lights flashed and 50 heavily-armed men popped out of the bushes.

One man came charging towards Luke, yelling and brandishing a gun that got larger as he got closer.

"Manos ariba, manos ariba (hands up)!"

These guys are pissed. thought Luke.

A violent rain and thunder storm had blown in. The intense lighting and cracking of the thunder followed by the smell of burned ozone indicated that the lightning was hitting close by. Luke plopped his trophy robalo and spear gun down in the mud, put his hands up and got down on his knees.

Chapter Two

SIX MONTHS HAD passed since Luke's award-winning stone shot had saved his mother Tina from certain death. During the world spearfishing championships, Luke had speared a 250-pound yellowfin tuna off the coast of Spain with borrowed gear and borrowed entry money. The $100,000 prize had bought the surgery his mother needed so badly.

Then it was time for him to heal.

Several months before making that magnificent stone shot, a terrible collision with an empty barge under tow in the San Diego shipping channel had nearly taken his life. All five aboard the small fishing boat had survived, but it was a mystery as to how. Their Coast Guard rescuers said they should have been dead five times over, if not from the collision with the massive barge, then from hypothermia as they floated in the dark, bobbing around like so much lost flotsam, as the bow of their smashed boat slipped slowly under, outlined by the lights of Point Loma, San Diego far beyond.

In that instant, the collision stole his love and desire to be in the sea, and substituted in his mind a formless dread and fear. Since then, he had taken painful baby steps to regain that love; which until then had nourished his soul. Each day he grew bolder, went a little further, a little deeper, a little longer. But the fear had never completely abated, and it took all the power of his soul to challenge the sea in the competition in Spain.

After the competition in Spain, Luke felt more remorse when he killed a fish. Maybe coming so close to death had instilled in Luke a new-found respect for all living things. Yet he continued to hunt for his dinner in the sea as often as he could.

On top of the barge collision and his mother's brush with death, the United States government had told his woman, Doctor Nici that she could not come back into the country for five years. Despite her medical credentials, she had got herself into a visa mess by uttering the word. "fiancée", at the wrong time during a routine check-out-of-the-country and check-back-in. She had tried to re-enter through Canada on the advice of an incompetent immigration attorney and learned, the hard way, not to attempt to outwit Homeland Security. She was fingerprinted, retinal scanned, handcuffed and bullied. It was traumatic. Her – their- world fell apart.

Nici, his beautiful Doctor Nici, who had nursed him back to health after his run-in with thugs in Haiti, (once his girlfriend, then his fiancée, today his wife) suddenly could not return to their cozy little home in Monterey surrounded by roses and a white picket-fence.

Nici, barred from entry to the United States, returned to her home country of Germany. For a time, business kept him in California and away from his fiancée. He stayed up nights puzzling over a solution. The post-911, United States immigration laws prevented Nici from even transiting through the U.S. to a third country.

Finally, Luke had had enough. He let the house go, left their dog with a friend, put everything in storage and packed his bags, dive gear and critical business material. Within a week he was in freezing, snow-covered Hamburg, Germany. With its twenty hours of winter darkness, Hamburg was about as far from the beaches of California as it was possible to get.

Nici picked Luke up at Flughafen Hamburg-airport looking just as stunning as the last time he had seen her. Nici had borrowed a Smart Car made by Mercedes-Benz; the tiny cars were all the rage in Europe. They sat only two people and got 80 miles to the gallon. It was as small as Europe rapidly began to feel.

They had contemplated relocating to Spain, where they stayed while Luke's mother, Tina was recuperating, but Luke was not yet ready for such a drastic change. Spain was seductive in her own way, with its grand seafood meals, a climate similar to that of California and the almost constant celebrations of one sort or another.

But he felt like a fish out of water in Germany: No sun, all snow and not much in the way of love between people. The German sense of humor perplexed Luke.

"I woke up this morning to find that I had put my shoes in the wrong cupboard," a friend of Nici's proclaimed, followed by a straight face and a pause. The man slapped his knee in cartoon fashion and let out a wailing belly laugh.

"Don't you get it Luke, cupboard, shoes? Ha ha ha, oh, I kill myself!" The man then wiped tears from his eyes, which bulged from his now beat-red face and said to Nici, "Nici, your American friend is nice, but he has no sense of humor."

The hardest thing to take was the constant verbal attacks from just about every variety of European regarding George

W. Bush's foreign policy. Comments ranged from: "Nine-eleven was justified. I can see why they did it and I can see why they will try again." To, "You Americans always have so much of everything, why can't you just leave the world alone?"

Luke had mixed feeling about the comments, as his love for the U.S. had grown into bitter disdain. After all, the U.S. had banished his fiancée from the land; from five years to, perhaps, forever for thin, incomprehensible reasons. Nonetheless, Luke questioned why people who claimed to be U.S. allies could make such hateful statements.

Luke and Nici spent several wonderful weeks catching up. Nici had taken a full- time position at an internationally-run children's hospital that specialized in early childhood diseases. Most of the patients were the less fortunate and from Turkish and Moroccan lineage. Nici performed her usual miracles, bringing health and hope to those who needed it most. Nici never inquired into or looked at her paycheck. She would have gladly done the work for free.

The ancient Hanseatic trading city of Hamburg was elegant and laid-out with typical German efficiency. Traffic flowed well, the trains ran spot on time and the food was eclectic. The main walking area in Hamburg was an eight-kilometer trail that circled the sometimes frozen Alster Lake. Luke and Nici spent an hour each day walking there. The cold was enough to freeze an exposed eyeball solid.

On one of their daily walks Luke spoke up.

"Nici, babe, I sure love being here with you, but we need a plan B. I can't stay in Germany, but I am not leaving you again. What do you think?"

Nici paused before responding.

"Yes. We should move. I don't even want to stay here. I know you need the ocean, diving and fishing. I know you must be near the water. It's like your blood. Let's see… what else do you need? What else are we looking for in a new home?"

"It would be nice to be closer to my business associates, family and the rest."

They crunched along the frozen path.

Luke said, "I have heard some good things about Panamá."

"Panamá?"

"Yeah. Central America, Panamá. Jungle. Panamá Canal. Relatively friendly natives."

"Well," Nici said. "Noriega is gone and there is no war -- put that in the plus column."

"I hear it has the best fishing just about anywhere, with a huge variety of species."

After talking to friends who had spent a year in Panamá and doing some Web research, Luke and Nici made their decision. Panamá it was. This tiny worm on the map was one of the few countries neither Luke nor Nici had ever visited. It was a decision made sight unseen.

Luke chose to go to Panamá City and scout out the situation, find some digs and get the lay of the land. The flight via New Jersey went smoothly. Luke read travel books and tried to anticipate his first task on arrival.

As the Taca Airlines 777 flight approached its destination, Luke spied dozens of islands and atolls awash with breakers surrounded by Caribbean crystal blue water. So far, his mental image of Panamá was on target. The sea ended, giving way to lush green rolling hills. The forest, a blanket of green, looked to be mostly virgin and uninhabited except for the odd clear-cut sections.

Twenty minutes later the plane had transected the narrow landmass that is Panamá. Now over the Pacific Ocean, civilization came into clear view: Panamá City. The city -- packed with high rise buildings -- abutted the shores of the meandering bay of Panamá. Luke was slightly disappointed to see that the blue waters he had just flown over on the Caribbean side of the land mass bore no resemblance to the mud-filled bay below. Even off in the distance far from shore, the water did not appear to clean up much.

The airplane circled over the sea on its final approach to Tocumen International Airport.

Luke prepared himself to meet the unknown.

Chapter Three

LUKE, HIS ROBALO confiscated, was in a fix.

The Panamánian Special Forces group apparently had enjoyed eating Luke's prized monster robalo. When he found out about it later, Luke guessed they had no need to preserve it as evidence. The thought cheered him a bit.

Luke, on the other hand, found himself thrown roughly into an ancient and fearsome, Panamánian jail. The jail, situated in the jungle on the Chagras river, which feeds the Panamá Canal, is a 17th century compound built by the Spanish to house runaway slaves, pirates and Indians who refused to convert to Catholicism. The jail - simply known as "La Modelo," or model prison -- is dank and just as wrought with slow death as it had been in colonial days.

Luke was stripped, cavity searched and blasted with a high-pressure hose. After an hour of shivering naked in his dark chamber, the wetsuit he had been freediving in, just hours earlier, appeared under the door. Luke understood that he would not be issued any prison garb. He slid the wetsuit back over his shaking bones. Not exactly Armani.

For 24 hours Luke sat on his cot, paced the floor and did push ups -- anything but sleep. His thoughts skipped around. "What did they do with my robalo? What was that yacht dumping outside the Canal? Will I ever see Nici or the light of day again?"

His wet suit amplified the sweltering heat and humidity. Luke dared not take off, though, as it provided a thin layer of protection against the mosquitoes buzzing around that carried dengue fever. A plate of something sloppy-looking made an appearance. Luke was hungry -- but not that hungry. He had no desire to get sick in this old Spanish prison.

Luke heard a slow but steady set of footsteps nearing his chamber. Next came a "jingle, jingle" of keys. The door creaked opened.

"Venga, ahorita!" the guard barked.

Luke was led down a long corridor. The other prisoners, looking insane, heckled him and threw garbage as he walked by. He clearly stood out from the others; standing six feet tall, sandy brown hair that he usually kept neatly trimmed, green eyes, a proud nose, light tan skin and a confident swagger.

He was amazed to see how crowded the prison was. There appeared to be no separation of quarters among the inmates. Murderers, pickpockets, men, women and even the children of inmates lived together. The prison provided no cells and almost no food. If an inmate wanted to live, he or she needed to find a way to buy food and rent a cell from the ring of thug inmates, and crooked guards that ran the joint.

Despite the unorthodox conditions, the prison had an element of humanity to it that First World prisons lacked; with money, one could buy almost anything. There were mini-restaurants, places to buy cold beer, even special quarters designed with a touch of kink for conjugal visits. Prisoners needed to be married to merit a conjugal visit, but if they were not, the guards would issue a temporary marriage license for $5. Rumor had it that some of the ex-Noriega gangs who had called La Modelo home for the past 18 years were allowed out on weekend furloughs.

The guard led Luke to a small interrogation room where he was told to sit and wait but given no additional information. It was hot and the rubber insulation of Luke's wetsuit was forcing beads of sweat from his brow.

An hour later the door opened. To Luke's surprise, in walked a man with short gray hair wearing a neatly pressed suit and ID badge that read, "D. Caucuss, Homeland Security, United States Embassy, Panamá."

Despite Luke's problem with authority and his lingering bad feelings about Nici's unjustified deportation, he was happy to see a fellow American. The two shook hands. Caucuss offered Luke a cigarette. Luke declined. Caucuss leaned back and   lit   up.

"Nice wetsuit."

"Thanks. It's Italian." Luke smiled in spite of himself.

Caucuss opened a manila folder. Luke could see a picture of himself on one side and a full page of data on the other.

"In your file, it says here that you are 32, single, self employed, have been living abroad for unknown reasons and have had several verbal altercations with border officials in Canada."

"Is that my dossier? Keeping dossiers on normal people was made illegal after Hoover."

Caucuss changed the subject.

"Mr. Dodge, it looks like you crossed the line with these guys. They don't call me unless a U.S. national has done something they deem to be a threat to the Canal. So, please explain yourself."

"It is not my fault that the best robalo diving in this country just happens to be in the Canal restricted zone, Mr. Caucuss." Luke said in a humble voice.

"You were just spearfishing? This why is your wetsuit is in camouflage? And why were you out there in the dark, in a storm?"

Luke took a moment to study Caucuss. Any wrong words and Luke would be making a life in La Modelo.

"The robalo come out at dusk. The camo is to make it easier to sneak up on the fish. And the storm... well, it just came in on me."

Luke contemplated telling Caucuss about the strange barrel-shaped items that the men on the tanker from Dubai had dumped. But he decided to let it go. Those barrels probably held galley grease and banana peels. Under the current state of paranoia, just the mention of terror might get him moved out of La Modelo and into some other more secure holding facility, Guantanamo Bay came to mind.

Caucuss grew serious.

"You see, Mr. Dodge, we have noticed a significant up-tick in the amount of global noise regarding terror and the Canal. We cannot afford to take any chances, especially with newly minted President Obama coming down for the tenth anniversary of the Canal handover in a few weeks. You know- for the 4th of July."

Luke remained silent.

Caucuss produced several 8 x10 inch pictures then flopped them down in front of Luke. The pictures showed a man bound, gagged and hooded. He was strapped to a board raised at a 45-degree angle. Another man dressed in a U.S. military uniform poured water over the man's nose and mouth.

Luke glanced and the photos, "What are you planning to do, torture me if I don't give you something?" Luke asked.

"Well, we don't like to use the word torture, we prefer, enhanced interrogation. These days, the ends seem to justify the means, if you get my drift."

"I think you would need a little more than water." Luke replied.

"That can be arranged." Caucuss leaned over and whispered in Luke's ear with a deadly serious, yet soft voice.

Luke calculated his words. "All right, you win but I swear, I have nothing to do with it."

Another man, who appeared to be Caucuss' superior entered the room. The man was short and portly. He stood silently in the corner, waiting for Luke to spill his guts.

"As I was getting ready to make my first dive near the Canal gates, I saw a fancy boat from Dubai. It was dropping strange barrel-looking things into the water. That's it, I swear, that is all I know and all I saw. Can I go now, please?"

Caucuss replied. "Dodge, I think you have been seeing things, there is no way a boat could dump anything near the Canal, security is just too tight."

"You mean the same the security I breached to spear that robalo?" Luke said as he flinched in disbelief that were implying he was making it all up.

"Look, you need to go look and figure out what they dumped." Luke pleaded.

"We do not have the resources to chase around your fish story."

The fat man motioned for Caucuss to come hither. The fat man whispered into Caucuss' ear. Luke's animal sense of self-preservation gave him bionic, deer-like hearing. He picked up every other word.

"Set him free, tail him, let him lead us to his terror cell, find out what he knows then throw him in the can with the pinheads in Guantanamo.''

Like focused on the word Guantanamo.

Caucuss sat back down, looking Luke in the eye said, "I am going to arrange to have you released on your own recognizance. However, due to the nature of the threat, if you are caught within 100 meters of the posted, "No Trespassing" signs near the Canal or Bridge of the Americas, you will be arrested, listed as an enemy combatant, sent to Cuba and held without trial on charges- indefinitely. I am sorry to have to take this measure, but nobody is kidding anymore when it comes to potential terror threats."

Luke decided that he would find a new robalo hole.

Caucuss nodded at the guard, who led Luke to the exit. Another guard gave him the rest of his dive gear, which was intact, including his spear gun, and sent him on his way.

Chapter Four

CASCO VIEJO" Luke told the cabbie.

"Mucho pescado (much fish)?" the cabbie asked after seeing Luke's spear gun.

"Just one." Luke replied.

The taxi drivers in Panamá are among the most aggressive, spastic, fearless anywhere. Some play 17-inch DVDs on the dashboard while driving. Movie choices range from the Little Mermaid to hard-core porn. The cabbies love to hustle just about anyone. They adhere to a slippery principal they call *Juega Viva*, or the game of life. It means- get what you can while you can.

Luke's tired head snapped back and forth as the driver swung around turns, zipping past other cars, honking the whole way. The taxi slowed as it entered Casco Viejo or "Old Compound."

This was the old town. The Spanish originally had founded the city of Panamá farther west, closer to a large river mouth near deeper water, where ships could approach the city easily to unload passengers, foodstuffs and take on the reason for the cities existence: Gold.

Unfortunately, the abundant pirates in the area also found that they could easily approach and sack the city. After suffering many losses, the Spaniards packed up most of the original city, bricks and all, and moved out to a narrow peninsula surrounded by shallow tidal flats. The shallow water made approaching this new city (modern day, Casco Viejo) by large ships impossible, thus protecting her from cannon fire and raiding.

The tidal flats at the foot of the high-rise Panamá City – now filled with raw sewage that the country cannot control – is the result of a natural geologic anomaly. The tidal flow in Panamá is counterintuitive. Although the Bay of Panamá is just 9.8 degrees above the equator, its tides rival that of Alaska, with a nearly 16-foot daily exchange. Oddly enough, the tide just 30 miles to the north in the Caribbean Sea moves just 20 inches with each exchange, it's a function of depth.

"Why you live here?" the driver asked Luke.

Luke looked out the window to see poverty, squalor, ten-dollar, 24-hour whorehouses, fishmongers, residents standing listlessly on the narrow sidewalks, children playing near exposed, tangled electrical wires and scantily clad people leaning over sagging balconies strung with laundry, watching the activities play out in their small world.

"For the ambiance."

Run down in parts, Casco Viejo was quickly being bought up and renovated by gringos, Europeans and Canadians. The architecture, a mix of Spanish colonial and French, combined with masterful cathedrals and cobblestone streets, was pleasing to the eye. One could almost hear Spanish horse hooves clomping down the streets.

The newer, wealthy residents lived side by side with third generation squatters whose radios blared salsa and reggae-tone during the week. On the weekends, the men often drank to excess and would piss right off their balconies.

Luke paid the driver $2 U.S. for the ride – 25% more than he would have charged a local.

As he scaled the four flights of stairs to his flat, Luke thought about how he was going to explain his absence to Nici.

As Luke went for his keys the door swung open. There stood his reason to be, looking as beautiful as ever. Nici reached out with a big hug and a firm kiss. Just seeing her warmed his heart. Nici, never hard on the eyes, was a thin, statuesque natural blond with glimmering blue eyes and a never-ending smile

"Not sure what to say, babe, other than it looks like we will need to buy fish for dinner."

Luke explained what had happened at the Canal. Nici made him promise never to dive there again.

The American who owned Luke and Nici's flat had transformed it from a squatters' shelter into a home fit for a king, complete with vaulted ceilings, exotic hardwood trim and a massive terrace over-looking Panamá Bay with its constantly growing crops of new high-rise apartment buildings. When Luke came on the scene, Panamá City was developing at a breakneck speed. Each day hundreds of new baby-boomers, eager to take advantage of warm weather and the low-cost living gobbled up new houses and flats. The city's infrastructure was falling behind rapidly, leaving near-gridlock traffic throughout the city at all hours of the day.

Luke had discovered that the average gringo or Canadian transplant living in Panamá usually fit a profile. The older couples generally had no children and tended be anti-Bush democrats convinced they were watching the U.S. become a police state. The younger ex-pats came from a variety of backgrounds; and were a mixture of Europeans, Americans, Canadians and the elite from other Latin countries.

Some had genuine reasons for coming to Panamá, such as UNICEF work or teaching jobs. But, by and large most expats under 50 who lived full-time in Panamá had a hidden reason for their protracted stay away from their homelands. The reasons ranged from that of Luke and Nici's visa issue to the blatant drug-running murderer who posed as a well-to-do real estate agent. As it was so eloquently stated in the Pierce Brosnan- Jamie Lee Curtis movie *The Tailor of Panamá:* "Panamá is like Casablanca without heroes, where no good deed goes unpunished."

The demographic of Panamá is a genealogist's dream. Panamá is a true melting pot with a much greater degree of racial harmony than in the United States. The Chinese were originally brought in by the French to work construction on the first, failed attempt to build the Canal. After the French were defeated by the rain and yellow fever, the remaining Chinese were left for dead. But as the Chinese will do, they rallied and eventually prospered. The Chinese in Panamá operate in an insular way with very little crossover to other races. They run almost all the small convenience stores known locally as *Chinos* and continue to assist their brethren back in mainland China to immigrate to the new world.

The rest of Panamá's three million inhabitants are made up of mulattos; the descendants of former West African slaves who populate the Caribbean side of the country, the European-blooded elite class, the Jews who are influential yet insular and the small but growing sector of white immigrants from the U.S. and Europe who come seeking a more pleasant life. The most recent migrants are the wealthy, yet desperate Venezuelans fleeing the heavy-handed, socialist regime of Hugo Chávez.

Panamá does not have a currency of its own. Although referred to as the Balboa, the legal tender is the U.S. dollar. The dollar and the Canal keep the economy stable. Panamá acts as sort of a Latin American U.S.A., attracting migrant workers from neighboring countries eager to work and earn dollars.

The largest immigrant class are the Colombians. Colombia, weakened by its never-ending battle with the drug cartels and neo-communist quasi-military outfits such as the Revolutionary Armed Forces of Colombia (FARC), has purged its best and brightest citizens. The Colombian immigrants seek places they can work and live without threat of extortion by the drug lords, so they come to Panamá.

Panamá seems like a Paradise for Colombians. It offers the U.S. dollar combined with ripe opportunity, low taxes and little, if any, government intimidation. The Colombians come to Panamá, set up businesses and work hard. They also tend to outwork the Panamánians on their own soil, thus creating some harsh feelings from the locals. It is tantamount to the person who hires on in a government job and decides to really work hard, making the rest of the lackeys look bad and forcing them to pick up their pace.

Native Panamánians have a poor work ethic and nobody seems to be quite sure why. Perhaps the Canal has always provided food for the people. Maybe they have always known that the U.S. would never let Panamá fall too far down into a crack. Maybe it's just the way things are.

In Panamá, it is presumed that if you are a Colombian woman under 30 working in Panamá you are prostitute, or "Pescadora," meaning fisherwoman. The concept may have some truth to it. The Colombian working girls in Panamá nearly all have children they are supporting back home and usually have a Plan B, such as a desire to save money and go to law school. This is a far cry from the drug-addicted prostitutes in many other countries.

This was Luke's country for the time being, perhaps for years, and he figured he might as well make the best of it.

Nici helped Luke off with his wetsuit, bandaged a few small cuts and poured him a warm bath to soak in while she readied the one dish that would make her man feel good -- Baja style, fish tacos.

They ate frozen fish that night.

Chapter Five

LUKE ENJOYED A nice long slumber and awoke the next morning to the sound of the
telephone ringing.

"'Alo, my name is Pascal. I saw your flyer in zee fishing tackle shop. Maybe we can meet today, say around three for a beer and talk fishing. I will be the one wearing zee white Polo…"

"Flyer?"

"Yes, zee flyer you put up asking for a fishing partner."

Luke wiped the sleep from his eyes while he recalled the flyer he had posted in a local tackle shop:

"Wanted -- fishing partner, must have a strong, fast boat and lots of free time."

The man on the other end of the phone turned out to be a 32-year old Frenchman originally from Bordeaux. His French accent came across thick and pretentious. Luke groaned inwardly and resisted meeting with him, but -- what the hell.

"Hey, OK. Let's get together."

"I will come to you. Where do you live?" Pascal asked.

"Casco Viejo. There is a decent pizza place on Los Bolvedas, across from the French Embassy."

Luke did not bother to give him an address. Addresses in Panamá are non-existent. The entire system of finding places is based only on landmarks and points of reference. Local knowledge is essential and can make finding anything an all-day task, but is suits the Panamánians just fine.

"OK. I will be wearing a white Polo shirt."

"See you then."

Later that day, Pascal arrived at the local Argentine-owned pizzeria. Luke had arrived first and ordered a beer. Pascal showed up soon after. He was a tall thin man with short brown hair and had a proud French nose. He spoke perfect Spanish. Pascal explained that he had learned it from his Spanish uncle.

Pascal was quick to point out that he was also of Spanish blood and not just a Frenchman.

The two sat down, ordered a small pizza and with a few sips of cold beer launched right into the topic of the day- fish. To Luke's pleasant surprise Pascal was the rarest breed of Frenchman, polite and non-opinionated when it came to U.S. geopolitics. Most Europeans, Luke had discovered, could barely choke down a few bites of lunch before launching into an anti-American diatribe.

"So, what brings you to Panamá?" Luke asked.

"For eight years, I was running exclusive guided fishing trips on Lake Nasser in Egypt, for the giant Nile perch."

"How big do they get?"

"They are pretty much the same fish as the Australian Barramundi. They can reach up to 200 pounds and they fight like hell. But the medium-size ones, until 80 pounds, have the most fight in them. They are native to the Nile, then when zey built the Aswan Dam in 1956, the Nile perch became land-locked in that massive new Lake Nasser."

Lake Nasser has more than 400 miles of empty shores, Pascal said, mostly clear water and a very empty feeling to it. The Egyptian government prohibited foreigners from fishing in the area until Pascal hired an attorney in Cairo to lobby the government, which eventually granted him a monopoly on sport fishing for the entire lake.

"Nobody fished these animals until I came along," Pasqal said. "They are too big for the small Egyptian fishing nets, and sport fishing in such an arid and hostile environment was unthinkable. As it is, we can only fish in winter when the temperature drops below 110 degrees."

"Are they good to eat?"

"The best in the whole planet earth, white, delicate meat."

Pascal gave a full description of what life was like living eight years in the barren Egyptian desert with only nomadic Bedouins and his guests for company. After eight years, he had had enough and needed a change.

"What was the main reason you decided to leave such a prosperous business?"

"Really, it was the religion," Pascal said. "When I first arrived in the early 1990s, Cairo was a progressive city with beautiful women in western clothing everywhere. By the time I left, the Islamic fundamentalists had a sturdy grip on the people. Sharia law was becoming the norm rather than the extreme. Women began to wear burkas and were allowed in

33

public only with a male companion. People were bullied into attending extremist mosques, and more and more I felt the eyes of anger upon me as white westerner. So, I left."

"My Father tells me they did the exact same thing in Beirut, so sad, such beautiful women in Lebanon. Then I went to Morocco – Casablanca -- where I fished for the White marlin for two years. It was fun but I wanted to see the new world -- so, Panamá."

"Now I want to set up a fish camp in Panamá. I have a 19-foot Mako and I want to explore all the possible areas to set up a remote fish camp. Will you come with me, Luke?"

"Mako is good boat -- unsinkable, they say. What the hell! When do we start?"

"I am ready right away. I have already seen much of the lower half of the country, San Blas in the Caribbean where the Kuna Indians live and the Darién jungle down by Columbia, but I think we should begin in Las Perlas. I hear there is an island there that might suit my needs."

Pascal and Luke traded knowledge of Las Perlas, an archipelago made up of some 50 islands and islets 30 miles offshore from Panamá City. Several of the islands have small, primitive villages made up mostly of descendants of former slaves and pirates. The islands were named after the pearls that can be found to this day in the rich oyster beds near several of the islands. One of the largest natural pearls in the world was taken from Las Perlas in colonial times. The Spanish king of the day was so impressed with the find that he granted freedom to the diver, an Indian slave who found the pearl.

The islands sat unmolested for years until the Islamic fundamentalists took over Iran. The CIA, eager to protect the Shah and his family, transplanted him to Contradora, the most habitable of the Pearl Islands. The Shah remained in his safe paradise-like haven until his death a few years later.

"Let me finish up some business and talk with my fiancée, Nici. I think we can go next week."

The fish species of the New World were still new and exiting to Pascal.

"Do you know what a robalo is?' Pascal asked out of the blue. "I saw a picture of one in a French fishing magazine. They live near the mangroves. Do you know where we can catch some big ones?"

Luke smiled and finished off his beer.

"The answer is yes I do, but we can't go there -- very restricted, especially for me."

Luke and Pascal shook hands and Luke paused, thinking, then said, "Do you have time to come back to my flat? My fiancée'; she makes great coffee."

If he was going to spend a week exploring remote islands with a man he had just met, he needed a second opinion. Nici was a better judge of character than he was.

The two men walked back to Luke's flat where Nici introduced herself with a smile and offered coffee. Pascal showed Luke and Nici on a map where they would be going and the approximate game plan.

"Luke, our destination is the gem of Las Perlas, Pedro Gonzales," said Pascal, tracing the island on the map. "Others have told me that it is perfect for my fish camp -- just some villagers, a really beautiful bay and many fish. It is pure and untouched. A virgin. A beautiful, lovely virgin, waiting for me."

Pascal finished his coffee, gave Nici the customary French kisses on both cheeks and left. Nici tried to hide her blush.

"I think he'll be OK," she said.

Chapter Six

IT WAS 6:00 A.M.

The day before, Pascal and Luke had loaded supplies and fuel onto the Florida-built white fiberglass Mako including: a 100-gallon deck load of gasoline for the thirsty 250-horsepower Yamaha outboard engine, 50 gallons of fresh water, myriad lures and other tackle, an ice chest full of food, mostly spaghetti, canned tuna and beer and several bottles of the finest red wine for Pascal.

Luke brought his spear gun, weight belt, wetsuit, fins and other freedive gear. Pascal would stick to the fishing poles.

Nici came to the launch ramp to wish them well. She had several children in tow. They were kids from the clinics where she worked and volunteered. Her care for them went beyond medical. Once they healed, she took great pleasure in teaching English to them and showing them a better side of life. This had the unfortunate side effect of sometimes creating dependency. Luke might be awakened in the middle night by throngs of serenading poor children standing outside his building asking for Mrs. Luke to give them some food and or money.

"OK, you guys. Catch lots of fish," Nici said as she blew Luke a kiss. The children and Nici stood on the dock and waved goodbye as the Mako sped off.

"Be careful, Luke Dodge." Nici whispered.

The humble launch ramp known as 'Diablo' was the only public boat-launch facility in Panamá City. The area adjacent to the ramp was full of chaotic Panamá- style marine storage and repair facilities.

The launch ramp was positioned on the estuary between the Bridge of the Americas and the entrance to the Canal. Pascal brought the boat up on to a plane and headed under the bridge.

Pascal glanced at Luke, who wore a pained expression.

"Why do you look so nervous?" Pascal asked.

"We are nearing the restricted Canal area. If I am found within 100 meters of the base of the bridge or the Canal gates they will lock me up and throw away the key."

Luke explained what happened a few days before on his robalo hunting excursion. He told Pascal about the strange barrel shaped items that the Emirate ship had dumped just yards outside the entrance to the Canal.

Pascal absorbed Luke's story and, studying the site with binoculars he had extracted from his bag, replied, "Very interesting, Luke."

Luke did not mention his lingering fear of the sea left over from the barge accident nearly three years earlier. He figured Pascal might consider him a jinx, so he kept it to himself.

Luke relaxed as they left the restricted area behind. They motored past the Amador Causeway, a five-mile, over-water road linking several islands together. Originally, the causeway was constructed to provide a secure place for defense of the Canal. Until the late 1960s, artillery lined the causeway, making it the most heavily fortified piece of real estate in the world.

Luke and Pascal traversed a line of more than 30 ships that stretched for 15 miles, patiently waiting their turn to transit the Canal. Ships would sometimes wait up to two weeks before it was their turn to enter the locks. For kicks, Pascal swerved close to the bow of the last moored ship, which loomed high above them like the barge that had almost taken five lives. Luke closed his eyes and played it cool.

Thirty minutes on, they reached the first of a series of inshore islands, the main one called Taboga.

As the mainland sank out of sight, Luke could feel the strength of the open ocean below him. Pasqal kept hard on the throttle as the Mako flew from swell to swell, the propeller clearing the water each time. Slam, slam slam! Pascal seemed to enjoy the kidney-jarring torture. They passed the midway point and for the next 30 minutes neither islands nor mainland were visible.

Pascal throttled back a bit.

"Luke, I was thinking about what you said earlier when you told me about the Emirate mega-yacht dumping things near the Canal. What do you think they were up to?"

"Not sure, but from the looks of it, probably no good."

"Luke, when I said I left Egypt because of the religion, I did not tell you the full story," Pascal said as he grew serious.

"I was in love, perhaps with the love of my life. Her name was Fatima. Her beauty, her natural beauty could not be over exaggerated. Hers was truly a face that could launch a thousand ships, with olive skin soft as butter, long black flowing hair, rich full naturally red lips and… and…" Pascal paused as he stuffed down emotion.

"Go on," Luke urged.

"She had such a magically wonderful way about her. I can still smell her hair, and hear her call my name. She was educated enough to know what freedom tastes like. She was a teacher. We planned to wed, but her Father, a man of some local stature, strictly forbade that she even to speak to a Western man. We would meet discreetly with the help of some mutual friends. Then, one night we could not stand it any more. We met in private and made love like we were the last two people on earth."

"What happened then?" Luke knew it couldn't be good.

Pascal took a deep breath.

"Somehow her father found out. Overnight, it became public knowledge about what we had done. She managed to come to me and begged me to flee for my life. I did not go. She said the Ministry of Vice and Virtue would force her father to avenge this deed. I pleaded with her to leave with me. She left, and I never saw her again. I was selfish. I am guilty. Soon after, her father took her life in what those people call an "honor killing." They should call it a "coward killing" instead. Barbaric!"

Pascal continued.

"He slit her throat in public, yelling that God is great as her blood spilled on the dirt and dust. That day my heart turned black. I am sure I will never love again."

Luke reached for words, but came up with nothing.

"Luke, I tell you this because if a boat from a Muslim nation is dumping strange objects in front of the Canal, you must warn the authorities, or at least go see what they are for yourself. These people are at war with anything Western and will stop at nothing to bring pain and suffering until every person on earth gets in line with their twisted, fundamental ideals."

Luke now understood why Pascal took it personally.

A lush green, S-shaped island with a large bay came into view.

"Look, there she is -- Pedro Gonzales, land ho!" Pascal exclaimed, his wretched story banished for a while into the realm of nightmares and never-ending regret.

The two grabbed their rods and sifted through tackle to find just the right setups. Both Luke and Pascal were relatively new to the marine ecosystem of Panamá. Both had years of fishing experience, but lacked knowledge about how to fish for local species such as the varieties of pargo, also known as true red snapper, a strong and highly aggressive fish with a sloped head and fan-like tail.

The pargo reaches 130 pounds and lives near ledges, caves and rocks. Another target species they hoped to encounter was the bojala, or amber jack, with its distinctive diagonal black stripe across both eyes. The bojala grow to 80 pounds and are known for their endurance and tough, fighting instinct. Its Spanish name is slang for 'pulls hard'. Luke was familiar with sashimi-style, melt-in-your-mouth bojala from all the best Japanese sushi bars he'd haunted.

Luke and Pascal also hoped to find some decent grouper and some blue water fish such as yellow fin tuna, wahoo and marlin near the outer edge of the island chain where the continental shelf drop off started.

"We can fish only until three o'clock, then we'll anchor off the village of Pedro Gonzales," Pascal said. "I have arranged a meeting with the *representarse*. He is like the elected official for the island. I want him to find me crew members and land for my fish camp."

"Look over there!"

Luke pointed excitedly to a disturbance not far away. Thousands of sea birds were gorging on an endless patch of what must have been sardiná, which is a type of shad bearing the head of an Anchovy and the body of a sardine. As the Mako sped over to the churning water, jumping game fish and diving pelicans came into clear view.

"Pascal, it's loaded. Let's throw some irons."

Luke went for his trusty seven-foot jig stick and tied on a blue and white Tady 45, which is a California-style surface lure that swims in a zig-zag pattern when reeled in from a long cast. Pascal, on the other hand, produced a silly looking lure. It was round with a truncated head, big glued-on eyeballs and two rusting treble hooks.

Luke tried not to laugh.

"What is that?" he asked, figuring it was some silly French thing.

"Zee Poppeergh (the popper). It floats on ze surface, like a bass lure. It is supposed to work well in zeese waters." Pascal's accent became thicker when he was excited.

Pascal tied the popper onto a long spinning rod and reel. The reel was hanging off the rod rather than mounted on top – a setup strictly for beginners, according to Luke. He had learned to laugh at such a setup as young boy, calling them coffee grinders. But technology had caught up with spinning gear and Pascal's Shimano 800 Stella reel, full of 40-pound braid line, was admirable, if not cool.

Pascal wasted no time in firing out his funny looking hourglass shaped lure. His cast was an amazing 75 yards. He flipped the bail over and with the very first turn of the handle, Wham!

"Oh, la la la! Fish on, Luke!"

The line peeled from Pascal's reel with lighting speed. Luke slung back his rod, gave a nice strong heave and let her rip. His jig landed a mere 30 yards off. Luke flipped his standard conventional reel into gear, took a few turns, but nothing. He could see right away that the silly looking French gear may have something to it.

Pascal was pulling hard on his fish and noticed Luke's focus of attention.

"What is it, Luke? What have I got?"

"Look at the fins!" Luke pointed.

A set of rooster-like fins sprang up where Pascal's line entered the water.

"Roosterfish-- *pes gaillo!* A fucking big one too!" Pascal said with the joy of 12- year-old on Christmas morning.

The monster fish tried his best to clear the water but only managed to get its massive thick body half way out. The fish submerged and peeled off another 100 yards of line. Pascal's rod tripled over.

"Oh fuck! I have a knot in zee reel!"

Luke waited for the snap of the line, but it never came. The hulking roosterfish broke the surface, this time showing off most of his white body with its diagonal gray stripes and erect rooster-style dorsal fins. The fish opened its mouth, thrashing its head from side to side, violently trying to shake the hooks loose, sea water pouring from its flared gills.

Thirty minutes later, the tired Frenchman finally pulled the big rooster alongside the boat. The two men hauled the fish aboard. Holding the flopping creature with difficulty, they took a reading on the portable scale they had brought aboard – a necessary item for bragging rights. Pascal struggled to lift the fish off the ground. He held the fish's head up to his chest while the tail remained touching the deck. It weighed in at a trophy, 84 pounds, almost at big as they get. They ceremoniously let it go free and watched as it slowly swam off.

Now it was Luke's turn. The patches of sardinás were everywhere. The normally bathtub warm waters of Panamá cool off from January through June. The chilly waters trigger the sardiná run. Schools of game fish concentrate in shallow water, gorging on nature's sardiná supermarket. Fishing can be outstanding during these months.

Pascal drove toward the next shoal of sardiná, which was being pummeled by hundreds of diving kamikaze gray pelicans, terns, marlin birds, frigates and sea gulls. The sardiná schooled so tightly they turned the greenish water black. As the fish and birds picked off the sardiná, the frothing water filled with glistening Sardiná scales and fish oil, leaving a diesel-like oil slick on the surface.

"Okay, Luke. Have at it."

Luke wasted no time. He refused to be out-fished by a European using funny looking gear.

"What do you do for a living anyway?" Pascal asked out of the blue.

"As little as possible. But when I must work it is in the import-export business, mostly seafood. Frozen stuff, mainly calamari, tilapia for the supermarkets back in the U.S., stuff like that. I used to trade in rare seashells and even shipped live lobster to the Orient for a year. In another life, I ran fishing boats for a living, charter and commercial."

Luke could see something large and red following his lure, then a big boil and wham! The fight was on. He set the hook by giving the rod a firm yank.

"Hook up!" he yelled.

"Looks like a big pargo, Luke. Nice going!" Pascal cheered.

The fish came in easy at first, and then woke up and smoked nearly 100 yards of line off Luke's reel. The fish fought hard, but more like the easily-winded White Sea Bass than the tougher jacks that were jumping and boiling everywhere.

Luke pulled hard on the fish for half an hour, twice almost losing it in the rocks. As the big red beast came alongside the boat, the two men grabbed the rail, stared at the fish and both let out a big "Wow!"

The pargo, a (*dientón*) dogtooth snapper, was bigger than any they had seen in photos -- nearly 75 pounds. The fish was aptly named for its rows of ragged K-9 looking teeth. The spent fish turned belly up.

"Looks like this one is dinner." Luke said. "I am sure the villagers will be happy to share it with us."

For the rest of the afternoon, almost every cast turned up a species new to Luke and Pascal. There were yellow jacks and the rare, yet beautiful blue jack with its psychedelic blue-and white-spotted pattern. Luke and Pascal boated several smaller broomtail grouper (*cherna*) and all were close to 40 pounds. They kept one of the broomtails for its delicate, oil rich meat.

"It always gets me – boating a new species," said Luke. "It's a big thrill, like the first time you sleep with a new girlfriend, there is only one first of anything."

Too tired to cast any more, the fishermen decided to troll towards the small village of Pedro Gonzales, for which they had set course. They secretly hoped they would not have to fight any more fish for the day. To ensure this, they picked the ugliest lures with the worst hooks that they could find in their boxes. But after just five minutes of trolling both the reels went off, clickers screaming, '*zzzzzzzz* 'and a nice sailfish nearing 100 pounds flew from the water. A second fish came off.

"*Pes Vella!* Your turn, Luke."

Luke reluctantly grabbed the rod, set his feet and pulled hard. He had heard that sailfish were a weak fish, but this one felt like a Mack truck. After 45 exhausting minutes and gaining very little line, Luke grabbed the line to pull in the fish   by   hand.

"Must be foul hooked," Pascal said.

"I think I snagged him in the ass, ouch!"

Finally, the tired bill fish neared the gunnel. It was beautiful, with a full sail-like dorsal fin and neon blue stripes. Pascal clutched the leader to bring the fish in close enough to grab. The hooks were buried in the fish's shoulder. Never intended for such use, the steel treble hooks gave out, freeing the fish. The shocked creature sank motionless for a few moments before kicking back to life and zipping off into the deep.

"I think I'm done for the day," Luke confessed.

Pascal regained the course for Pedro Gonzales, twelve miles to the west. They passed an attractive jungle-covered islet with a perfect white sand beach. From nowhere, a helicopter with a camera mounted on the nose cone rose from what looked like the middle of the island.

"Must be *Survivor*. They are filming out here." Pascal said.

They learned later that *Survivor* had hired nearly all the local islanders, paying them a whopping $15 a day. The press generated from the filming directed the attention of developers onto the mostly virgin, islands that, up until then resembled the untouched Alaskan wilderness, only with palm trees instead of evergreens.

They pulled into the bay in front of the tiny village of Pedro Gonzales, anchoring the Mako in shallow water. As they waded into the seashell strewn white sand beach, several local children came running down to meet Pascal and Luke. Apparently, the island did not see many gringos or Europeans. Left to their own devices, the villagers or Gonzaleros, scraped out a humble living from lobster diving and fishing. They all dreamed that a tourist project might find their island, bringing jobs, opportunity and food. The children, all black, had oversized heads with bulging eyes mounted on skinny frames. Luke could see that malnutrition was an issue here.

On the beach were several fiberglass fishing pangas in various states of disrepair, and a large wooden vessel that appeared to be under construction. The boat, nearly 50 feet long, was made entirely of local materials. Taking several years to construct, the yet-to-be-named vessel would work as a tender bringing building supplies, fuel and food from the mainland and return with seafood to be sold in Panamá City.

Next to the wooden boat were the jail and two policemen, Luke observed with a knowing nod. No matter how small a community may be in Panamá, one can always find a jail, police, a church, a school and a medical clinic. In this case, the jail was no more than a 6x6-foot cement room with a bar-covered window. A smiling inmate looked out at Luke as they passed. The policemen stared down at Luke and Pascal.

Juan, the island's *representarse,* appeared with a big smile and a firm handshake. Juan was well fed and slightly better dressed than the other villagers. Juan showed Luke and Pascal around the village, which consisted of a single paved street, a broken-down Church, a small School, two humble cantinas and about 30 simple waterfront homes, mostly painted in pink, purple and green pastels. Each house had at least two hammocks strung up near the front porch, always with somebody napping in them.

Juan was proud to say that his Father, Pedro, had come from a nearby island in the 1950s to found this village. He said that in those days, they lived in simple palm leaf huts and had no motors for the boats, only sails. From his point of view the crumbling road, brick houses and a fickle generator that supplied electricity for a few hours a day were serious improvements. Juan directed Luke and Pascal to the humble, clean house where they were to stay for the night. They were happy to have a bed to sleep in.

Luke gave Juan a bottle of Abuelo, a good Panamánian brown Rum. Soon, Fofoo appeared. Juan told them that Fofoo was the best man in the village to work as a deck hand or *marinero.* Pascal gave Fofoo the job of watching the Mako during the night.

Despite the intense heat of the brick house and welt-size mosquito bites along with dozens of screeching roosters, Luke and Pascal made it through the night and were ready to continue their research expedition the next morning.

Fofoo was the only able-bodied man not working with the *Survivor* crew. Eager to prove his worth, Fofoo had spent the entire night on the deck of the Mako. At first light, the three men headed off for another day of intense fishing action. Pascal asked Fofoo to direct them to the best spot for big bojala.

"Necesitio carnada vivo," Fofoo said.

"We need live bait for the bojala." Pascal translated.

"OK, let's catch some. Gotta be some bait fish around here," Luke said.

They loaded up the bait tank with small Cohinua, a lively, silvery colored jack that lives well in a tank and swims good with a hook through its nose.

Fofoo was happy to the direct them to a wash rock about halfway to the neighboring, but much larger, Isla Del Rey. Isla Del Rey, nearly 30 miles end to end, was covered with old growth trees and had thus far been spared from the destructive hand of developers. Their research had revealed that the island sported numerous white sand beaches, coco palm tree-lined creeks and an inland reservoir that provided water for a small fishing community. Gasoline could be bought on the island at a serious premium and needed to be strained for sludge before use.

Fofoo offered his employers some advice. Roughly translated, he said, "We do not trust the villagers here. They cheat you every time."

Fofoo motioned to start fishing at the approaching wash rock. Luke, having been raised on live bait fishing in the San Diego tuna fleet, cherished the opportunity to pin on a Cohinua.   Luke scampered to find the best bait. Pascal, unfamiliar with live bait fishing, watched with a "wait and see" expression on his face.

Luke hooked a fat, lively bait through the nose and let it rip. The strong little jack peeled line from the reel in a free spool. Like a Porsche shifting from second to fifth gear, the emptying line went from a steady clip to a screaming peel. Even with heavy thumb pressure the spool did not slow. The bite was solid. Luke flipped his reel into gear, took one fast turn and set the hook, yelling his instinctually loud, "Fresh one!"

Some fish have only one or two strong runs in them, some jump, some charge the boat before getting into the fight. But the bojala just pulls, solid and steady until the gaff (a large, sharp hook used to the pull big fish over the rail) hits it. A true fighter to the end, the Bojala is not a quitter.

"Pull hard, Luke!" Pascal coached, pointing into the water. "I think I see the fish."
Luke pulled hard on the fish and gained as much line as he lost. After thirty minutes and six laps around the boat, the mighty amber-colored jack neared the surface.

"This is too much work. Next time I will get in the water and just shoot one of these things."

"Biojala!" an excited Fofoo proclaimed.

Fofoo went for the gaff. Big fish seem to know what a gaff is, making it necessary to conceal the gaff from the fish's view until the very last moment. Fofoo dangled the gaff over the side of the boat. The fish eyed the gaff and fought to keep its distance.

"Hide the gaff," Luke barked.

With the gaff hidden behind the rail the fish finally broke the surface.

"So beautiful, with its brown body, yellow tail and look at that dark stripe on its eye," Pascal said.

Fofoo sank the gaff into the fish behind the collar and heaved her into the boat. The Boajala -- near 90 pounds, Luke guessed -- kicked violently on the deck and finally had to be clubbed.

"Muy bueno!" Fofoo cheered.

"Do you mind if I take a rest and then get in the water for a bit?" Luke asked Pascal.

"No problem, Luke. Let me just fish for an hour, then we can head to the blue water."

In the next hour Pascal, using the live bait, boated three more respectable Bojala between 30 and 40 pounds.

"I guess the live bait is working these days. Okay, we go offshore now."

The trio headed toward the inner edge of the Continental Shelf and the first place where deep water could be found off Panamá. After running for an hour and 15 miles past Isla San Jose, the last island in the archipelago, the water abruptly turned from an off-green to a crystal-clear blue. Other the main island, the chart did not show any islands or wash rock in the area. But several reefs with breakers could be seen off in the distance. Fofoo, an island native, had never seen these waters just 30 miles from his home village.

Where to start was anyone's guess. Luke took charge and asked Pascal to drop him by the first set of wash rocks. They had been told it was a prime area for deadly Bull sharks. Luke took an extra long look around for dorsal fins. The bull shark, although smaller than the great white, has more testosterone per pound of body weight that any other animal in the world. The testosterone gives the shark what is essentially constant steroid rage and it eats absolutely anything that crosses its path -- birds, turtles, rubber tires and occasionally humans. Luke was accustomed to the semi-predictable great white sharks back home that used the gray light of dawn and dusk to sneak attack their sea lion prey. Attacks on humans by Great Whites were considered a case of mistaken identity. The bull shark on the other hand, eats 24/7 and would be more than happy to intentionally chow down on Luke's tasty flesh.

The concern about Bull sharks faded as dreamy thoughts of giant tuna, wahoo, Dorado, grouper and pargo filled Luke's head as he slipped on his wetsuit, which was still damp from his night in jail. He was grateful to be free, not in jail, and out doing what he loved.

Luke cleared his mind of all thoughts. He did this by saying the alphabet backwards and forwards until he could visualize all 26 letters in a neat line, each with a corresponding numeral above each letter to indicate its place in line.

Luke rolled over the rail and loaded the spear gun that his friend, Scott Merlo, had made for him back in the states. The gun had a beautiful, thick 58-inch zebrawood and mahogany stock and was powered by three 5/8-inch power bands. The big gun was tough to cock, but once loaded, the good engineering and balanced stock forced the arrow to travel straight and fast.

Ready to roll, Luke worked through a few warm up dives while spotting for baitfish. He came across a mass of baitfish and some smaller jack. With visibility near 60 feet, the bottom was still out of sight. Luke breathed-up, taking 15 slow and deep breaths, then descended. The bottom came into clear view about halfway down.

Luke could see the tip of a pinnacle sticking up from the edge of a shelf with one side plunging into an abyss. As Luke neared the bottom he could make out shadows another 20 feet down the slope. He pushed on as a cornucopia of life came into view. Hanging near 80 feet was a swirling mass of several different species of pargo ranging from 30 pounds to what looked to be close to 130 pounds. The more aggressive but less tasty dogtooth snapper patrolled the perimeter and showed little fear of Luke, while the yellow tail snapper stayed closer to the middle of the swirl. Each member of the local jack species paraded by in mini-schools of two and three. The most beautiful and rare of the jacks, the Blue Jack, was present. Near 30 pounds each, they sported bright blue bodies accented by electric white and purple spots on their dorsal side.

This spot was *happening,* and anything in the sea could appear at any second. Luke, still new to these waters, marveled at the plethora of unfamiliar species. Accustomed to diving in the kelpy waters off California, Luke generally worked at depths of 40 to 50 feet, although he was capable of diving past 100 feet. He was mindful, always, that working and shooting fish past a depth of 60 feet -- unless one had vast experience -- posed a serious risk of shallow water blackout. The clear, deep water has a hypnotic effect to it. "Just a few more feet," you tell yourself, then just seconds into stalking a game fish, you look up and find yourself 100 feet down and already fighting for air. Add a fighting fish to the equation and death is never far off.

Luke dropped a small marker buoy on the tip of the pinnacle so he could find it again easily and glided towards the surface.

"That is fucking deep," Luke murmured while catching his breath.

After three minutes of relaxing and breathing up, Luke gulped air and let himself slowly sink to meet the tip of pinnacle. Adding to the allure of the deep, once down on the bottom, the visibility opened to an unlimited 200 feet. As Luke leveled off, he took notice of several large looming shadowy masses off in the periphery – maybe sharks, maybe whales.

No time to fret about it. Luke eyed the largest pargo of the school. Then he zeroed in on his quarry, careful not to lose the tree for the forest, he locked his heat-seeking eyes onto a dime-sized spot behind a certain fish's shoulder where he hoped to plant the spear and break the fish's spine. At this depth only a perfect stone shot would allow for the possibility of getting the 100-pound pargo that was now in Luke's sights. Taking aim, Luke softly squeezed the trigger. The powerful Merlo gun was so well balanced that it had little recoil, throwing all expendable energy into the accurate forward momentum of the spear. But the clear water blurred Luke's sense of distance. He had taken a maximum range shot of 25 feet. The shaft struck the fish but sank in just enough to miss the fish's spine, hitting it dead in the shoulder meat. The angry pargo zipped off into the depths. Luke held onto his float line, which was moored by a single red float.

Quickly being pulled past the point of no return, Luke let go of the line. With his gun in hand he made for the surface that seemed to be a mile away and at the edge of visibility. Luke tried to slow his rate of kick and manage his spastic craving for fresh air. As he reached the half way point, stars started to dance around Luke's head. Still at 60 feet, Luke had no choice but to dump his weight belt. He gave the buckle a firm tug and watched as his belt tumbled to the bottom. Free from weight, Luke rocketed towards the surface. He broke the surface with a gasp and deep breath.

"Are you okay, Luke?" Pascal asked with wide eyes.

"My float -- get my float -- the fish is on there... huge pargo."

"Tengo, yo lo tengo" ("I have it.") Fofoo yelled.

Luke's heart sank as he saw a smiling Fofoo pulling and jerking with all his strength. Before Luke could blurt out to go easy on the fish, the line went slack and Fofoo sadly announced, *"Se fue."* (He left).

With no weight belt, stars in his head and no fish to show for his trouble, Luke sadly collected his dangling shaft with a huge chunk of pargo meat on the tip.

"I have no weight belt. I'll stay shallow." Luke told Pascal.

"Bonne chance, Luke," Pascal said, preparing to start line-fishing again.

After floating for 20 minutes Luke felt recharged and ready to dive again. Staying shallow, less than 20 feet, Luke hovered over where his marker told him the reef was.

Suddenly a mass of maniacal baitfish began plunging into Luke like small missiles.

Something is coming...

Before Luke could complete his thought, a small school of large wahoo, aiming to make dinner of the baitfish, zoomed inches past his face. There was no time to appreciate the Wahoo's long, slender body with horizontal tiger stripes and a mouth designed to tear smaller fish to shreds. From the surface, Luke swung his gun around and fired from the hip. Luke tagged the last wahoo in the school just forward of its tail. The long narrow fish zigged then zagged several times but never sounded for the depths. After pulling Luke around for 15 minutes the feisty fish slowed down enough for Luke to grab him by the gills and plant his knife firmly in its skull.

"Nice fight!" Luke thanked the fish.

As Luke swam back to the boat he could see Pascal hooked up to something big. He could hear Pascal's "Oh, la, la, la, la." When he made more than two "Oh la, la's," it apparently meant, a fish over 50 pounds.

Luke handed his wahoo to Fofoo then entered the boat from the stern to see a massive, tired pargo lying on the deck.

"Nice work, Pascal."

"Nice work, Luke."

Chapter Seven

PASCAL AND LUKE had boated enough fish for dinner. As the wind kicked up past 20 knots they decided to head back to Pedro Gonzales and start the evening early. An hour later the Mako approached the small point and village. Fofoo motioned to anchor the boat on the leeward side of the bay to protect against the building swell. He also signed that a big storm was on its way. He pointed at the ring around the moon as a sign of the impending bad weather.

As they unloaded their catch for the day, small children crowded around. Loud music blared from the town center. The *representarse* came down to invite them to the party. The men from the village had returned from a day's work filming *Survivor*, apparently with cash in hand. A drunken fiesta was sure to follow.

Pascal made the mistake of paying Fofoo his wages for the day, and Fofoo faithfully promised to keep watch on the Mako the whole night through. But before long, the guide found himself drinking beer and chasing several village girls into the wee hours of the night, eventually passing out in a bush.

Pascal and Luke headed back to their rented house, made a hasty meal, had a few beers and fell into bed.

As 3:00 a.m. rolled around, the tide abated and the swell picked up. With the entire town dead asleep, the Mako began to drag anchor. A six-foot swell planted the Mako firmly onto a coral head. With just enough water to float the boat, the Mako sang back and forth over the coral head, grazing it each time. With every pass, chunks of fiberglass were torn from the hull. The propeller and cavitation plate on the motor were destroyed.

By dawn, the hull of the Mako looked like it had been pounded on a reef during a hurricane. With first light, Fofoo woke from his stupor and headed out to the Mako. When he saw the damage, he fell into shock. He had let the Mako, his grand responsibility, become hamburger meat.

In his state of panic, he made up a hasty story. He told Pascal that he had slept all night on the Mako and a commercial fishing boat from Panamá City came into Pedro Gonzales late at night to buy marijuana. He further explained that the boat had a special rack on it that grazed the bottom of the Mako, creating the damage.

Pascal thanked him for telling the truth, and asked, "Why is a boat coming here to buy marijuana?" Pascal asked.

Fofoo thought for a moment, then motioned for Luke and Pascal to follow. After a short hike up a goat trail they reached a clearing. There stood acres of fully-grown pot plants, each with multiple 12-inch long banana-shaped buds dangling off the plants.

"Panamá Rojo," Fofoo said with a smile as he caressed one of the buds.

He explained that the government allowed them to cultivate the plants as long as they did not try to export. They sold it cheaply, usually for a $100 a pound. Without the pot, they would starve or have to leave the island. Fofoo explained that sometimes *narcotrafficos,* driving very fast boats came from Colombia and tried to use their island as a stop-over point. He added that usually the islanders chased them off, but sometimes they were forced to let them stay because the *narcotrafficos* have big guns and like to kill people for fun.

Despite a damaged boat and bad weather, Pascal and Luke concluded it would be best to make for the mainland.

Luke made a quick dive under the Mako to asses the damage one last time. The damage was borderline severe. Luke told Pascal that it looked bad but they would make it. To be safe for the ride home, Luke tied empty fuel jugs together should they need a makeshift life raft. Luke told Fofoo to send out boats to look for them if they did not check in within three hours.

"That is not needed," Fofoo replied. "*Jesús es su co-piloto*" (*Jesus is your co-pilot*), he added with confidence.

As they readied the boat for the 40-mile crossing the *representarse* came down to give them avocados as gifts. He begged Pascal not to abandon the idea of the fishing lodge, as they badly needed the income. Pascal glanced at Fofoo as he said, "Thank you for your hospitality. I will think about it."

Pascal then changed the mangled propeller, fired up the motor and pointed the damaged Mako toward Panamá City. Luke's job for the trip was to be sure that any new leak did not flood the bilge during transit. The thick, double hull construction of the Mako really paid off. The two men returned safely, tired but unscathed.

Chapter Eight

LUKE COULD HEAR LOUD voices from the street as he approached his building. As he dragged his tired legs up the flight of stairs to his flat, he heard two unusual noises emitting from behind his door -- a barking dog and the thundering voices of two seemingly intoxicated men. Not knowing what to expect, Luke unsheathed his knife and loaded his spear gun. After taking a deep breath, Luke flew through the doorway yelling as he charged into what he thought was a break-in and possibly rape situation. He went charging for the first man as the dog barked excessively at Luke. Before Luke could slit the man's throat, Nici screamed.

"Luke! Stop! It's John!"

Luke was like a deer caught in the headlights.

"Hi Luke, meet my friend, Rob," John said.

John, a middle-aged man of average build with dark hair, was an old friend of Luke's from California. John, now worked as a cargo pilot for Global-Fast Airlines. Global-Fast, formerly Air Americana, had been a civilian general cargo carrier with ties to the CIA dating back to operations during the Vietnam war that called for non-military airlines to make "humanitarian runs" into Laos and Cambodia.

The name was changed after heroin transport operations were uncovered that lasted for years after the war ended. After the second Gulf war erupted, Global-Fast had just one client, the U.S. Department of Defense. They were technically still a civilian airline, so they could breach the no-fly zones over Iran and North Korea. But in reality, the CIA wrote their paychecks for the purpose of delivering ordnance to battle theaters and bringing home fallen soldiers in U.S. flag-draped coffins.

Rob, John's friend, was a tall, blond man from the Florida Keys. He had been drinking and shook Luke's hand with an overly firm grip.

"Hey Luke, I wanna thank you for putting us up on short notice," John said. "I was transiting to Europe on my way to… well I can't tell you. Anyway, Rob came down with me. We wanted to see what you have been doing."

Short notice? I never knew they were coming, Luke thought.

"Babe, meet Chewy, too." Nici then held up a beautiful mid-sized black dog that appeared to be a pit bull and border collie mix. The dog was jet back with just a touch of white on his forehead and chest. Luke walked over to the dog, locked eyes with it and stared intently.

"Chewy, huh? Nice name. I won't ask why you decided to call him that or even where you got him."

Chewy gave Luke a big kiss on the nose, instantly sealing the bond.

"I was hoping you could show me and Rob around tonight. I hear there are some good strip-joints in this town." *Same old John.*

Luke paused.

"Nice to see you guys, really, but this town takes energy that I just don't have. I'll be glad to recommend some places, though."

Luke knew that John and Rob most likely were going to visit every brothel in Panamá City. With prostitution being legal, their night was sure to be a long one. Wenching was their hobby and that was why they had come to Panamá.

"Hey Luke, you gotta join us," John said with a slur.

Nici looked on with an encouraging smile. European to the bone, Nici was never the jealous type. At times, she almost encouraged Luke to go sow his oats. He never tested the waters, but the mere thought of such liberty was enough to keep Luke faithful.

"Naw, guys, really I just can't, not tonight," Luke replied.

"Come on, Luke, go have some fun with your friends, it's okay with me." Nici said.

"Babe, you know where they want to go, El Zona Roja, booze, broads and gambling…"

"Sounds like fun. Luke, there are other ways to have fun besides just shooting fish. Go have fun."

Luke was cornered.

"Okay," he said while staring into his new dog's eyes.

"Does he fetch, or swim?" Luke asked.

"So far, he just barks, but I will teach him all of that as time goes on," Nici said.

"Ruf, ruf, ruf." Chewy introduced himself and rolled over, panting with his tongue hanging out.

Luke showered and insisted that his buddies let him sleep for at least 100 hours. They gave him just two.

"All right, you guys, you asked for it and I am gonna give it to you. *Jefe, Bodeguita por favor,"* Luke instructed the cabbie.

The night was young and the Bodeguita ("little warehouse") was mostly empty.

"Where did you bring us, Luke?" John cynically queried.

"Most people don't start to party in Panamá until after eleven... then this place is wall to wall, red-hot Latinas just waiting for a you to ask them to dance."

"I hate dancin'," Rob slurred.

Yelling over the blaring Salsa music, Luke changed the subject.

"So, where are you flying off to next, John?"

"You know I can't really say too much. But the Muslim extremists have beaten a path in Egypt. The normal people there are terrified that the Taliban might resurge near Cairo, leading to civil unrest and even war. So, let's just say I will be taking some pictures of the pyramids next week."

John, never an emotional man paused, tears showing in his eyes.

"Each time we fly those boys home in their coffins, they make us re-ice the bodies mid-flight. If I used to be a moderate, now I am extreme. I really hate those ragheads over there, killing our men and women for who knows what reason. They are evil to the bone and need to be killed. I used to do my job for money, now I do it because I believe in fighting the Islamo-facists. Really, our future depends on it."

Luke thought back to the story Pascal had told him about his beloved Fatima, then he thought again about the tanker from Dubai he had seen dumping the barrels. He recalled agent Caucuss telling him about the up-tick in intelligence regarding the Canal and terrorism. His own conscience was quickly eroding any chance of remaining a bystander.

John told Luke about more horrible atrocities that he had been privy to in the Middle East. "When are people going to realize that the radical Muslims want us all dead, or converted to Islam. It's so simple," he sighed.

The men's attention was soon diverted by a throng of single women pouring through the door. The women wore mini skirts and low-cut blouses. Some sported fishnet nylons. All had visible G-stings sneaking up the small of their backs accented by tattoos that implied sexual innuendo. The girls all looked to be under 25, their skin color ranged from jet black to almost white. They came in all shapes and sizes - tall and athletic to short and busty. No niche went unfilled in the highly competitive world of sex-workers in Panamá. A sex worker earning dollars in Panamá could save enough money to buy a house, a car and take care of their entire extended families.

"I like the ratio," Rob said as he downed a little purple pill. John did the same.

"Hey, guys, we have a long night ahead of us. Take it slow. There will be plenty more."

A band took center stage. The bar-goers applauded and whistled loudly as the singer grabbed the microphone. A clean-cut man in his late 20s, the singer moved and sang like Ricky Martin. He opened with a song written about the bar in which he was now singing.

The dance floor instantly filled with excited people.

"What is going on? No dancing," Rob said with a plea for mercy as a pretty girl appeared out of nowhere, grabbed him by the arm and began leading him to the dance floor.

"Just go with it, Rob," John laughed.

The Bodeguita was the most renowned salsa dance club in all Panamá. Most of the *pescadoras* were from Colombia, namely from the cities of Cali or Medellin. Cali boasted more internationally known Salsa dancers than any other city on the world. The Colombians take their Salsa seriously. The gyration also helps to put chum in the water, thus helping the *pescadoras* to hook gringos for a trip to the "push buttons."

Push buttons were readily available small hotels based purely on infidelity and the sex-trade. Offering complete anonymity, the patron would drive into a closed garage door, exit the car and push a button. Payment was made through a turnstyle. The key was then dropped through a mail slot in the door. Nobody could see the patrons come or go. The rooms were generally tidy and cost eight dollars an hour.

Actively avoiding the oogling girls, John pointed to one girl in her late twenties who lit up the dance floor with lighting fast, Salsa moves. The girl with kinky long hair and extra tight jeans seemed to be content with dancing alone.

John took a shot of liquid courage and worked his way over to the girl he had spotted.

Looking like a typical gringo in a Hawaiian shirt, John blurted out his only Spanish.

"Hola, tú es muy bonita." (Hello, you are very beautiful).

The girl paused, smiled and replied in English, "Thank you, I like the way you dance."

The music stopped and the lights temporarily came on to reveal the girl's face. John stood in momentary shock as he could see that her entire left eye had been lost in some sort of terrible violence.

"It is okay to look at my eye. Buy me a drink and I will tell you the story. I am
Veronica."

"John. Nice to meet you."

After a few rounds, Veronica told John that she had been the head girlfriend of a dangerous drug lord in Medallin, Colombia.

"He did a lot of *ya-yo* (cocaine) and became insanely jealous. One day he caught his friend walking me to my car, so he pulled out his 9mm and shot me in the face while he called me a *puta*. As you can see I lived, but moved to Panamá as soon as I was able. I learned English from the computer and now my only fun is Salsa."

Luke intervened.

"There are lots more than this place, so let's get a cab."

So far, Luke had imbibed slowly, but it was catching up with him. Everybody is a different type of drunk. Some get mean. Some get stupid. Luke became loud and funny, but developed a sense of overconfidence that sometimes led to apologies over the phone the next day.

Luke tried to tear John away from his one-eyed maiden but the pilot insisted that she come along. Rob saw them leaving and followed. The four grabbed a cab.

"Clube Miami," Luke said with a smile.

"Sí, señor."

A few minutes later, Luke, John, Robert and Veronica arrived outside an inconspicuous building with just a few red lights. They were checked for weapons and Veronica was asked to show ID.

"Ella es Colombiana, no permite." (She is Colombian, she must go...)

The guards refused to allowed Veronica entry. It was assumed that as a Colombian she was prostitute and the club did not want to give their own girls any competition.

Luke begged John to keep his cool. John walked Veronica to a cab, paid the driver and exchanged numbers with her, swearing he would call her.

As they entered the club they were treated to every man's dream. Dozens of young, beautiful women vied for the men's attention. The girls all wore the same outfit: Three- inch long white mini-skirts, laced-up, white knee-high boots and skimpy white tops. They laughed, giggled, wriggled and acted coy. But after several of them had danced in the nude on stage, the mood changed. As the girls took turns dancing on stage, they generally took all their clothes off, but kept one hand over their privates. If they chose to do anything overtly sexual they would wear a mask to hide their identity. After dancing, the girls assumed that the men's blood was boiling and became more aggressive, grabbing, touching and caressing until something gave.

John was the first one to cave. He picked a demure, short, native Panamánian girl and took her to one of the back rooms. Forty minutes later and 90 dollars poorer, John emerged with a tired look and a smile on his face. The girl, who called herself Fanny, gave John her number, begging him to be her boyfriend.

Robert followed suit, going off with a taller girl with straight hair and a confident walk. Luke stood vigil at the table. As soon as Luke rebuffed one girl, another one would come in her place, trying a slightly different tactic. Feeling bad that he had to turn them down, he bought each one a drink. By the end of the night his bar tab exceeded $300.

Three a.m. rolled around.

Drunk and burning through cash, Luke insisted that they call it a night.

Chapter Nine

TWO DAYS, LOTS OF sleep, 45 glasses of water and ten aspirin later, Luke was past his hangover and ready to get back on track. John thanked Luke then exchanged emails addresses. Rob, who decided staying drunk was easier than dealing with a crippling hangover, gave Luke and Nici bear hugs.

"I love you both," Rob gushed. "I had the time of my life."

As Luke watched John's jet depart his thoughts once again centered on the discussions he'd had with Pascal regarding the wave of Muslim-backed terror threatening free people everywhere.

"Hey babe, please take me to the Ancon. I need to do some thinking." Luke said to Nici.

As Luke and Nici began negotiating Panamá City's perpetual gridlock, they passed one of the many public busses known ad *Diablo Rojos* (Red Devils). The buses, (mostly retired U.S. school busses) are ubiquitous in Panamá and cost only 25 cents to ride. The drivers love to honk their loud horns and take great pride in air brushing images on the back of their buses. The images are usually family members or movie stars who the owners admire.

Luke's eye caught one such image, but it was not the driver's son or daughter, it was Osama Bin Laden and the paint was fresh. Luke rubbed his eyes in disbelief that anybody would be so out-right supportive of the Al Qaeda, especially in harmonious, neutral, peaceful Panama´. In addition- to be sure he got his message across- the owner of the Red Devil had written, 'O. B. Laden' right on the bottom of the image. The message was anything but subtle and it sent shivers down Luke's spine.

An hour later, Nici dropped Luke and Chewy off at the top Ancon hill. The Ancon is the highest point in Panamá City and provides an amazing 360-degree vista of the Bridge of the Americas, the city, the dense rain forest, the Pacific Ocean and the Canal. For years, this prime spot had been locked down by the U.S. military. But now it proudly displayed the world's largest Panamánian flag, which made a waffling sound as it flew in the breeze.

"I'll be home in a while okay? I've got some thinking to do." Luke repeated.

"Okay, honey pot, whatever you need." Nici was not one to pry.

As Nici drove off, Luke took a deep breath, then another, and looked down at Chewy.

"Well pup, what do you think I should do? If I go back to the restricted zone to see what that big Dubai yacht dropped and get caught, I will never see the light of day again. If I do not, and the bastards *are* plotting some sort of terror plot here, I will never be able to live with myself. Looks like Homeland Security is not going to do anything…"

"Ruf, ruf," Chewy counseled.

"Really, you think I should do that?"

Luke walked to the top of the of the vista, then took a seat on an old
log. He stared hard at the Canal. He replayed the events of September 11, 2001 over in his head. Like most American, that day was seared into his brain.

On 9-11, he and Nici had stopped over in Stuttgart, Germany on their way from California via London to Cape Town, South Africa. They'd planned to make business connections, dive with great white sharks and catch some tasty waves at the famed Jeffery's Bay.

They did everything they'd planned, but in light of the attacks and canceled Atlantic flights, they stayed for three months exploring Mozambique, the wild African Tundra and the stark desserts of Namibia.

Luke recalled as their Lufthansa jet left Heathrow London, the airplane telephones had ceased working and the flight attendants became rigid and white as ghosts. He'd figured they were just German women and that's they way they behaved. But upon landing, the whole flight was literally pushed out of the airport doors, bypassing all customs and immigration, and their bags were delivered later that day.

Nici's sister Jasmine picked them up at the Stuttgart airport and promptly explained in broken English that a big bomb had gone off in New York. They arrived at the restaurant that was owned by Nici's parents, Vlado and Anna. Anna served Luke a traditional German dish, dripping with tasty sauces. They turned on CNN and saw the passenger jetliners slam into the Twin Towers.

Never having been an extreme patriot, Luke was surprised at his own reaction. He watched the airplanes hit the towers two or three times before it hit him. The tears came slowly at first, and then built into a semi-hysterical wail. Luke could not believe how badly he personally grieved the loss of souls he'd never met.

Perhaps it was a sense of intense vulnerability, perhaps it was latent patriotism and perhaps it was a more primal sense of having really been stepped on. Whatever the reason, that day had left a lasting scar deep in Luke's psyche. Never again would he take his freedom for granted and he vowed to hold the perpetrators' hands to the fire if he ever had the opportunity. He knew that nothing would ever be the same, and that the noose would tighten in the future, hurting both his friends and foes.

But after Nici was deported forcefully and banned from entry to the U.S. for at least five years, Luke figured, that was it! He came to resent his country and the taxes he was still forced to pay it. He was convinced he would never get over his fear that tyranny and injustice had taken hold of his home.

The pendulum swung back somewhat after living in Panamá for several years. The passage of time had softened the bitterness Luke felt for the U.S. He temporarily set aside his trepidation about his country and focused on his family and those he loved. He knew he had to do it for them.

"Well Chewy, looks like I have no choice. But Nici, maybe she will object to such a risk."

Ruf, ruf, ruf."

"Yeah, you are right. She is a fighter too and will push me to find out the truth, no matter what the cost. Let's go, but if it all goes bad, I'm blaming you." Luke patted Chewy on the head.

Luke and Chewy walked the several miles down the hill and through the dangerous neighborhood called Chorillo. He blocked out everything as he thought about how he was going to break the news to Nici.

He practiced what he would say… "Babe these guys dumped some explosives in front of the Canal and I need to see what it is."

No. No, that won't work! Luke shook his head.

After sufficient mental ping-ponging, Luke came up with a plan for breaking the news to Nici. His tired legs finally delivered him home to Nici, who was waiting with a warm meal.

Luke took a few bites of the breaded fish with vegetables she had made for him.

He walked over to the stereo and picked out their favorite song, *Mariposa Traicionera* by the group *Mana*. Grabbing Nici by the hand, they began to slow dance, hip to hip cheek to cheek. Nici played along as they both sang the lyrics.

"Mariposa, ya me mariposa, no regresso contigo…"

Luke played the song twice, holding Nici tighter with each passing moment. The two danced and moved like a single person, in perfect Latin rhythm. When the song ended, without uttering a single word, Luke led Nici upstairs into their bedroom.

He slowly undressed her, kissing her ankles, working his way up.

"I love you more than the son, the sea, the air and the earth," Luke said in a soft voice. He kissed her passionately on the lips several times and forehead until neither of them could stand it any longer.

Two hours later, Luke sat flushed and smoking his favorite Monte Christo cigar as he watched the tourists and locals shuffle down his historic street. He said nothing of his plans, but as women sometimes do, Nici knew for sure that he was up to something that would put him mortal jeopardy.

Like a condemned man on his last walk to the chair, Luke ate the thickest steak he could find that night. He asked for it rare, so he could taste every bite. Nici obliged and poured him two bottles of Chateau Lafitte 1981 that she had brought from Germany and had been saving for a special occasion.

Luke headed off to bed and asked Nici to stay by his side, close by his side the whole night through.

Chapter Ten

"LET'S DO THIS," Luke said out loud as he approached the exact place he had been arrested just two week earlier.

This time there would be no pausing to slip on his booties or wet suit. He had arrived by taxi already fully suited up in his camo wet suit. He figured early morning would be the best bet to avoid the authorities. He paid the taxi driver two dollars and instructed him to stop and wait a mile from his entry point. Luke exited the taxi with haste as the driver crossed himself while wishing Luke a sincere *"Via con dios"* (Go with God).

Luke approached his entry point, bush by bush, hedge by edge, hiding and pausing along the way. He slung his spear gun behind his back, thinking he could use it to defend against crocodiles, or in a last-ditch effort against the Panamá defense forces that prowled everywhere. This was a do or die mission with no points for second place.

Luke's adrenaline glands went into overdrive, giving him animal-like reflexes. His hearing and sight became clearer and time compression kicked in to allow him to see each passing second as if it were ten. This natural amphetamine forced a suppression of all fear and produced an overwhelming urge to accomplish what he had started. He had not felt so alive or so acute since he had jumped for his life during the barge collision years earlier.

Luke could see the bank where he would enter just past the next set of bushes. The only problem was the electrified, razor-wire fence between him and the water. Luke had let his wet suit completely dry out, thus providing insulation between him and the 10,000 volts running through the 20-foot high fence. With a neoprene-gloved hand he touched the fence, waiting for the shock to come. It never did.

As the sound of electrical current whizzed through the fence, Luke cautiously scaled the first side, then gingerly parted the razor wire to slip through. The razor cut his glove, exposing the flesh of his hand to the electricity. Even with the minor exposure, his hand flew off the wire and his whole body jerked back. He let go of his fins, mask and spear gun then dropped twenty feet, landing in a pile of mud. The impact knocked the wind from his lungs.

"Fuck! Keep moving, Luke, move!" his brain yelled.

With no formal military training, Luke had only his instincts and cheesy war movies as guidance. He reached the water's edge.

"Shit." A fast aluminum patrol neared his position. Luke dove into a nearby bush, hoping his camouflage would conceal him.

The boat passed. Luke donned his mask and fins. He said a quick prayer before sliding down the short muddy bank and into the water.

The water under the bridge was the same off-green color and faintly salty taste as the last time he had been here. Luke floated behind some debris while he caught his breath and loaded his gun. As he did this a large shadow approached from his left side.

Oh shit! A bull shark, his brain screamed.

Bull's had the rare ability to adapt to brackish and fresh water, making them deadly to estuary, river and even lake swimmers.

On second glance, the shadow was a massive Panamá robalo, probably over 70 pounds, a world record. Luke readied his gun, took aim. The fish paused as if to dare him to pull the trigger.

He lowered the big gun. Stick to the program, he reminded himself.

"Okay, you win this time. I have work to do."

Luke poked the fish with his spear tip and started his swim toward the Canal gates where he had seen the yacht dump the barrels. The tide was ebbing at a fast three knots. Luke quickly grew tired fighting the strong current. As he approached the spot, he tried to relax and recapture his breath but it was no use. After a short rest on the surface, Luke found himself blown 50 yards off course. He decided to kick upstream, closer to the gates of the locks. This way he could rest and breath up while drifting, then dive just before he neared where he thought the objects would be.

His plan worked and he achieved the maximum bottom time of three minutes. With the morning light filtering through the water to the depths, he scoured the bottom for anything suspicious. Fifteen dives later, and coming up empty each time, Luke was growing relieved.

Maybe the barrels were some sort of markers that have already been removed, he thought as he swam back upstream for the 16th time. With each swim and dive- ten minutes passed. Luke had been diving steady for more than two hours. As the tide changed the current went slack, allowing Luke much more ease of navigation once he was on the bottom. As the dust on the bottom began to settle, the visibility opened to a clear 25 feet.

Luke took his time breathing up. He wanted to make this one count. He gulped air to top off his lungs and glided to the muddy bottom below. A tingle grew in his belly. The same tingle he had felt before his Harley was stolen in Europe and before he had to jump for his life when the fuel barge cut the boat he was on in two. Before he could cognate on the butterflies in his bowels, canister-shaped objects came into view. Luke suppressed his emotion in the same way he did when sighting a trophy fish. He kicked over to the first barrel, which was halfway buried in the mud.

At first blush, the white 55 gallon drums appeared to be nothing more than a petroleum by-product of some kind. Luke grabbed the rim of a barrel. The white paint appeared to be fresh and was clearly not the original coating. With no clue as to what was inside, Luke unsheathed his trusty, kill knife. He scratched the barrels in several places until he could see traces of marking under the paint. He scratched and scraped as if it were a winning lottery ticket.

"What is that?" Luke thought as a large symbol under the paint became discernable. Out of air, Luke went back to the surface where he saw the gates to the locks slowly opening. A small, armed Panamánian defense force vessel approached. They did not appear to see Luke. The doors came to rest in the fully open position as the small vessel acted as a guide for a giant cargo ship that was about to clear the locks. A loud horn blasted to signal the vessel to move ahead. Luke did not want to leave his find, as he had not yet uncovered the mystery of what was in the barrels.

He dared not swim too far as he might not be able to find the spot again. He stayed low in the water, breathing heavily, waiting until the small vessel – the cargo ship not far behind -- bore down on him. To avoid detection, he dove and held onto the first barrel, he could hear the small vessel pass overhead. Then the looming shadow of the tanker approached and Luke could feel the thud, thud, thud of the massive propellers in his chest cavity. As the 700-foot Dutch-flagged car carrier passed directly over Luke he got his first clear view of the symbol on barrels.

"I am in deep shit!" his brain yelled as he realized that the symbol was the international radioactive waste warning.

Hoping it was a fluke, Luke dove a dozen more times, scraping paint off each barrel. Every barrel carried the radioactive waste symbol. On the second to last dive Luke uncovered a slightly smaller barrel but with the same white paint. As he scraped, each letter revealed itself: S-E-M...

Is it cement, spelled wrong? he wondered.

He kept scraping to find more letters: S-E-M-T-EX.

Luke discovered rubber coated detonation cables linking all the barrels together. Three of the barrels were loaded with SEMTEX. Designed by the Russians, SEMTEX was among the world's most powerful plastic explosives.

Luke made one last dive. As he approached the last barrel of SEMTEX, he could see a faint red glow. He rolled over the barrel to see the same sort of timing box with antennae protruding from it. For fear of setting it off, Luke dare not try to disarm the bomb or cut any cords.

I will tell Caucuss and everything will be okay, he thought as he jetted towards the surface.

To remember the location of the bombs, Luke took a triangulation of three prominent land marks and committed them to memory.

In all, Luke counted 17 barrels of radioactive waste and three barrels of SEMTEX enough to destroy the entire bridge and the locks. This bomb was a much more sinister than just an explosion. This was a dirty bomb. When exploded, such a bomb would destroy the Canal gates, the bridge and contaminate the entire greater Panamá City for months, if not years, and would certainly result in catastrophic loss of life. Shipping routes would be altered permanently, throwing off the balance of trade, send the cost of consumer goods through the roof and, no doubt, result in some sort of major reprisal or war by the USA and maybe China. Such an attack would surely derail the recently approved 5.5 billion-dollar, eight-year plan to double the capacity of the Canal.

There was a lot at stake.

Chapter Eleven

AFTER FOUR HOURS of continuous diving, Luke's legs felt like noodles. With the current picking up, he barely had the strength to maintain a steady position over the barrels. Using his last ounce of energy, Luke set a course with his mental compass back toward his entry point nearly a mile to the east. As he kicked hard to stay ahead of the current his mind raced with anticipation and fear.

Why am I doing this and what the hell and I going to tell Nici? This is starting to feel really stupid His mind was starting to doubt.

He switched to denial.

"Maybe it is an elaborate hoax. How could they be dumping such things right under the nose of such a heavily-guarded facility?"

Trying to keep his mind clear for the difficult task of evading capture, Luke let his mind play one his favorite songs; "Sweet Home Alabama," by Lynyrd Skynyrd.

Now just 20 yards from the riverbank, Luke could see a Hummer motoring slowly near the fence he had scaled earlier. The Hummer stopped. Out stepped Capitán Gomez. Just five feet tall, he was young and ambitious. Gomez had a real hard on for working his way up the ranks by viciously pursuing any criminal activity in his patrol zone. Gomez approached the fence, knelt to investigate the footprints Luke had left, looked up and instinctively pulled out his pocked binoculars. Luke swam silent and low until he reached the thick mangroves. In three feet of water, he lay quietly watching, praying that the Hummer would drive away soon.

The tenacious Gomez continued to scope out the fence until he settled on the small bit of razor wire Luke had parted to slip through. The depression Luke had made when falling in the mud was the final clue Gomez needed to sound the alarm. Well concealed in the mangroves, Luke held steady as a general siren blared. More than a dozen military vehicles appeared and spread out to patrol the surrounding areas. Three river patrol boats zoomed past Luke's position and a helicopter hovered near by.

Gomez took charge of a dozen men, leading them along the Canal bank. Again, by instinct, like a bloodhound on the scent, Gomez stopped directly in front of Luke's hiding place. The soldiers hacked through the edges of the mangroves with machetes while Luke sat motionless just inches from their combat boots. As the soldiers slashed away, Gomez gave the order to go slower and not to miss anything.

Luke prepared himself to be caught. Then Capitán Gomez gave the order to stop, wait and listen. It was dead quiet. Gomez put his hand to his ears and looked intently at the mangrove. Luke suppressed panic. Several tense seconds crawled by when a large animal with rough skin slammed into Luke from behind. The crocodile surfaced just inches from Luke's face. The creature and the man locked eyes. Luke kept his cool while the croc sized him up with its hungry yellow eyes and their evil-looking horizontal slits. The croc was so close to Luke that he could smell its stinking reptilian breath.

Stuck between a rock and hard place. Luke had to choose between engaging the crocodile and dozens of Gomez's highly motivated soldiers waiting on the bank. Out of options, Luke slowly unsheathed his knife, pausing to take stock of the six sets of boots on one side of him and hovering croc on the other. Luke gripped his knife, inched over to the croc and threw his weight behind a swift, noiseless upward thrust. His small six-inch kill knife must have felt like a pinprick to the big croc. Luke held the knife firmly implanted into the crock's upper chest while he gripped the animal's mouth closed. As the beast threw him from side to side, the commotion gave his position away.

The croc dragged Luke offshore as the soldiers watched in amazement while the crock rolled Luke over and over again, pulling him down for ten seconds at a time. After a five-minute bucking bronco fight, Luke felt the animal acquiesce. Only then did he pull the knife out. The beast floated for several seconds before swimming dejectedly off into the murk.

Gomez grabbed a rifle from one of his soldiers, firing twenty shots into the air and another dozen into the ground, shattering Luke's momentary sense of elation over saving his own life.

"Venga, Venga!" (Come, come) Gomez shouted.

With nowhere to run, Luke made his way toward the men.

"Here we go again," he thought somberly.

Luke sat and removed his fins, eyeing his loaded spear gun that was sitting on the bank.

A shiny black Lincoln Town Car joined the jolly gathering. The helicopter hovered closer.

"Whop, Whop, Whop, Whop." The blades cut through the thick, humid air.

Out of the Town Car stepped Mr. Caucuss – the inquisitor of El Modelo and the same man who warned him that entering the restricted area would mean a one-way ticket to a concentration camp in Cuba.

Caucuss removed his glasses and shot Luke a withering look.

"I'm screwed. Run!" burst in Luke's head as his body switched into fight or flight mode. He dropped his weight belt and fins then lunged for his spear gun. The soldiers scrambled and shot wildly in Luke's direction. Luke rolled under the nearest Hummer. After two revolutions, he found himself under an open driver's door of a running armored Hummer. Luke threw his gun in the back, scrambled in and floored the pedal.

"Sorry!" Luke yelled as he careened past two soldiers who were in the process of taking aim.

"Tiren!" (Fire!) Gomez screamed. The troops opened fire on the Hummer. The helicopter gave chase, firing its 50-caliber anti-tank Vulcan cannon directly into the fleeing vehicle. Several rounds penetrated the hood, wiping out the radiator.

Steam erupted form the hood as Luke's visibility dropped to near zero.

Luke smashed through the security fence as the other Hummers and chopper struggled to keep up. Driven by a mania for survival, Luke careened around street corners at 40 miles an hour, crossed red-light intersections and narrowly missing a dozen people in the crosswalk. He stayed ahead of his pursuers but as he entered the rough Chorillo neighborhood, Luke's radiator gave out.

With a sputter, the mighty Hummer came to a stop. Luke Dodge grabbed his spear gun, exited the Hummer and ran flat-out. Still in his wetsuit, it was not long before the 100-degree heat took its toll of the badly dehydrated young man. The fine custom spear gun that was so elegant in the water was awkward dead weight on the run, all 17 pounds of it.

"Hola, necessitas ayuda?" (Hi, do you need help?) asked a man who stepped into his path.

Thinking he was hallucinating, Luke continued stumbling into nowhere.

"Hey gringo, I think you better get in." A silver-haired man driving beside Luke in a Toyota Land Cruiser was speaking.

The chopper had spotted Luke and had called in the other troops. Moments later, a convoy of reinforcements closed in on Luke and the Toyota.

"Looks like you really pissed these guys off. I think you better get in," the man said as he opened the passenger side door.

Unable to form a sentence, Luke looked at the smiling man and glanced at the back seat, on which was lying several spear guns.

Luke took one more look at the approaching military and jumped into the SUV.

"Hi, my name is Hernan. You better hold on."

"Uhhhh…aahhhhh" was all that came out of Luke's parched mouth.

Hernan performed an act of miracle driving unlike Luke had ever seen. As he sped through the poor neighborhood, Hernan smiled and laughed as if the pursuit was some sort of game. He had a strange ease about him.

Hernan was no stranger to outrunning the military, Luke was to learn. The bullethole scar on his leg bore testimony to his days as an anti-Noriega rebel. Now at age 65, Hernan still knew all the best escape routes in town. Hernan put some distance between their car and the military. His slick driving and intimate knowledge of the area paid off. Hernan pulled into a ramshackle building that had been set up as an anti-Noriega safe house 20 years earlier. Out of fear of a new dictator repeating the same inhumane methods as Noriega, Hernan had personally kept the safe house in operation. The house had the façade of a normal slum dwelling, but the double doors in front opened enough to allow a car to enter.

"Welcome to my humble abode, well, my second home," Hernan said in near perfect English as he exited the car.

"After Noriega went to jail, I kept this place going in case we ever needed to take back our country again. But really, we use it as a club house. So far, the wives have not been able to find it, ha, ha. ha. Shhh, I hear them coming. Quick, downstairs."

The Panamá defense scoured the surrounding area for over an hour before letting up and moving on.

Hernan's downstairs dwelling was a veritable fraternity party replete with a full size nude wall hangings of Pamela Anderson, a pool table, a full bar, a 52-inch plasma TV and of course a humidor fully stocked with the best Cuban cigars.

"What did you say your name was, and what the hell were you running from?" Hernan inquired as he took his time lighting a foot-long Churchill.

"The name is Luke, Luke Dodge. Lemmi pull this wetsuit off."

Luke removed his suit, unloaded his gun and gulped a full liter of water.

"Ah, that's better. Well, seeing how you risked your life for a perfect stranger, a gringo at that, I think I can tell you what the deal is. If I do, you will be the only other person on the face of the earth to know the truth."

Hernan's face flushed with interest.

"Tell me boy, what is it?"

"In short, some Arabs are planning to blow up the Canal using SEMTEX and radioactive waste. Enough to throw a toxic cloud for a 20-mile radius. I know. I saw it with my own two eyes."

"Why don't you just tell the authorities?" Hernan asked.

"I was caught robalo diving in the Canal a month ago, thrown in jail overnight and warned by my Homeland Security, if they ever caught me in the restricted zone again I would be listed as an enemy combatant and sent without bail, trial or due process to Guantanamo Bay, Cuba… maybe for life. I told HS about what I saw, but they did a funny thing, they blew off the threat as fish story. They still decided that I was a threat. I saw a super yacht from Dubai dump the barrels, I knew I had to check it out and … well here I am. I never thanked you for saving my life, so thanks. Why did you do it?"

"I saw your spear gun, your wet suit and the army chasing you so I figured it must be a misunderstanding. Plus; old habits die hard. I still love to taunt those fuckers. Here, check out my quiver of guns. Made them myself."

Hernan led Luke over to the rack on the wall holding three spear guns. He held them up one by one and described the aspects of each and told stories about some of the amazing fish he had speared in the Pacific and the Caribbean.

"We started back in the 1950's when there were just five or six guys diving in the whole country. We started the whole thing. Do you see the detachable spearhead? We invented that for the 1000-pound grouper we have here. This small gun here, I have had for 30 years. I shot a massive pargo in the Pearl Islands with it- maybe 140 pounds. When I went down to free the fish from the rocks, a 20- foot tiger shark swam between the pargo and me. The shark just kept coming and coming, slow and steady inches from my mask. It was the only time I have ever felt beads of sweat inside my mask."

Hernan held up Luke's gun.

"Wow, nice shape and great balance," he said with admiration.

"Thanks. My buddy Scott back in the states made it for me. I was not going to leave that bad boy behind."

Luke felt as lucky as privileged; to be alive and in the company of a freedom fighter and one of the first freedive spearfishermen in Panamá.

"Luke, we need to decide what to do with you. Eventually, they will come here, so we cannot stay long. I have a house on the Caribbean, near the border of a large Indian reservation called the Kuna Yala. If I can get you there undetected you might be safe for a while. But at some point, you will have to face the music. We leave at dawn."

That night Luke and Hernan stayed up sharing dive stories and drinking Chivas Regal blue label whisky and puffing on cigars.

"Noriega's men grabbed me one time when I was coming back from diving, just like what happened to you. They knew I was against them so they shot me in the leg, and then loaded three bullets into a six-shooter revolver and played black roulette with me until I promised to give up my efforts. I had to sleep with an Uzi under my bed sheet while I recovered in the hospital." Hernan went on telling stories for hours.

As first light peeked through the ceiling boards, Hernan and Luke woke, yawned and stretched. Hernan peeked out the door before backing into the street. The two men, nearly 35 years apart in age, headed off with chuckles and laughs the likes of which Luke had not enjoyed since he successfully robbed and sold hundreds of pounds of lobsters from poacher's traps more than a decade prior. Luke hid under bed sheets as the car made its way through town and then onto the road that transected Panamá leading to the Caribbean coast.

"Are we there yet?"

"It'll be a while Luke, sit tight."

After three hours of potholes and near misses with Mack trucks the duo reached the coastal town of Portobello.

For 400 years, Portobello had remained the stronghold and main disembarkation point for Spanish galleons laden with gold, silver and emeralds from the New World. The ruins of the moss-covered citadels and fortifications stood vigil over the once heavily contested, picturesque turquoise bay.

Protective walls were built and dozens of cannons were put in place to protect the royal gold from such famous pirates as Sir Francis Drake and Captain Henry Morgan. With the demise of the Spanish empire, Portobello was eventually abandoned, leaving a few former slaves, pirates and Indians to make it their home.

On this day, the usually sleepy town was full of Panamánians. Most of them had walked more than 22 miles, some of them on their knees, to reach the church that housed the "Christo Negro," or Black Christ. Once they served their penance from the grueling walk in the midday sun, they would parade the beautiful effigy of the Black Christ around town. The day's events culminated with everybody getting drunk and passing out in the bushes.

"You see these guys, Luke? They are mostly criminals. They do this walk once a year in the hopes of redeeming all their criminal acts for the year. So, it is good we came today because the police are too busy busting them. They will not be looking for us, I hope."

They approached a police roadblock.

"Luke, just stay cool. Play dumb. Do not speak Spanish to them. Say you are on vacation and you lost your ID. There is a gun under the seat just in case."

A stern-faced policeman approached.

"IDs, *por favor.*"

"Just on vacation," Luke said with a feigned smile.

Hernan showed the cop his ID and slid $20 along with it. The cop took Hernan's ID back to his motorcycle, pretended to write something down then returned the ID, less the cash.

"Passe." (go ahead). The guard waved them on.

"That was a close one." Luke said.

"Yes, I love it the most. Now we go to my place."

Hernan loved the close shaves.

After two more hours of negotiating the worst road in Panamá, Luke and Hernan passed through the village the of Nombre de Dios (name of God). Hernan explained that the town was the site of a verified miracle a century ago. Finally, they turned left onto a skinny dirt road that cut through dense rain forest. The road made a few switch-back turns until it terminated at Hernan's place.

The home sat on its own private lagoon that filled with fish during the Sardiná run. He called the place Leticia's Aquarium. Leticia, Hernan's wife and, back in the day, a fellow revolutionary, loved to watch the fish in the lagoon, hence its name. Hernan's land sprawled for nearly a mile, giving them absolute refuge for the time being.

Hernan proudly showed off his boat, a fast 27-foot fiberglass panga with Twin 115 HP Mercury outboards.

"Let's take a rest. Tomorrow we can go out in the boat, there are some good reefs here just offshore, tuna, wahoo…"

Luke was amused that Hernan, a man who had risked everything to save the skin of stranger, was more interested in spearing fish than worrying about hiding out. It was as if he knew that no harm would come to them. Maybe he had connections that would ensure their safety or maybe he had lived life on the edge for so long that it just felt natural to him. Either way Luke counted his blessings.

While Hernan slept, Luke found a pen and paper and wrote a note to Nici.

"Babe, well if you have this note it means Hernan has found you. He is a good man who saved my life, so I want you to make him a big dinner with your special chicken dish. I

cannot tell you what I found when I was diving as it would put you in danger. But please trust in me that I am doing what I have to do to be free. It seems like we never stop fighting to be free. I may be gone for a while and I cannot tell you much about where I am or where I am going, only that I love you from the bottom of my heart and I promise to return home as soon as I can. Please hug the dog for me and tell everybody I just went fishing for a while, no need to make people panic. Stay strong and I will come home soon.

We will finally tie the knot when I get back.

Forever in love with you,

Luke.

"Luke, hey, if you dive on the far side of the lagoon after dark you'll find lobsters. Maybe you can catch some for dinner," Hernan said as he awoke from a short nap.

As soon as it started to get dark, Luke swam to the far side of the lagoon. In stark contrast to the Pacific, the water was so clear it looked like pure air. An octopus exited its hole, elongated its head and shifted electric color patterns as it eyed Luke. As much as Luke loved to eat Octopus *ceviche*, this enigmatic creature was simply too beautiful to kill. Just over the next set of coral-covered rocks sat a Caribbean spiny lobster. Luke learned quickly that this animal had much nastier, sharper spines covering its body and antennae than its California lobster cousin.

Luke's thin glove was no match for the hardened spines. Grabbing the lobster as it kicked, the creature's spines pierced the glove, planting two puncture wounds in his index finger. As Luke jerked from the pain he backed up into a purple sea urchin that was clinging to a rock. Also, a cousin of the California sea urchin, this prickly pear had über-long spines that moved in unison, tracking the motion of anything that hovered near it. It also had the ability to eject its spines and deliver a non-lethal but blindingly painful dose of venom.

The urchin shot ten needle-sharp, brittle spines into Luke's left shoulder. The pain forced a girly scream from Luke's lungs.

That embarrassment over, Luke stuffed the pain and persisted in his quest, bagging three more decent lobsters before heading in.

"Hey, show me the lobster pot," Luke called to Hernan as he entered the house. He boiled the hapless bugs and seared the juicy, tender meat in a frying pan with butter and some greens Hernan had on hand. Luke liked to cook lobster with celery, but it was not always available. Hernan rustled up the rice.

After dinner and a companionable drink and cigar, Luke fell into bed, passing out before he hit his pillow. The next morning, Luke awoke to the noise of cranking outboard motors. He looked out his window to see Hernan test-starting his twin engines as the boat lay at anchor in the crystal lagoon. Luke saw the name on the transom: "Popoocho."
meaning old granddaddy.

"Get up Luke, *andale* –we have fish to kill."

"Man, this guy has a lot of energy," Luke thought.

Luke waded out to the boat.

"What is "Popoocho?"

"Old granddaddy."

"Is that you?"

"That's me. I am the granddaddy of a big wild family. Okay -- *vamanos!*"

Hernan laid into the throttles, bringing the long narrow boat up onto a plane.

"Where are we going?" Luke asked.

"First, we have some fish to spear at a wreck I have been diving for decades. I figured it is best to keep you on the move so I have some friends I am going to hand you off to."

Luke was treated to a rare vista of miles of virgin beaches abutting rain and palm tree forests.

"We are entering the Kuna Yala," Hernan said. "It is an entire state that belongs only to the Kuna Indiana since they won their independence in 1921. They originally lived in the mountains bordering Colombia, but war and treaties pushed them to the coast. They had to re-learn life as lobster divers, coco harvesters and now eco-tourism. They are good people and have a healthy distrust of the government so I think you will be safe there for a while. Anyway let's get some fish."

Hernan pulled up to the single most post-card perfect islet in the world. Just three feet above sea level, "Dog Island" was just one of the 365 white sand-ringed islands that make up the unique San Blas archipelago, a geologic phenomenon that stretches two hundred miles and ends near the Columbia border.

The mast of the wreck protruded several feet above the small lapping waves.

"This wreck, I forget the name, has a special place in history," Hernan said. "In 1958, a Panamánian man named of Juan Guzman recruited 40 Cubans to try to launch an amphibious attack here in Panamá. Emboldened by Castro's recent takeover of Cuba, they figured they could do the same in Panamá. Instead of launching a glorious revolution, they wrecked here on the reef and they were all shot or arrested within hours of landing here. The Panamánians, with the help of the CIA knew they were coming. It was their very own *Bahia de los Cochinos* (Bay of Pigs) but not many people know this. "

Hernan continued, "Today it's a good place to dive. Go down -- there is little hole near the wreck's port stern, put your body all the way inside, wait, be patient and a big snapper or grouper will come to see who has intruded on his home. Then you can give him the news, olé!"

Hernan punctuated his speech with a flurry of Flamenco steps and a loud, "*olé!*"

"I hope I still love life like you do when I am your age," Luke shouted as he rolled back into the water.

Luke was happy to see that the water shone an amazing, crystal clear 100-foot visibility. He gazed at the entire outline of the wreck, the 80-foot tramp steamer that had been broken into two parts by the elements over the past six decades. Luke made an initial dive, swimming along the gunnels of the vessel using mono fin strokes and thrusting his body like a dolphin. He tried to imagine the vision of the ship's doomed leader, the hopes of his comrades and the chaos that must have ensued when the ship foundered.

Luke made for the surface 30-feet above. As he rested, he thought about the men who had manned the ship that now rested in deteriorating hunks on the bottom of the peaceful bay.

They must have been true believers and really loved the Communist ideal. Or maybe they wanted the Canal....

He took ten deep breaths before descending to the small hole Hernan had described. Luke found the opening and stuffed his body into the aperture. With dim light Luke could see the myriad snappers of various species and sizes but nothing worth shooting at. Just as he readied himself to emerge from the hole, a red snapper zoomed into sight and charged toward Luke. The fish stopped a foot from Luke, flared his gills and showed its teeth.

"This is my hole, get out!" the snapper told him.

"This is my spear gun and I need to eat tonight. So sorry."

He then took aim and let the arrow fly, scoring a perfect head shot that stopped the fish cold. He grabbed the 30-pound snapper by the eyes and headed towards the surface.

In the distance, he saw Hernan struggling with something. Luke strung up his fish and jetted over.

"Luke, *mira, un grande*."

Luke dove down to find that Hernan's shooting line had disappeared into the rocks. Luke stuck his head into the hole and saw the white eyes of a large grouper that looked to be more than 200 pounds. Luke kicked to the surface.

"Shit, Hernan, that is a big fish. I'll zap him in the head."

"After you do, close his gills so you can get him free from the hole."

Luke loaded his gun and took a deep breath. He came eye to eye with the grouper. Before he pulled the trigger, he said to the fish, "Mero, I am sorry I have to take you now. You have been a good guardian of this wreck, but I am sure you have many niños that will watch over it. Anyway, the man who shot you is older than you, so it's okay."

With that, Luke pulled off, killing the fish instantly. Just as Hernan advised, Luke closed the fish's gills, pulled out its fat body and headed up.

"Aye, chihuaua!" Hernan exclaimed. "I have not shot one of those for a while, we call it a few fish or *mero*. The meat is so full of flavor. I love it so much. So does my wife!!"

With plenty to eat and a great experience under their belts, the two new friends swam back to Papoocho.

They ate a quick lunch of crackers dipped into garlic tuna, pulled anchor and set off into the freshening wind.

Chapter Twelve

NEARLY AN HOUR passed in companionable silence. As they ran into the wind, Luke studied the vacant coastline, the countless islets and the intent look on Hernan's face. Motoring with no modern electronics, Luke was unsure what they would find or what they were looking for. Trusting Hernan so far had been a good bet for Luke so he decided to trust him blindly some more, wherever that took him.

"Look, big shark! The Chinese have not yet cleaned these waters of them. Maybe they try to eat you or me, but they are the cleaners of the sea and deserve to live," cried Hernan, pointing to the angled dorsal fin of a large Hammerhead off the port bow.

A pod of spinner dolphins zoomed in to ride the bow wake. "Luke, whistle, loud!"

Luke stuck two fingers in his mouth in a "V," uncorking his loudest whistle. Several dolphins broke the surface like cruise missiles.

"Look at them spin, like tops," Luke shouted as the dolphins spun in the air for the shear joy of it. The dolphins sped off, disappearing into the blue as fast as they came.

"Lucky guys," Luke said as he waved good bye to his pinniped pals.

Hernan pulled back on the throttles as they neared an island. It appeared to be inhabited and connected to the mainland by a small footbridge.

"This is Plyon Chico, Luke. It is a stronghold of the Kuna People. They live here in a mostly traditional manner. They really have held onto their native ways. The Kuna love their land and appreciate all that nature gives them. You see, the government has tried to eliminate them -- all of them -- several times. Each time they fought back and won.

The Kuna are old allies of mine. During Noriega's time, I had to hide out here a couple of times. They took me in, hid me, fed me and befriended me – and asked nothing for themselves. They are some the world's last true human beings. Now that I have some political influence back in Panamá, I go to meetings and argue on their behalf, make sure nobody tries to step on them."

Hernan pulled up to a small makeshift dock. Already several Kuna stood waiting ashore with smiles and open arms. Hernan tossed an older man the bow line.

"Hola, Morgan, mi amigo," Hernan said with reverence.

Morgan was a local tribal leader whose height was, at most, four feet, six inches. He had wide, splayed, shoeless feet and a square build. He had a humble looking, dark brown face that one might mistake for Mongolian in a different setting. Morgan wore cut off Levi shorts and no shirt. Hernan towered over the Indian.

To Luke's surprise Hernan spoke fluent Kuna. It sounded like a sing-song noise with no discernable individual words and always ended in an up note. Kuna was faintly reminiscent of modern day Korean. The Kuna language had no alphabet and was not written down until the late 1950's when American anthropologists came to study the tribes.

Hernan and Morgan shook hands, warmly hugged and spoke for about five minutes before turning to Luke. Hernan, Luke surmised, had explained to Morgan that Luke needed to lay low for a while and asked if he could stay with the Kuna. Morgan studied Luke for a full five minutes, before saying with a smile, "Yes, of course."

Luke was officially introduced to Morgan and several other tribal elders. The commotion of the meeting was drawing the attention of the children and women of the tribe. Morgan turned to his people and announced with brevity that the man to his right was a friend of Hernan's and would be treated as family if he desired to stay. Morgan gently grabbed Luke by wrist and motioned for him to walk with him for a tour of the village.

The village of Playon Chico occupied 99% of the small island on which it sat. The tribal elders led Luke down the main dirt road. All the habitations were made of split bamboo and palm fronds. The only structures made of cement were the three churches and a Mormon temple. A recent invasion of competing missionaries from Catholics to Presbyterians to Mormons had left the Kuna confused and at times at odds over certain fundamental beliefs. To counter this, the Kunas had set weekly council meetings that all Kunas were required to attend. Among other things, they were reminded that above all, they were Kunas and any new beliefs must be second to their traditional belief system.

The Kunas took great pride in introducing Luke to every one of the 220 Kuna on the island. He was taken into more than twenty small homes and asked to drink tea in each of them. The Kunas loved to keep pets; parrots, monkeys, cats and dogs roamed every corner of the island. The cats and dogs seemed to get along and be the best of friends.

"Luke, it's getting dark. I need to get back. After dark, many Colombian drug boats run through these waters." Hernan said.

With smiles and hugs, Hernan said his good byes to Morgan and the other villagers. As Hernan was untying his boat Luke thought of what to say. Hernan brought along a spare set of dive gear. "Luke, you look a little light on gear, grab what you need." Hernan said.

In his great escape, Luke had dumped the heavy stuff and was glad to borrow a weight belt, fins, mask, snorkel and most of all, a 55-inch teak and mahogany spear gun with a reel on it. 15 years earlier, Hernan had spent two months making the gun by hand. As Luke studied the gun, Hernan chimed in," She has taken many big Jew fish (groupers). One was nearly 900 pounds."

"Hernan, I will never forget your kindness. Thank you."

With a smile and a wave, Hernan brought his boat up onto a plane and headed off into the sinking sun. Luke and the tribe watched until the small boat sank into the horizon.

The Kuna made their living primarily from lobsters. They sold their catch to a Jewish guy who flew down in his bright red, twin prop private plane each week to collect the live animals for export to the U.S. They also harvested coconuts that they sold to Columbian collecting vessels. Luke did not speak a word of Kuna, so he had to rely on his broken Spanish and Morgan's broken English. This made communication tough, as the Kunas also had limited Spanish skills.

Luke showed Morgan his dive gear.

"Enorme," (Huge) Morgan said with admiration as he held up and caressed Luke's gun.

Luke showed him a dive light that he had been borrowed from Hernan.

"Para la noche." (For the night) Luke said.

Luke asked if he could tag along on a lobster hunt the next day.

"*Sí,* " Morgan said. "Okay, Senor Luke. *Con gusto.*"

Morgan took Luke to the dwelling that would be his home for the next few weeks. – a communal home that housed several families. The elder instructed a woman to string up a hammock in a prime spot near the back.

The Kuna women lived topless and adorned their bodies with beads and fancy printed garments called *molas*. The girls were not given names until their thirteenth birthdays. The Kuna society tolerated a high level of promiscuity. They shared everything, food, clothes, diving gear and sometimes each other. In the old days, marriage existed but the idea of keeping a mate all to yourself was seen as act of selfishness and frowned upon. A recent influx of missionaries steered the Kuna towards a more monogamous, Catholic existence.

Luke watched as the children played around the fire and the old ladies roasted maize. His thoughts turned to Nici and her well-being. He concentrated on sending a message telepathically.

"Don't worry. I will be home soon, babe."

The roosters started crowing at 3:00 a.m. Just one or two at first, then every rooster on the island joined the chorus.

"RRRRRRR. Okay, fucking rooster! I'm awake!"

. Blasted awake, Luke walked outside and was surprised to see the Kuna readying their canoes for a day's lobster diving.

"*Buenos días*, Luke!" Morgan greeted him with a big smile.

Luke grabbed his gear and gingerly boarded the tippy canoe. He was fortunate to be on the chief's boat which was outfitted with an outboard engine. All the other canoes were powered by traditional-looking single sails. Luke recollected the fantasies he'd had as young man in which he would travel back in time to fish and dive with the native Chumash Indians in his original home of Malibu California. This was as close to that dream that Luke had ever been. The feeling of excitement in his belly made him forget all about the fact that the U.S. government was full-throttle after him, plus the possibility that some terrorist gang had intercepted his APB. He really had no idea how bad it actually was. But, so far in the little canoe on the little island everything seemed ironically tranquil.

Morgan pulled the engine rip cord. The 45-foot canoe, which had been sculpted from a single ancient hardwood tree was holding Morgan, Luke and three of Morgan's cousins. They chugged off into the gray of early dawn. After a two-hour run the canoe magically found its mark. A seamount rose from 2,000 feet below. The spot they were on was a circle of reef that arose about three feet out of the water, forming a crystal clear, coral-filled lagoon, 200-feet in diameter. Land was 25 miles toward the northeast and had dropped from sight 20 minutes earlier.

The isolation and distance from land had little effect on Morgan and his crew. One by one, the Kuna donned crude lobster diving gear – an old-style plate glass rounded mask made with a hard rubber skirt, a homemade snorkel with no purge valve, a wire noose used to snag unwitting lobster and short stubby fins.

Luke figured they would be diving inside the shallows of the lagoon and was surprised to see the first Kuna roll over the canoe while still on outer edge of the reef. The man named Dulup (meaning "lobster" in the Kuna) began to hyperventilate heavily through his snorkel. After sucking in deep breaths and fully exhaling for more than three minutes, Dulup turned and dove off the canoe. The long boat rolled side to side but had enough mass to prevent capsizing.

Dulup sank out of sight. After several minutes, Luke grew concerned. He packed his lungs with air, flipped into the water and kicked towards the bottom. Nearing 80 feet, Luke could see Dulup working 20 feet below him, snagging and stringing up lobster like he was going for a walk in the park. Dulip gingerly placed the wire loop of his homemade lobster grabber around the midsection of each lobster, then cinched it tight, giving the lobster no way out.

Luke could not believe Dulup's lung capacity and his ability to stay down for so long. Luke, already starving for air, made his way to the surface. Luke did his best to keep up with the Kunas, but their extraordinary ability to stay down was simply outpacing Luke. The Kunas were the best natural breath-hold divers he had ever seen. They dove to excessive depths all day with the grace and ease of marine mammals. Not bad for a people who had, 100 years earlier, occupied the highest mountains of Colombia. Luke set off to explore the lagoon. With the swell up to six feet, he had to guard against being slammed against the jagged rocks as he entered the lagoon. He was treated to the rare sight of coral reefs bearing no signs of human impact. The staghorn coral stood five feet off the bottom and spread out for acres. The zig-zag patterned brain coral accented the massive table top coral and purple sea fans waved in the gentle surge. The reflection off the glistening white sand on the bottom was so bright that it hurt Luke's eyes. He bagged a few lobsters, but the Kunas were doing much better in the deeper water. Luke was never one to be out-dove so he swam back to the canoe, slid over the rail and asked Morgan if he could take a rest. The bottom of the canoe was filling with clicking three- to five-pound lobsters.

Luke dug around for his dive light, then clicked it on to show Morgan. He asked in polite Spanish if they could stay until after dark so he could have a try at the lobsters in the night.

"Sí, pero hay muchos tiburones grandes en la noche," (Many large sharks in the night), Morgan warned.

"They don't like the way gringos taste. Too salty," Luke plugged back.

Luke spent the remainder of the day shading himself from the scorching tropical sun and watching as the Kunas made dive after dive, all deeper than 90 feet, coming up with at least one lobster each time. With each ascent, Morgan would look intently at his fellow Kuna, awaiting a report. As the divers announced their catch -- "One!" Two!" "Three!" or even "Four!"- Morgan, the divers and whoever was resting in the boat would let out yelps of joy as if it were the first lobster they had ever seen. Each lobster meant additional money and sustenance for the diver's families.

The gentle afternoon wind kicked up as the sun disappeared into the Caribbean Sea amidst a backdrop of purples, pinks, reds and yellows. As Luke had always done in California he suited up again, said a quick prayer and entered the water about 20 minutes before absolute black. He started by making a few dives on the outer edge of the barrier reef. He was pleased to see that a small school of decent-sized pargos were out hunting. Luke loaded just one of the three bands on his gun, closed the gap and shot a 30-pound Pargo behind the gills. Aware that shark could be near, Luke put on the brakes, stopping the fish in its tracks. As he kicked toward the surface with his catch a gray form appeared off to his left.

"Uh oh, the landlord is here," Luke said to himself.

He broke the surface and tried his best to pull the fish up before the 15-foot Bull shark could make quick work of his wriggling dinner.

"Tiburon abajo!" (shark below) Luke screamed as the Kunas looked on.

With no moon, the sky had gone ink black. Luke dare not bring the fish close to his body as the shark might enjoy a gringo and fish sandwich. Luke handed his gun up to Morgan and motioned for him to haul in the pargo. The bull shark made its move. With lightning speed, the shark swooped in and snatched the pargo from the spear shaft. The violent motion jerked the gun from Morgan's grasp. Luke dove fast and deep to try and save his gun before it sank into the depths. He caught up with the sinking gun 50 feet below. He grabbed the wooden stock as the Bull shark zoomed in. Using the mahogany butt of the gun, Luke batted the inquisitive beast away with a smash to the nose. It backed off.

Luke kicked his way to the surface, climbed into the boat, stealing a glance at Morgan. He and the other Kuna were too polite to say, "I told you so," but their bemused faces said it anyway.

Luke asked to be dropped in the center of the protected inner coral reef where the *tiburon* would not be lurking. Luke collected himself and the rolled off the side. The beautiful coral he had seen during the day was even more electric during the night. The various species of coral had extended their nocturnal polyps to feed. Several fat grouper poked their fat heads from their holes to check on Luke. He saw them but decided he had learned his lesson and spearfishing in the Caribbean so far from shore at night might be a bad idea. Luke swam for ten minutes and spun around in the water to locate the canoe. He saw nothing but a star-filled black sky and the purple phosphorescence of the breaking surf. Luke did not stand a chance at survival should he lose track of his ride home. A dark colored canoe with no lights in the black night was a needle in a hay stack.

"Morgan! Where are you! Morgan!" he shouted as he prepared to make a sweep with his dive light.

"Estoy aquí, Luke." (I am here, Luke) came the firm reply.

The canoe was just feet from Luke but was completely concealed by the darkness.

Luke came across a line of lobsters walking in the sand. Marching as if on a mission, the line of more than 20 lobsters were easy picking for Luke. He swooped down and grabbed them, throwing them in the canoe one by one. The Kuna crew celebrated as the individual lobsters plopped into the writhing mass at the bottom of the boat.

Happy that he could add to the Kuna's bounty, Luke pressed on looking for more. A large red crab came into view. He closed in to see that he had found a species of warm water King crab known as centollo. He figured his best was strategy the old, "grab it by the ass" technique. He launched his arm at the ten-pound crab. The crab, to which nature had given lightning-fast reflexes, countered by using its massive pincers that looked like they could crack a coconut and for sure break Luke's wrist or finger. Luke saw the incoming claws and backed up.

"Congrejo grande,." (big crab) Luke shouted toward the canoe.

"Cuidado, Luke, el congrejo le gusta lucha." (Be careful Luke, the crabs like to fight).

Luke went down for a second try. This time he lunged straight for the crab's claws, grabbing both with all his strength. Luke was amazed at the animal's raw power. Luke struggled to keep the claws under control as he made his way back to the boat.

The Kuna let out an extra-excited set of catcalls as Luke rolled the monster crab into the boat.

Concluding he had adequately proved himself to his new Indian friends, Luke signed that he was ready to go home. Luke counted the day's bounty: 54 lobsters, one king crab and a lost pargo. Luke threw a victory fist upward and Morgan returned the   gesticulation.

Morgan fired up the small outboard. With no moon, no lights on the mainland as reference points, no compass or GPS, Morgan steered the canoe straight and fast toward home more than 30- miles to the east. Luke sat just two feet from Morgan. As the crisp pollution-free air filled Luke's lungs, he gazed up to the stars.

"Look there -- a satellite." Luke said in English.

Unsure what Luke was talking about, Morgan pointed out constellations, calling them by their Kuna names. Morgan explained they believe that all Kuna originated from outer space. They believe, he said, that three tall black women came to earth with a single child and that child was the first Kuna.

Luke thought it made as much sense as any other creation story.

"Sí verdad," (Yes, it's the truth) Luke replied reverently.

More than two hours later, Luke and his new friends touched shore in Playon Chico. Morgan oversaw his men put the live lobsters into underwater holding cages where they would stay until the lobster plane arrived to buy their catch. The crab, however, was on the menu that night. The Kunas boiled the animal in a steel drum over a blazing bonfire. When it was ready to eat, Morgan tore off a claw and presented it to Luke, while saying something in Kuna. Luke was not sure what it meant but by Morgan's smiles and the gift of the claw it may have been a big welcome to the tribe. Luke crunched the heavy shell of the claw with his teeth, exposing the meat, which he plucked from the exoskeleton and ate slowly with his fingers. He closed his eyes in gastronomic ecstacy.

"Ooh, ummmmm," came the groaning sounds of pleasure.

The delicate, sweet meat was the single most succulent, delectable morsel Luke had ever tasted from the sea.

The community meal became an evening of celebration. The women beat drums and the older men sang Kuna songs while dancing in place. The music and motion was hypnotic and primitive, bringing forth a vision of life at its purest.

Although, he had been with the Kuna only one day, Luke felt more at home and more familial with these people than at any time in his 32-year life.

The next morning Luke slept through the chorus of crowing chickens. The gaggle of children by his hammock pointing, laughing and poking at Luke finally woke him up. Luke responded with open arms and bear-like sounds, sending them smiling and running off onto the corner. Amazingly, Morgan and his crew had awakened at 2:00 a.m., had gone lobster diving, collected their catch and had already returned. Luke rubbed his eyes, put on his shirt and made his way to the beach to watch them unload. Morgan explained that they had to come in early because they were expecting the plane to come in by noon to buy the lobsters.

"Vuelo" (Flight), Morgan shouted as he pointed at the sky.

Luke held back his smile as he thought of the French little person named Tattoo from the TV show Fantasy Island who would always point and yell, "Zee plane! Zee plane!"

The double engine beach craft landed on a short, weed-lined airstrip. Luke kept his distance as he did not want to draw any attention his way. The Kunas rolled their prize lobster up to the plane in wheel barrows. One by one the pilot, a middle aged Jewish man wearing a yarmulke cap weighed the lobsters, wrote down the weights and loaded them into coolers for transport. After the final tally was taken, the pilot announced the amount to be paid. He handed the Kuna fishing line, dive gear and a small outboard engine. He deducted the supplies from the tally and paid the Kunas the balance in cash.

With six other Kuna villages to collect lobster from, the pilot wasted no time. He loaded back into the plane waved goodbye, taxied down the rough strip, rose and circled over the water.

Luke watched as the Kunas rejoiced over their new pile of cash. Until the mid 1990's the Kuna knew nothing of hard currency and traded only in coconuts. The idea of cold hard cash was still new to the Indians and was sure to have an intoxicating effect on them.

Morgan went to Luke, put his arm around him and threw him an ear-to-ear grin. The two walked through the part of the village that Luke had not yet seen. Luke was surprised to see this side of the village was home to a medical clinic and a small garrison of soldiers that were of 100% Kuna blood who enforced Kuna tribal law on Kuna lands. Their main purpose was to protect the tribe from the abundant drug traffickers in the region. They also had a proper school with solar energy panels and a basketball court. Next to the court was a small raised stage where the Kuna made public announcements and held the weekly congress of tribal affairs.

Luke dropped his water bottle as his jaw fell open. His gaze focused on the backdrop behind the stage. To the left was a painted profile of man who appeared to be Caucasian and to the right was a larger and more distinct image of a woman. In the center was a ten-feet by ten-foot swastika. This was not the Native American or Buddhist version the symbol. It was the real Nazi deal. Luke paused and collected his thoughts as he did not want to seem erratic and scare off his new friends. Being the son of a Jew, the symbol had deep meaning for Luke, so he chose his words carefully.

"Que pasó, el segño?" What is up with the sign? Luke asked.

Morgan explained that a man by the name of Richard Marz had come to the Kuna during a time in the 1930's when they were being wiped out by the Panamánian government. Mr. Marz came here with his wife, who was more motivated that he was, and showed us how to fight, how to organize and how to stay strong. The Marzes are our heroes, Morgan said, and the symbol in the middle is the symbol of revolution and justice.

What happened to the Marzes?"

"They returned to Germany and we never saw them again, but we remember their contribution," Morgan said reverently.

Luke pondered the situation. He resisted telling him the true meaning of the Nazi swastika. How could he tell them that their heroes were involved in killing six million Jews and many others and that they were responsible for the most calculated atrocities in history? Would they have any concept of what it all meant? What good would it do to tell them the truth?

These people had helped save the Kuna people and Kuna culture. The German couple might have come to Panamá fired with good intentions.

Luke recalled hearing about Hitler's plans to take over Panamá and seize control of the Canal. He figured that maybe the Marzes's job for the Nazis was to gain support from the Indians then using them to take control of the country. Either way, it was all ancient history. Luke simply said:

"Entinedo." (*I understand*)

C.F. Goldblatt

Chapter Thirteen

THREE DAYS HAD come and gone. Back in Panamá City, Nici was doing her best to ward off her growing worry. She had reported Luke missing to the local police but they simply filled out a report and asked her for twenty dollars. To keep her mind off her missing lover, she folded all of the clothes twice, smelling Luke's shirts as she handled the garments. She swept the terrace several times.

Nici put down her broom to answer the knocking at the door.

"Who is it?"

"Ruf, ruf ruf," Chewy barked.

"My name is Hernan. I am a friend of Luke's and I have some news."

Nici composed herself, then, to hide her anxiety opened the door slowly.

"Welcome to my home. Come in. Can I get you something to drink?"

"Agua, please."

Hernan took a seat on the wide terrace and looked out over the bay. Nici studied the man through her kitchen window as she poured him bottled water with ice and a twist of lime.

Nici gracefully presented the drink to Hernan and waited for him to speak.

"Nici, here is a letter from Luke. He is okay. For your safety and his I cannot tell you where he is or what he is running from. All I can say is that he is good hands and needs to lay low for a while."

Nici read the note with haste and laughed when she reached the end, disconcerting Hernan.

"What has my Luke got himself into this time? If there is a pebble blowing in the wind it will find his eye, my sweet Luke."

Her laughter turned into concern. "I must go to him. It will be okay. Let's go," Nici demanded.

Hernan restated firmly, "I am sorry, he must stay hidden for now. I will try to bring news when I can. Please destroy that note. If anybody comes here tell them that you do not know any Luke Dodge and that they have made a great mistake, do not mention my name either, por favor."

Hernan gulped his remaining water, thanked Nici for the hospitality and made his way towards the door. Nici spoke. "Are you sure you do not want some food? It says in the note that Luke wants me to make you my famous chicken Cordon Blue. It is really good. Please stay a while."

"Mrs. Nici, I am honored really, but I must take a rain check. I go way back with this government and if they knew I was here they would know right where to look for Luke. "

Hernan pulled his baseball cap low over his ears and put on dark sun glasses.

"*Via con dios,* Mrs Nici," (Go with God) Hernan said with a smile as he left the way he came.

"Wait! Will you tell me how to get hold of you?" Nici shouted as Hernan made his way down the flights of stairs.

"Lo siento," (*Sorry*) Hernan said. Before exiting the building, he looked both ways to be sure that he had not been spotted or followed.

Nici set the note aside. She knew that dwelling on the situation would not make things better. All she could do now was trust in Luke's ability to land on his feet and get himself out of whatever trouble he was in. Nici looked at her watch. She realized that she was late for her volunteer duties at the local Hospitál de los Niños.

Nici jumped into the way-too-large-for-the-narrow-streets Black Dodge Quad cab pickup truck that Luke had imported and headed off to the low-income children's hospital. She walked to the emergency room entrance as she slipped on her doctor's scrubs and name tag. She swung open the bay doors to behold a sight that she had not seen since her toughest days in the Sudan. In triage sat more than fifty sets of weeping hysterical parents all holding children foaming at the mouth, shaking and barely conscious.

Not knowing what to make of it, Nici asked the nurses if they had any details. The nurses replied that the children had taken the same bad batch of government-issued cold medicine. Nicky later learned that some unscrupulous person in the health ministry had mixed the cold medicine with Glycol. Glycol, commonly known as anti-freeze has a sweet taste, and causes kidney failure in the very young, the sick and the old.

Nici worked through the night and into the next day alongside her colleagues. They managed to stabilize most of the children but the three that were too far gone slipped away as Nici performed CPR. Hardened to useless deaths of innocents, Nici did her best not to let it get to her. Finally, she went outside to cry. She lit her first cigarette in more then ten months.

"Fucking, stupid drug companies, what were they thinking?"

With that, a tired Dr. Nici fired up the pickup truck and headed back to the flat. On the short drive home she fantasized that Luke would be waiting for her with open arms and a cooler full of fish.

No such luck.

Nici parked the truck, exited and stretched.

"*Hola,* Juan." She said to the doorman.

"*Mucho trabajo hoy?"* (A lot of work?) Juan inquired.

"Yes, too much."

Nici dragged herself up the flights of stairs while dreaming of a nice long bath and a slumber in her bed.

Nici entered her previously locked flat to find two men standing in her dining room reading the note from Luke. To the left was Mr. Caucuss. He was dressed neatly in his pressed navy-blue suit. To Nici's right was Gomez of the Panamá defense force. Wearing his army fatigues, shiny combat boots, Aviator glasses and sporting his mack-ten mini assault rifle, Gomez was an ominous -looking character.

Nici tried to be cool as Caucuss went into a brain twisting line of questioning.

"Mrs. Dodge, it says here."

"My last name is Zadravec and what the hell are you doing in my home?" Her stint at the hospital had worn her nerves paper thin.

"Calm down. My name is Caucuss. I work for the Homeland Security, anti-terror unit and this is Gomez. He heads a special forces unit charged with maintaining Canal security. Now, your friend Mr. Dodge is on our most wanted list and our records show that you have been his girlfriend for years."

"What list? What else do your records show?"

"It says here that you lied to a federal agent while attempting to illegally enter the USA via Canada, then were summarily deported. So, we have reason to believe that you would harbor a terrorist bent on hurting the US of A. So why don't you tell us what you know?"

"I don't know any Luke Dodge and you have made a big mistake…"

Caucuss then read aloud Luke's note that she had accidentally left on the coffee table.

"Look, Luke has done nothing wrong and I don't know where he is or what you think he has done but you have made a big mistake by coming here."

Gomez then cocked back his ring-covered right hand and back handed Nici across the face.

"Mentirosa!" (Liar!). *"Hija de puta"* (son of a bitch), Gomez yelled.

"All right, Gomez, calm down," Caucuss demanded.

Caucuss re-read the letter and focused on the small print at the bottom of the page.

"This letterhead belongs to somebody named Hernan Guzman," Caucuss said aloud.

"Guzman, did you say?" Gozman asked intently.

Gomez grabbed the paper, gave it a quick study then motioned to Caucuss that it was time to leave. Gomez rushed Caucuss out the door. With no further words, the men left quietly and with no apology for the intrusion or the assault.

"Shit! It was Hernan's letterhead," Nici realized. By the look in Gomez's face, he knew where to find Hernan or worse, Luke. Nici had to warn him.

Chapter Fourteen

LUKE WAS EARNING the respect of the Kunas. He began to forget his worldly troubles as he set out each day before dawn to help Morgan and the others harvest lobster. Luke's fast hands were adding significantly to the Kuna's take each day. Doing what he loved and contributing to the tribe's welfare made Luke happy as a clam. Luke could have assimilated easily into the Kuna way of life and stayed there forever. Each day he took a moment to reflect on the Chumash Indians that were decimated so long ago in California. With the Kuna, he was privileged to have a taste of a forgotten way of life. The days came and went while Nici plotted the best way to get word to Luke that he may have some unwanted company coming his way.

Nici hired a private detective to find Hernan. It is a challenge for anyone to keep secrets of identities and whereabouts in small Panamá. Within two hours of requesting a search, the PI hand-delivered Hernan's home address to Nici.

She hopped into her truck and headed off to the address she held in her hand. After an hour of driving in circles she relented and paid a taxi driver to show her the proper street. She had him stop a block short of Hernan's place so she could survey the situation. As she suspected, a Military Hummer was parked outside. Caucuss and Gomez had beaten her to the punch. Nici cautiously approached the home and squatted behind the front hedges. She could see Gomez yelling at Hernan, then pulling back his hand and belting him just like he had done to her. Working the good cop- bad cop routine Caucuss predictably intervened.

"I know you know where Dodge is! He is a threat to the Canal. If you do not help us you will be a traitor to Panamá," Gomez yelled and pointed in Spanish.

Cuacuss and Gomez issued Hernan an ultimatum. If he continued to hide Luke's hiding place, he and his wife would be brought up on charges and arrested. Frustrating their efforts, Hernan remained stoic and said nothing.

"You guys are going to have to do better than that. If that puta, Noriega, would not break, neither will I! Now get out," Hernan yelled back, raising a defiant fist.

"We will be watching you, Guzman," Caucuss said as he and Gomez headed for the car.

Nici waited until the Hummer was out of sight and made for   Hernan's   front   door. She banged loudly.

"Hurry let me in, let me in," she pleaded.

Hernan looked through the peep hole then opened the door. He was not happy.

"I told you not to look for me, but I understand why you came. I am strong, but they might come back and really apply some pressure to me or my wife, so we better make a plan. I think the best thing would be to get a message to Luke. He needs to move but we cannot know where because if we do, they will surely beat it out of us."

"What is the best move? And thank you from the bottom of my heart for helping my Luke."

"He has been hiding with the Kuna Indians in the Caribbean. Tomorrow, early, I will take my boat to the village and warn him. If you want, buy a back pack, put in a few things it and I will take it to him. It's too dangerous for you to come along. Plus, my wife would think I have mistress." Hernan never missed the opportunity to crack a joke. Nicky laughed.

Hernan then went for his gun locker, pulled out a 9mm pistol and a sub-machine gun, loaded clips for both of them and chambered rounds.

"Luke might need these," Hernan said.

Nici went off to the sporting goods store and bought a heavy-duty rucksack that she filled it with as many survival gizmos as she could find: Water proof matches, raincoat, Swiss army knife, water distiller, a small tent, energy bars and flares. Nici topped off the back pack with several homemade tuna sandwiches and a note that read simply.

> *"Luke,*
> *You are the love of my life. Do what you must, but stay alive and come back to me. I will wait as long as it takes- Love Nici"*

Nici dropped the overflowing rucksack with Hernan, thanked him again and headed back to her flat on the other side of town.

Hernan woke early and bee-lined it out of town. Watching his rear view the whole time, he sped through the dawn until he, once again, reached his home on the Caribbean. Hernan said a quick hello to the young Indian couple that took care of his home then launched his boat. He fired up his outboards and maxed out the throttles, bringing the boat up to a fast 34 knots. The glassy early morning water made travel easy and fast. In just under two hours Hernan neared Playon Chico. Hernan passed a canoe with several lobster divers aboard. He did a double take on the white, tall Indian in the middle.

"It's Luke," Hernan said aloud.

Hernan spun his boat around and pulled up alongside the canoe.

"Hola Luke, Hola Morgan." Hernan said. "We do not have much time. They are going to find out where you are very soon. Here, tie this line on. I will tow you in so we can get you going."

Luke did not argue. He tied the tow line to the bow.

"OK, hit it," Luke shouted.

The canoe looked unnatural, peeling through the water at 30 knots. The Indians laughed and smiled at the unusual feeling of speed.

At the village, Hernan hurriedly told Luke the situation and handed him the rucksack. He uncovered the guns and handed them to him. The Kunas all took a deep breath.

"Hernan, I really love it here. This is the best place I have ever been and these people are better than family. I will be okay here," Luke naively responded.

"Luke, you are very mistaken. These security people think you are some sort of terrorist. Now, I am going to ask Morgan to take you far, far away and not tell a soul, not even me. It is the only way you will be safe."

Hernan turned to Morgan and made his request. Luke knew the deal was sealed when Morgan grabbed Hernan's forearm and shook firmly.

"OK, Luke, it's a deal. Listen to me. Do not let these guys catch you for any reason. Also, there are Colombian drug trafficking rebels in the Darién rain forest, real banditos. Morgan will take you deep into the Darién. It is a truly wild place, the last frontier of virgin rain forest on the Panamá/Colombian border. She is beautiful with animals and plants never seen by human eyes. She harbors many secrets and dangers. So, keep your eyes open, shoot first and ask questions later. Do not get taken prisoner, for any reason, they have no mercy. You can thank me later. I must go."

Hernan jumped back into his boat and sped back up the coast. Based on Hernan's unusually high level of anxiety, Luke knew he had to take this seriously. Luke riffled around in the rucksack to find the note from Nici. He paused to think of her.

Morgan was giving his family hugs. He grabbed his bow and arrow, a machete and a small shoulder satchel. Luke made a quick round to thank his Indian brothers.

The man named Dulup approached Luke. In broken English, he asked for a favor. Luke thought, "Oh no, here it comes, the hustle."

Dulup produced $200 cash and put it into Luke's hand.

"Thank you for the diving lobster, for your journey," Dulup said.

Ashamed that he had misjudged Dulup as a beggar, Luke was taken aback by the gesture. The $200 was Luke's cut of the lobster sales. Luke was as grateful as he was surprised.

Luke put on a pair of shorts, tennis shoes and a T-shirt that Nici had packed in the rucksack, and just like that, Morgan and Luke headed over the small footbridge that met the trailhead at the base of the jungle-covered hills. Luke took one more look back at the idyllic village, waved good-bye and followed Morgan into the thick crackling jungle.

Chapter Fifteen

AFTER A FEW MINUTES, Luke felt the forest close in on him. Morgan ambled along with ease while Luke carefully chose each step. He paused to look back, but the thick forest clogged his view. Luke's legs were soon covered with insect bites. The repellent Nici had packed for him proved ineffective. The virgin rain forest they were trekking through was known to be home to malaria, yellow fever, dengue fever and several other mosquito-borne diseases-to-be-named-later, any one of which could kill a person with a compromised immune system. Luke slapped his neck and his legs incessantly.

Morgan, watching Luke behave like a bull with mad-cow disease, produced the foulest smelling herb Luke had ever taken a whiff of. The small reddish looking herb smelled like the mackerel that Luke had left in his car for two weeks while away on a fishing trip. Morgan motioned for Luke to eat a small piece. Reluctantly, Luke plugged his nose and sucked down the root. Luke smiled hopefully.

"Not so bad… No, wait… plah, plah, blaaah,"

Luke puked his guts up.

"Plah, plah."

The barfing went on for twenty minutes.

"Tome agua," (Drink water), Morgan said, handing him a bottle.

Luke sat, panting and drinking water.

"Nice herb."

"Otro," (other*)* Morgan said, handing Luke a white herb.

"You must be kidding," Luke choked out.

Luke resisted. Morgan insisted. Morgan won.

Reluctantly, Luke swallowed a small piece of the tasteless herb. To his delight no side effects ensued.

"No mas mosquitos," Morgan said with satisfaction.

Luke collected himself, gulped more water, stood up and gave Morgan the thumbs up. Luke took a few more steps and realized that he was overloaded with gear: Two guns, ammo, a 17-pound spear gun, dive gear, water and a rucksack. It was a heavy load hiking uphill in 97-degree heat with near 100 % humidity. Morgan saw Luke struggling with his gear and was kind enough to grab the spear gun and the dive gear. The lighter load allowed Luke to get back on his feet and keep moving.

An hour later, to Luke's absolute astonishment, not only did all the mosquito bites cease, the smaller "invisible" biting bugs called, *no-see-ums* also stopped their feast on Luke's flesh. He figured that the first, stinky herb was some sort of purging medicine meant to cleanse his system. The second herb must have been the active ingredient in the natural repellent that was now oozing from Luke's pores and fighting off the bugs better than any spray western science could produce.

"Luke, diré el inglés y usted dice el español. Aprendemos mejor aquel camino." (Luke, you speak Spanish and I will speak English. This way we both learn.)"

"Acuerdo," (Deal) Luke replied.

Morgan spoke and understood more English than he originally had let on. The missionaries- eager to mold his mind had taught him the basics of the language.

"Luke, look, watch, many good things in forest, all things are good things, just some good things bite," Morgan said, pointing in the trees and the soil. He pointed at specific things. Luke tried to focus but saw only more jungle. Luke figured the whole jungle ecosystem was like the giant kelp forests of California: eerie, thick and full of hidden life that only the trained eye could detect.

Luke understood Morgan's words to mean that all things, plants and animals in the forest had a use, but some could hurt you.

After marching for several hours, mostly uphill, the trail ended at the edge of a small creek. From here on out it would be dead reckoning through the seemingly impenetrable forest.

"We sit, rest," Morgan stated.

More than happy to obey, Luke dropped his heavy rucksack and plopped his overheated carcass into the cool flowing creek. Morgan also took the opportunity to cool off and fill his small goat-skin bladder with water. Luke refilled his three one-liter bottles and added several drops of iodine to protect against giardia.

Morgan spied something, then quietly let the stream wash him towards Luke.

"Quiet, look."

Morgan motioned to stay low while pointing off into nowhere.

Luke stayed low but saw nothing. Then, a big black cat materialized. In a crouched position it slowly approached the water's edge. Before drinking it turned its head toward Luke and Morgan. The enigmatic creature's deep yellow eyes with vertical slits momentarily fixed onto Luke. The Puma lapped water as if Luke and Morgan were not even there. Now sated, as if reveling in its supremacy over these two-legged creatures obviously out of their element, the cat backed up, curled into a ball and proceeded to lick its paws. It paused every so often to check on the humans floating in the creek. Knowing they could not stay there all day, Morgan made his move. Luke was startled when Morgan lunged out of the water and threw his arms high while emitting a piercing scream. The trick sent the cat scampering up a nearby tree. Luke and Morgan continued upstream while the cat glared at them from the branches.

Luke had no idea how long the trek would last or where they were going. When Luke asked Morgan how much further or details about their destination Morgan simply replied, *"Lejos."* (far)

With each hill, Luke fantasized about finding some sort of civilization around the bend; perhaps a cool blue swimming pool, margaritas and bikini-clad Hawaiian Tropic girls who had just flown in for the Ms. Rain Forest contest. As Luke and Morgan crested a particularly high hill, a breathtaking view of jungle stretched as far as the eye could see in every direction. The afternoon mist gathered around the tops of the tallest trees and sounds of tropical birds and mating calls of Jurassic-sized insects filled the air.

Luke looked at Morgan.

"Muy lejos!" (Very far)

Morgan smiled, then looked to the sky and smelled the air as if it would tell him the correct direction they needed to travel.

"This is going to take a while," Luke thought to himself as the reality his situation set in like the hook in a fish's mouth.

Morgan pointed in a direction which felt like west to Luke. With the setting sun in their faces the pair descended the grassy hill back into the thick of the primeval jungle.

Luke took notice of the little things first, like the ants that walked in single file lines stretching for a mile or more. Each ant carried a small piece of leaf to be taken to its mound to feed the queen or add to the fortification. Most of the leafy plants close to the forest floor bore scars from the ants' handywork. The ants marched and worked with the purpose and cooperation of a Chinese railroad construction crew.

Everything seemed to be oversized, from the hulking trees with ten-foot diameters to the bamboo that grew in clusters 30 feet wide and shot up more than 100 feet from the earth to the sky. As they walked, new groups of birds loudly announced the arrival of Luke and Morgan. The bird songs varied from the melodious to chirping to ear piercing squawking. Luke rubbed his eyes as he watched a leaf jump. On closer inspection, it was a small frog that had a perfect dried leaf color pattern, making it impossible to see unless it moved. The whole jungle was like that, full of unseen life that did not reveal itself until it flew, crawled, hopped, ran, slithered or swam.

The sense of being watched by thousands of pairs of eyes was palpable. Because of his novice, untrained jungle eye, Luke could see only the foliage.

The huge trees were not just trees. They were entire ecosystems with vines on top of vines swirling up and down the trunks, ending in a web-like base whose roots spanned the blood red soil for twenty feet in every direction.

The overhead canopy allowed scant sunlight to hit the forest floor. This had an insulating effect, making the air seem like hovering water. The canopy broke up the intermittent rain, keeping Luke and Morgan almost dry during the afternoon showers.

Luke and Morgan marched along what could be either a foot trail or an animal pathway. The trail, which zig-zagged back and forth across a small creek, could have been made by other Indians, animals or more frightening; another group of people altogether...

The palm trees grew in groups of three and four. They bore clusters of bright red berries that Morgan took the opportunity to harvest. The palm fronds stretched thirty feet in every direction giving the forest a pre-historic Jurassic-like feel. Luke laughed as he recollected the jungle ride at Disneyland he had enjoyed as a kid.

Hanging on every branch, every leaf, every twig and in each divot of soil that Luke kicked up was some kind of life. Luke felt as if he were walking through the lungs of the planet. The forest seemed to breathe in and out. It was a single dwelling, living thriving organism.

Luke poked at each pile of dried leaves before crossing it. He checked for the infamous Fleur-de-lance, a well-camouflaged, highly venomous brush snake what was responsible for hundreds of deaths each year.

Luke let his instincts take over. He tried to connect with the jungle in the same way that he connected with the sea.

"Don't fight it, don't fear it, use all of your senses," he murmured.

Around each bend, with each passing of 100 yards or so came new batches of sounds, different bird calls and insect noises and most noticeably, different smells. The base odor of the jungle had a pungent, funky organic aroma. This smell was accented by the ever-changing flora and fauna, producing myriad smell mixtures. The smells imprinted on Luke's brain so deeply that if were blind-folded and asked to walk the same trail again he could identify his location just by what his nose told him.

The appearance of an ancient automobile jolted Luke from communing with the jungle. The car looked like a Chevy from the 1950s. It was covered with a light, greenish moss and was home to several small green tree snakes and a lizard. With no roads nearby, it was anybody's guess how the old car had come to rest in the middle of the rain forest. Luke did notice one small piece of graffiti that simply read *'rebelde'* or rebel. Not sure what to make of it, Luke and Morgan carried on.

Luke's thoughts returned to the well-camouflaged frog. He figured that everything in the jungle made use of some sort of disguise.

Maybe this is why the jungle feels so alive; like you are in the belly of whale. Because everything is not what it appears to be, everything is hiding, but everything sees you, he thought.

The three toed sloths living high up in the canopy could only been seen when they moved, otherwise they looked like balls of nuts or berries.

The whole forest was eyes, just staring, watching.

As Luke worked his way deeper into the jungle, he began to feel part of it rather than an alien being walking through it. He felt like an extension of the trees. As he breathed in, the forest breathed in and as he exhaled, the forest exhaled with him. He become more in tune with the natural rhythm of the jungle and began to see some of what Morgan could see. It was like learning to see all over again. Luke learned what might hurt him and what to stay away from.

Luke pondered the thought that, *Maybe it was just such an instinct along with trial and error that led the Indians to know what plants to eat, what herbs to use as medicine, what could be used as poison or even as hallucinogenic drugs. It was this sixth sense that may have served the Indians well for generations, making them part of the forest and not something apart from it. Perhaps the Indians knew their own forest like the rest of us know our own bodies.*

Luke's companion interrupted his jungle reverie. Morgan held up his hand for Luke to stop and motioned for him to come over. Morgan pointed to several fresh boot prints in the soil. These were not the bare feet of Indians or the hooves of game. They were deep impressions made by some sort of military combat boot. There appeared to be six or seven sets of boot prints in all. Morgan knelt, touched the soil on the tracks, paused for several long minutes then looked up at Luke. Morgan said nothing but conveyed the need for vigilance. They were not alone. Luke recalled what Hernan had told him about the guerrillas, the Columbian rebels known to dwell in the Darién.

Two hours passed while Morgan remained on high alert. He stopped every ten feet to listen and watch before moving on. At one point, Morgan stopped to inspect a machete notch on a tree trunk. He turned to Luke.

"Luke, keep gun ready."

Morgan readied his small but accurate bow and arrow. They continued to walk. Darkness was approaching. The nocturnal creatures of the forest began to show themselves. Blood-sucking bats filled the air, owls hooted and frogs ribbeted loudly. Luke pulled out his flashlight and directed it into the jungle. More than twenty pairs of eyes of various sizes glared back at him.

Morgan gestured that they should make camp in a clearing.

With unwanted company, possibly near them in the jungle, they declined to shoot and kill their dinner, settling for Power Bars and water.

The creatures of the night roamed everywhere. The nocturnal denizens had evolved over the millennia to see and hunt at night for one purpose -- because their quarry was asleep and easier to kill. Consequently, Luke and Morgan determined to sleep with one eye open. Morgan's short stature allowed them to share the small tent that Nici had packed for Luke. Morgan added some dry brush as bedding, Luke did the same. Exhausted, the two men dozed off. The snapping, shuffling sounds of the forest continued until 2:00 a.m. when a different type of sound woke Morgan.

"Luke. Listen." Morgan whispered.

The forest had gone dead silent. The men heard footsteps. Listening intently, Morgan reached for his bow. Luke reached for his 9mm pistol. The footsteps stopped, and the crackling of the forest resumed. Luke slept the rest of the night with his pistol in his hand. For a moment, he thought he had heard voices speaking in harried Spanish. Morgan did not seem too concerned, so Luke wrote it off as his ears playing tricks on him.

They awoke early, crawled from the tent and were shocked to find boot prints just outside their tent door. They packed up hastily and kept on high alert. Luke locked and loaded his Mack-ten sub machine gun. He offered his pistol to Morgan.

"No like guns, too loud," Morgan smiled.

They skirted a coffee-brown swamp. Morgan cautioned Luke not to go near the edge, making the biting motion of a crocodile. Luke could see the dorsal fin of a giant, long, slender Amazonian arrowanna fish skimming just under the water and healthy-looking turtles floating in the middle. Several ancient, dead trees rose from the middle of the swamp. The smell of the forest near the swamp was extra rich, it over-stimulated one's olfactory sense much like super-saturated colors confuse the eye.

It was almost as if there was too much life in the air. The 100-degree heat pulled the water from the soil, to be rained back down to earth the same day, creating a never-ending cycle of water evaporation and replenishment. This water cycle ensured that the thicker-than-natural smells of the forest remained ever hovering in the air.

Luke's nerves settled down as the day went on. Morgan hacked away at the brush and vines without rest or water throughout the day.

Luke watched as Morgan swung away at the foliage with passion. He pondered:

"Man, Morgan is a wild man. Something is really eating at him. Maybe he has past experience with whoever is out here. Must have been bad, whatever it was."

"Come Luke, come." Morgan said firmly each time Luke lagged. Around 3:00 p.m., not able to keep up the frantic pace, Luke insisted that they make camp atop a high summit. The mountain-top plateau would give them a good vantage point to protect themselves and keep the bugs at bay.

Morgan kept vigil. He looked intently into each part of the forest as if he had some sort of X-ray vision. He wanted to see what was out there before it saw him.

"Can I help, Morgan?"

"Maybe find some food, look near the water."

"Morgan why are you so afraid of the people out there?" Luke said, pointing to the woods.

Morgan frowned at being called afraid. It was the worst insult in the Kuna culture.

"These people, they are not people. They are worse than animals. They come to my village and hold guns to the heads of our children to force us to store their drugs for them. One time, when I refused they shot and killed my Goddaughter."

"Oh," Luke was nearly speechless at this revelation. "Morgan, I'm so sorry."

Luke went off into the woods to find something for dinner.

"No use gun, Luke, too loud," Morgan said.

Luke grabbed his spear gun. About a mile up a small creek he came upon an unusually clear, large pool of water. Floating near the banks were several large Capybaras. The large rodents stood three feet tall and resembled guinea pigs on steroids. Luke recalled when he was a boy seeing the Indians in Brazil eating Capybaras.

On mock hunts, Luke would practice sneaking up on one of the wary animals. He tried to recall the proper method of stalking. Luke removed the spear tip from the shaft and cocked his gun, using just one of the three power bands. He lay down on his belly, slowly advancing using the army crawl. He closed the gap with the Capybaras to ten feet. He took aim at the largest one and squeezed the trigger, bracing against the powerful kickback, which was much stronger in the air than under water.

The spear struck the beast in the shoulder. The others scampered away as the wounded Capybara dragged Luke from the bushes.

The grunting animal tugged on the line and Luke dug in his heels and tugged back. He was not about to let go. The Capybara splashed to the middle of the pond, pulling Luke to the water's edge. Luke could see the tail of an approaching crocodile. He turned on the gas, just managing to haul the animal away from the predator. Not willing to give up, the croc followed the Capybara up onto the land. In proper cave-man style, Luke picked up a rock and heaved it at the hissing dragon's head, sending it back to where it came from.

"Damn gators." Luke worked his way down the shooting line to the less than dead giant rodent at the end. He lunged, grabbing the animal's snout, planting his knife in its throat. With one firm slash the animal went limp. Luke dressed the animal and headed back to camp, carrying the choicest pieces and leaving the rest for the forest creatures.

Morgan, standing lookout, seemed content that they had not been followed. He was happy to see that Luke had slain such a protein-filled dinner. Luke started a small fire. Morgan said a Kuna prayer of thanks to the Capybara's spirit before he cooked the delectable thighs and drums.

Morgan and Luke, while keeping all their weapons handy and at arm's length, feasted like kings on the charred meat of the Capybara. Morgan made a paste from the palm tree berries that he had picked earlier. He dipped his meat in the paste and Luke did the same. The taste was bitter but the fruit provided the men with critical vitamins.

The men sat back, rubbing their drum-skin tight bellies. Luke indicated they should throw the bones far away and wash themselves so as not to attract something with fangs.

As the full moon glowed over the vast forest below, Luke and Morgan crawled into the tent and fell fast asleep. That night no strangers came prowling.

With a good's nights rest, a rich meal and no signs of the bad guys, Luke and Morgan headed off the next morning full of renewed assurance.

"Donde vas?" (Where to?) Luke asked as Morgan scanned the horizon.

A flock of loudly squawking green parrots filled the sky.

"Parrots fly to the sea." Morgan said as he pointed in the direction of the parrots' aerial pathway.

Luke recognized the parrots as seabirds and agreed that they were heading toward the sea. The two plotted a mental course matching that of the birds and headed off into the thick. Before long, large wasp-like insects buzzed around Luke's head. Each time he swatted at the bugs they seemed to grow angrier and buzz louder. Eventually, Luke had to run and stick his head in a pool of water to get the bugs to leave him alone. Morgan laughed, as he thought that was pretty funny.

They continued their walk.

"Luke, stop."

Morgan placed his hand across Luke's chest to halt his forward motion, pointing at the ground. A flat, greenish, angular head slid out from the bushes. The men let the snake slide across their feet. The fat snake just kept coming and coming until nearly 20 feet of snake had crossed their feet.

"Buena comida," (Good food) Morgan said while miming eating, pointing at the tail end of the python. The men walked on, leaving the massive snake to its pursuit of jungle animals.

They came to a stretch of tall grassland that kept them concealed. It made for easy crossing and much less machete hacking. Morgan seemed relieved to have the relative rest. Luke and Morgan ambled along, side by side.

"Morgan, gracias por su ayuda, usted es mi hermano de otra madre," (Thank you for your help, you are my brother from another mother.)

"Egualamente," (The same for you) Morgan smiled.

"Manos arriba! (Hands up!)

Luke looked up. Just ahead of them in the clearing stood the answer to the mystery foot prints.

"FARC," Morgan said softly.

Luke mistakenly thought he had said, "Fuck."

"FARC, Colombianos, banditos!"

Luke focused. The men ahead were Columbian neo-communist anti- government, drug running, kidnapping rebels who called themselves the Revolutionary Armed Forces of Colombia. Initially, FARC was a Che Guevara inspired people's army designed to fight off the corruption of their despotic leaders and to bring perceived equality to their legions of poor through the communist ideal. However, the corrosive quality of the billions of dollars that their organization had gained from drug running had made them nothing more than coca growing, armed capitalistic bandits.

Several splinter groups also dwelled in the Panamánian Darién rain forest. This allowed them to sneak into Colombia and carry out kidnappings, bombings and extortion. They would retreat into Panamá, safe from the heavily armed U.S.-aided Columbian military. This rebel "safe zone" in the southern-most section of Panamá provided a good place for the FARC to rest, but fire-fights among the different factions were common. Critical supplies such as ammunition, medicine and even food were scarce and logistically difficult to get to the troops in the dense road-less jungle. Scarce supplies often led to sickness, malnutrition and dementia.

On one occasion, the Panamánian defense force attempted to oust FARC from their land. Several FARC and a dozen Panamánians were killed in the process. The FARC took action by hijacking the airwaves feeding the evening Panamánian news. Masked guerilla fighters came on screen and issued a stringent warning that any further attempt to evict them would be met with the bombing of a major Panamánian bank. Panamá relies heavily on the revenues generated from their robust offshore banking system; no further action was taken by the Panamánian government, thus allowing FARC and other armed rebels to roam the Darién with impunity.

Luke was not eager to engage these jokers.

Eight FARCs pointed their well-oiled machine guns towards Luke, who turned to check on Morgan. His friend was not there.

"Morgan, Morgan where did you go?" Luke said with his hands in the air.

Morgan had vanished silently into thin air, leaving Luke to contend with the situation.

"Drop your guns!" the leader commanded in English. Luke dropped both of his guns onto the ground while keeping his hands high.

"Easy boys, I am sure we can work this out. I have $200 in my pocket, take it, plus my guns and go. Nobody will know about this. You have my word," Luke said while keeping his tone low and controlled.

The FARC stood there looking like they had just knocked over and stolen the Colombian drug guerrilla wardrobe from a Hollywood costume warehouse. They wore head-to-toe camouflage. Two of the men wore red bandannas and smoked cigars. All had three-month beards. Each man carried two machine guns and 500 extra rounds draped over their chests. They were thin and seemed to be weak and slightly confused. Several of them looked to be about 14 or 15 years old.

The FARC held a field meeting to determine Luke's fate. Luke could here both sides being aggressively argued.

"Kill him."

"No, keep him alive so we can ransom him."

"No, let him go. We don't need to aggravate the Americans any more."

"I have to finish paying for my new boots. We need the ransom," one man joked.

"OK, we kill him," the leader said. They all nodded in agreement.

Luke readied himself to make his move. Three of the men brandished their guns while walking towards Luke.

"On your knees, gringo, now!" one of the kids shouted in near perfect English as he slid a bullet into his pistol.

Luke suppressed panic. Were they bluffing?

Suuuuup!

The arrow came flying through the air, and sank halfway through the neck of one of the FARCs. Firing from behind the trees, Morgan had scored a perfect shot.

The speared man lay gurgling and twitching on the ground as he tried to grab and remove the arrow. His body collapsed.

Morgan began to rapid fire his arrows at the FARC. Luke went for his pistol. He grabbed it and fired wildly until the clip was spent. The FARC retreated, dragging their dead comrade.

Luke ran over to check on Morgan.

"I got one, he dead," Morgan said with a raised fist. "They not bother us again. Let's go."

Luke collected several of Morgan's arrows off the ground and gave them back to him.

"Maybe you will need these."

The shock of the attack slowly wore off as the men continued their epic forest transect. Having covered more than 50 overland miles Luke grew impatient, always pushing Morgan to tell him how much farther and where they were going. Morgan remained silent. To ease his aching muscles, cut and bitten flesh and edgy psyche, Luke whistled tunes, Colonel Bogey's March and several advertising jingles.

Morgan strode on with a renewed confidence.

"Maybe the FARCS scare easy," Luke thought to himself as he watched Morgan move through the bush as if he were on a Sunday walk at the beach. Morgan's cool nerves seemed to spread to Luke, giving him a sense of calm as well. Luke was once again able to enjoy the stark raw beauty of the rain forest. He could tell that he was entering a new microclimate. There were several new species of gold, red and brilliant blue-colored tree frogs.

"No touch, poison." Morgan said as he pointed to the gold frog.

Luke's mind drifted as he began to fantasize about the ocean in an almost erotic way. He closed his eyes and listened to make-believe crashing ocean waves. He saw himself diving into the cool waters of his native Malibu. He wanted to swim in the sea, any sea, and feel the refreshing, cool energy. Luke needed to feel something familiar. The loud squawking parrots that he had seen two days prior pulled him from his dream. Morgan saw the birds and removed a leather strap from his satchel. He strapped it around the tallest tree he could find. Using the strap as leverage he shimmied up the tree trunk in seconds.

"La mar!" (The sea) Morgan exclaimed as he pointed.

Yes, the sea. I must have smelled the salt air, Luke thought.

"How far?"

"Lejos."

"Oh, great. 'Lejos' again."

Luke's fantasy of an afternoon swim in the sea slipped away.

That night, after a delectable boa constrictor dinner, all Luke could think of was swimming in the ocean again. His dreams were nothing but water, water, water. He dreamt that he was a dolphin swimming freely and spinning through the air. In his dream Nici came to him in the form of a female dolphin and they swam side by side. The dolphin that was Luke stunned sardines with his tail so Nici could eat them as they sank to the sea floor. The dolphin that was Nici said nothing but conveyed that she loved him, that he needed to stay the course, and be free. The two dolphins hovered as they gazed into each other's eyes.

Luke woke up with a start. Morgan was gone. Before he had a chance to react Morgan appeared and climbed back into the tent.

"Making peepees." Morgan said.

The next morning, Luke was eager to get moving and reach the sea as fast as possible. As beautiful as the jungle was, its confining foliage along with the FARC lurking about was working on Luke's head, making him antsy to finish the trip.

For the next two days, Luke and Morgan plowed a steady zigzag pattern, crossing streams and muddy ponds. Every time Luke thought that he had logged all the various forms of jungle life, something totally new came into view. The seemingly endless array of different life forms stimulated the hunter-gatherer in Luke. His primal instincts for survival had been honed by his years of pursuing game in the sea. The first thing any underwater hunter learns to do is recognize all the species in the food chain and learn what they act like under different conditions as well as their eating and breeding habits. Luke soaked in jungle and all its nuances in the same way he soaked in his surrounding when diving and spearfishing in a new ocean or on a new reef.

A good hunter will develop a sixth sense, a way to mentally file and later make use of this data without even thinking about it. This skill is what many refer to as *instinct*. Perhaps genetics is why people still feel the need to hunt and fish. In ancient times, throwing a spear and hitting your game was a real cause for celebration. Your family and tribe would survive, thus increasing your chances of passing on your genes. Plus, it must have always been, as it is now, the guy who kills the biggest fish gets the woman, every time. Perhaps the stand-in for fish these days is money.

Nonetheless, Luke had inherited the gene to hunt. His mind soaked up as much new bio-data as possible. Luke's ears remained wide open to the sparse advice that Morgan offered. Morgan only said things that were important. Idle chat was not his game.

Back in Panamá City, Nici lit her daily candle that offered her hope that Luke would return home soon. She wrote letters to Luke in her diary.

"Luke, last night I had the strangest dream. I dreamt that we were both dolphins and you kept feeding me sardines. Not sure what it meant but I loved it."

Nici kept in touch with Hernan, hoping to hear any shred of news. They both maintained a look-out for signs of Caucuss or Gomez. Nici paid the local *barrio* kids to watch and warn her by ringing bells should either of the government men come looking for her.

***

"Come, Luke!" Morgan whispered.

Luke jogged to catch up.

"Look. Iguana. Ocean is close, good food."

Morgan opened his eyes wide and fixed his stare dead into the blinking eyes of the four-foot long bright green and black striped iguana. The small dragon was well concealed high up in the forest canopy, invisible to the untrained eye.

Luke looked on with curiosity. Several minutes went by. Morgan continued his staring contest. The giant lizard began to shake nervously until it could no longer clutch the branch under it. The iguana lost its grip, plummeting 20-feet to the forest floor. It landed with a thud. Before it could get on its feet to scamper away Morgan pounced on it while biting the back of its neck, causing the lizard to go into paralysis.

Luke was impressed.

"Nice trick, now we have dinner."

"Es un regalo." (It's a gift) Morgan said.

Morgan was not a lizard hypnotist. Apparently, Luke learned, the green iguana simply does not like to be stared at. Sort of a killer case of stage fright.

Luke heard the unmistakable sounds of waterfalls in the distance. Luke and Morgan followed the sound until it grew into a thundering roar. As they approached the ledge, swirling mist cooled Luke's sweat-covered face. Luke and Morgan took a few more steps to behold the sight of millions of gallons of tropical fresh water cascading down more than 100-feet into a large pool that led to a river below.

"Muy lindo," (Very nice) Morgan said as he breathed in the misty air.

"What is the name of this place?" Luke asked.

"Uhm, big waterfall." Morgan replied.

After letting the white noise of the falls lull them for a while, the two men worked their way to the base of the falls on a narrow trail. Luke filled his water containers, then slipped into the water and floated on his back with his eyes closed. The cool river water brought his core temperature down. He opened his eyes to see another Indian standing on the river bank. The man wore fierce-looking blue tribal paint on his face, legs and arms. He had on a T-shirt and traditional blue loin cloth. He held a small fish spear in his left hand.

Morgan waved at the man. The man waved back as if they knew each other. Morgan went over to the man and in customary rain forest manner they showed genuine happiness to see each other. They spent twenty minutes conversing, smiling and laughing paying no mind to Luke whatever.

Morgan finally waved Luke over.

"Luke this is Jimmy, Jimmy Carter."

Luke shook the man's hand. "I'm sorry. What is the man's name again?"

"Jimmy is Embera´, a different tribe. They live here, on the Pacific side of the Darién. On the rivers and coast. They like to be named for famous people. Jimmy Carter is famous, right?"

"Yep, a real super star. Do you guys know each other?"

The newcomer spoke. "Kuna and Embera´ made fierce wars for a generation. I was Kuna, then my grandfather gave me to the Embera ´when I was small boy. In this way, we make peace."

"I am sorry, Jimmy. I did not know you spoke English," Luke said.

"Spanish, some French, Kuna and Emberá ´. I speak many linguas," Jimmy said proudly.

Luke stupidly asked, "What were the wars about?"

Morgan and Jimmy exchanged looks as if they were hiding something.

"Kuna people used to eat Emberá people, so they fight."

Luke asked no more questions on that topic.

"Emberá too chewy anyway, no good food." Jimmy joked.

"Morgan, did you know that Jimmy would be here?" Luke asked.

C.F. Goldblatt

"Jimmy always here. Jimmy will take you to his village on the Sombu river. Two more days from here, tough walking, uphill. You will be safe there. Watch out for the FARC and the jaguars. Both hunt in the night."

Luke reached for words of thanks, but knew any long speech would seem trite, so he simply did a full forearm shake with   Morgan.

"If you ever need anything, for the rest of my life, I will give it to you, thanks! *Gracias para todo*." (Thank you for all).

Jimmy grabbed his small spear and water bag and started down along the edge of the river. Luke followed. He stopped after just a few minutes to give Morgan a goodbye wave, but the Indian had disappeared into the forest.

Jimmy was more vocal than Morgan and asked seemingly endless questions about Luke and where he had come from. Luke assumed that Morgan had told him what he was running from.

"What your favorite music? Do you have a wife, kids? What do you do for work?"

Luke patiently answered all of Jimmy's questions. The Embera' lived a far more traditional lifestyle than the Kuna. The Embera' were a tough people who relied on and desired cash money far less than the Kunas. They existed in remote rain forest villages that saw few, if any, outsiders. For a period of time the U.S. Air Force hired the Embera' to teach pilots jungle survival skills. Luke provided Jimmy with a rare glimpse of the modern world.

Jimmy moved through the forest with great speed and ease. Each time he looked back, Luke was digging himself out of thickets of tree branches, stuck in the mud or catching his breath. The increasing grade and heat was pushing Luke to the edge of heat stroke. Jimmy sat down on a rock and waited until Luke caught up.

"Need to show you a few things." Jimmy said while handing Luke his machete.

"Take off shoes and leave some gear, too heavy."

As the altitude increased, Luke's ability to negotiate the knee-deep mud decreased. The tennis shoes Luke wore acted like suction cups in the gooey mud. Luke reluctantly took off his shoes and set down his 75-foot spear gun buoy line, his wetsuit and his extra long freediving fins that he had borrowed from Hernan.

"Whoever finds that dive gear here, in the jungle, is going to be confused."

Despite the weight, Luke insisted on keeping his spear gun, mask and snorkel.

"Okay, I think I'm ready to keep going," Luke said with renewed optimism.

Sad to leave it all behind, Luke slung his gun over his shoulder, said goodbye to his gear and continued his slog up the hill.

Jimmy slowed his pace so Luke could keep up. Jimmy began to pick and point out seemingly endless numbers of different plants. The Embera´ have a very strong tradition of using native plants and herbs for everything from making powerful dyes, to curing cancer, to poison, to making their breath smell fresh. He allowed Luke to touch and smell each one then explained their use. One plant had a large leaf that, when cut, emitted a noxious skunk-like smell. Jimmy said it would make you blind. He waved it in front of Luke's nose. One sniff caused Luke to spit his water out.

Another shrub that looked like a marijuana plant Jimmy said would enlarge both male and female genitals and "make you really want to have sex when made into a tea." Luke tried to store the showers of information but it was enough just to keep going. Many of the most potent plants blended into the scenery and were inconspicuous.

"My grandfather, he has more than 100 years, no teeth and knows every plant in the forest. He can teach you everything."

Three hours into the trek and about halfway up mountains covered with 1,500- year-old hardwood trees, Luke's vision blurred.

"Do you want to know more about natural medicine, Luke? Luke? Luke…"

Jimmy looked back. Luke had fallen face down into a soup of mud and animal dung. Jimmy turned Luke over and poured water on his face that had drained of all color. Jimmy felt Luke's pulse and opened his eye lids.

Luke came to, coughing up mud and saliva.

"Enfermo," (Sick) Jimmy said.

"Jimmy, I am a mess. You go on. Leave me here," Luke pleaded.

"You, silly man. We stay here for the night. In the morning, you feel better."

Luke spent the night shivering like a wet dog in the snow, puking his guts out and heaving explosive diarrhea that came every 15 minutes on the money. Jimmy covered Luke's body with leaves which alleviated some of the deep muscle aches. Luke curled up into a ball. The pain was so severe he wished for death or at least some relief. Then the burping began.

"Burp, buuurp, buuuuurp…"

Luke belched and belched uncontrollably, purging volumes of air from his gut and lungs. Drinking water was futile, as it came back up as fast as it went down. Luke was in serious danger of dying from dehydration.

"Tell Nici, I love her," Luke whispered between belching spasms.

Jimmy grabbed Luke and his spear gun, leaving the rest of his belongings. He strapped the gun to Luke's back. In the dead of night with only a sliver of moon for light, Jimmy wrestled Luke into a piggy-back position. Luke had lost 20 pounds since he had been on the run, making him a slightly lighter load. Wearing Luke's 165 pounds like a heavy rucksack, Jimmy mustered up and huffed up the steep hill. Luke continued to vomit and belch as they went. They stopped only when Luke had to defecate.

Jimmy drank no water while he hauled Luke up hill for more than fours hours. They reached the summit at daybreak. One there, a delirious Luke beheld a vista so beautiful it would normally have made him cry. Down the other side of the tree - covered hill was a long flowing river that snaked back on forth as far as the eye could see. The river was flanked by an ocean of green on either side of it. Far off in the distance was a slight sparkle that was Pacific Ocean. The faint trace of ocean breeze gave Luke a spark of life. Luke managed to briefly stand on his own and swallow a few sips of water. Luke tried to take few steps, but his knees gave out. He grabbed a branch to prevent himself from falling again. His momentary reprieve was met with worsening symptoms of his unknown illness. The water he drank came back up but this time with foamy blood.

"You really bad, need to get you to *Abuelo* (Grandfather)."

Before Luke could curl back up into a ball Jimmy saddled him onto his back and trudged down the 1,000- foot hillside. Luke slipped in and out of consciousness as his head bobbed back and forth with each painful step that Jimmy took.

Four hours later they reached the base of the hill and the river's edge, where a small canoe waited. Jimmy refreshed himself and Luke in the cool river water. Jimmy supported Luke as he floated face up. Luke's vision was almost gone. He could only see the bright sun and some of the shapes on Jimmy's face.

Jimmy then sang a traditional healing song which sounded like a lullaby. The inexhaustible Embera´ loaded Luke into the dugout canoe then grabbed a long wooden pole. Hugging the river bank, foot by foot, he piled the pole into the river bed, forcing the canoe upstream against the fast rushing river water. Jimmy stopped only briefly to again cover Luke's shivering body, which was curled up and covered with leaves.

"Hold on, Luke. We are getting close."

To try and stay lucid, Luke focused on Nici and everyone he loved.

As dusk approached, Luke felt the hull of the of the canoe skid over river rocks then come to a stop. He heard voices speaking softly in Emberá . It sounded like Kuna but had a much more pleasing tone. Several pairs of painted naked breasts flopped down into Luke's face. As sick as he was he managed to laugh. The topless Embera´ women lifted him out of the canoe and carried him to the home of the village medicine man. It was the 100-year-old toothless man Jimmy had spoken of. He was not actually Jimmy's blood grandfather, but all older men in the village were referred to as Abuelo.

The Emberá houses were built on sturdy hardwood stilts to keep them above the water when the river flooded and to keep the mosquitoes at bay. They were open-sided with slit bamboo floors and palm frond thatch roofs. The only access to the homes was a ladder made from a single notched log. Abuelo wore only a traditional, blue loin cloth. He had a hunched back, crazy white hair and his eyes did not appear to be sharp or clear. His wife, who was nearly 90 with long black and silver hair, was topless, with painted designs on her skin. She remained beautiful even at her age.

Abuelo removed Luke's clothes and inspected each part of his body carefully. Luke could barely comprehend Abuelo's Spanish, as his lack of teeth muddied his words. Several of the adorable village children gathered around to look on as the Abuelo inspected Luke. Abuelo stopped when he got to Luke's big toe on his left foot. He spat on his hand then rubbed Luke's toe to clean it. A small, barely visible entry wound could be seen.

"Gusano." (worm) Abuelo said, shaking his head.

Luke learned that after he had removed his shoes in the jungle he had stepped into a pool of standing water where the larvae of a tapeworm bore into his flesh, finding their way to a home in his intestines. The parasite, which generally kills its host in less than a week, reproduced inside of Luke. The new larvae had feasted on Luke's large intestine and worked its way into his stomach cavity. Next, would be his heart and then his liver.

Luke struggled through another agonizing night. Life was draining out of him at both ends; the parasite was destroying him from the inside.

At first light, Abuelo grabbed a reed basket and secured it to his body with the attached headband. With Jimmy along to help, Abuelo walked deep into the forest, picking a dozen types of plants, including the one that smelled like a skunk. Abuelo carefully captured a red poison dart frog which was gaily colored with black and red spots. The Indians extracted drops from the creature to envenomate their deadly blow-gun darts for killing monkeys.

Back at Abuelo's home, Luke continued writhing in pain. Abuelo twisted the herbs together in his hands then put them into a pot filled with boiling water. As he did so he sang a healing song and rocked back and forth. The herbs cooked for twenty minutes. He gingerly added a single leg from the poison frog and let it cook for another five minutes.

Luke watched as Abuelo took several gulps of the elixir before handing him a cup of it. With no warning, Abuelo poured the scalding hot tea all over Luke's body.

"Shit, that burns!"

What more agony could he endure? Barfing and burning – Luke was ready to die.

Abuelo's wife helped Luke sit up. She pried his mouth open to make him drink nearly a liter of the herb and frog concoction.

Luke gasped for breath and waited for the bloody vomiting to renew, but it never did.

"Now you take a journey and become better," Jimmy said.

Abuelo continued his healing song.

Luke passed out from the pain and he awoke in the jungle. He was 13-years-old again and found himself running from a jet-black puma. Luke had the endurance of a strong adolescent.

He ran and ran but the puma gained on him. Confused, he turned to his left and there stood his long-dead father, Larry.

"Face the puma," Larry said in a voice that he had not heard for more than 20 years.

Luke ran some more, then turned as the Puma lunged with open claws, a nasty growl and glistening white canines. Luke calmly stuck out his hand and grabbed the puma by the throat. He squeezed hard until the cat went limp.

"Well done, son. Now, wake up."

"Uhhh," Luke gasped.

"Where am I?" Luke shouted.

"Did you kill the puma?" Jimmy asked.

Luke felt that his spirit journey had taken only a few minutes but, in reality, more than five hours had passed.

"I killed the puma," Luke said. "My father was there. He spoke to me…"

"Good. Sleep now."

Luke's belching, vomiting and other symptoms abated. He was finally able to stand up slowly and move around, even drink water and eat some bread.

Within a day, Luke passed the pesky parasites.

Chapter Sixteen

WITH EACH PASSING DAY, Luke grew stronger. After ten days, he was back with the program and in good shape. He spent his days with Abuelo in his simple home. Luke's bed consisted of a naked floor and a wood block on which to rest his head. Abuelo's wife, whom Luke called Abuela (Grandmother), would go about her daily chores of pounding rice into meal with a hardwood pestle and mortar, killing and cleaning chickens or fish and helping Abuelo when he needed to make herbal remedies. When there was time, she told stories to the children or worked on weaving intricate and beautifully-crafted baskets which sometimes could take a full year to complete. She kept the cooking fire perpetually burning by feeding four long hardwood logs into the heated center of the fire pit. They burned slowly and hot and created a stable place to support pots and pans for cooking.

The children all had big brown eyes, smooth, even brown skin, and black hair. The children did not seem to mind having mouths full of rotting, falling-out teeth. They played in harmony; swimming in the river, digging in the sand, dancing and singing. They needed no adult supervision and rarely, if ever, cried or complained. The children roamed freely around the village which consisted of about 150 people and 20 homes, a communal center for tribal meetings and festivals, a brick school house and an open field for playing games.

The village was named Pavarondu. As isolated as it was from the modern world, it was nonetheless still in the world. The Emberá had long ago given up sustenance hunting and taken up crop and livestock cultivation. The baskets that they so carefully crafted were all sent to market, leaving them to use Tupperware in their own homes. They cooked almost everything with lard and vegetable oils, leaving the women on the heavier side. The women started having children around 15 years old and generally had more than ten in their lifetime.

Marriage was informal. A man and woman simply agreed that they were married and the agreement was binding from that point forward. The barrage of different types of missionaries; Seventh Day Adventist, Catholic, Latter Day Saints, Presbyterian and others had obliterated traditional religious beliefs and left many of the formerly topless women feeling uneasy about their nakedness. They often donned shirts when a white person came to visit.

Povarondu was more than 100-miles up the Sombu River and was the most remote of eight Embera' communities that existed along the edge of the river. The Panamánian government had implemented a program of building schools and offering other sorts of aid. The government was attempting to assimilate the Emberá, who were more than happy to accept any new change that came along, so long as it made their lives easier. Like the Kunas, the Embera´ people originated in modern day Colombia and still have ancestors there. They migrated to Panamá about 100-years ago and have lived there ever since.

Each time Abuelo came back from a jungle forage, Luke studied the different types of plants, berries, leaves, animal parts and seeds used for each concoction. It became clear what type of illness the different elixirs were supposed to treat; they were a custom formulation based on the complaint and body-type of each patient who came to visit Abuelo. One man might display joint pain indicating arthritis, or a woman might show that she had severe menstrual cramps.

The remedies appeared to be highly effective, even for such things at nightmares and depression. No payment was made for the service, but generally a gift was left as consideration.

Luke asked Abuelo to show him more about the natural medicines. With time, Luke became familiar with the different types of treatments. When he was well enough, Abuelo took Luke into the forest to show him where the different plants, berries and herbs grew and how to identify them. Certain plants were hard to find and required hiking for hours up to higher altitudes and even turning over rocks and mucking around in caves with bats and cockroaches. Abuelo sometimes would study two different plants that looked identical to Luke for half an hour, finally settling on one. Abuelo made sure that Luke understood that choosing the wrong plant could make a condition worse or even kill a person or make them go crazy. This was not child's play.

In the afternoon, Luke enjoyed hunting for fresh water shrimp with the teenage boys of the village. They would dive in the holes along the riverbank. The shrimp had one strong pincer, making them tough to handle. The Embera´ countered this by using small wooden spears powered by surgical tubing. A good diver could spear 20 or so shrimp and a few small Tilapia fish in an afternoon.

"John viene con gringos," (John is coming with white people), the children yelled with joy.

Still cagey that somebody might find him out, Luke watched from Abuelo's home as a well-dressed Embera´ man helped three white men unload professional-looking camera gear. The three men, two Germans and a Mexican, were based in Mexico City and worked for a German TV news station. They had paid John, the tribe's so-called representative, $1,000 to film a documentary of the village.

John, whose chosen last name was Travolta, spoke good English and had spent a year living in Van Nuys, California. He had learned the value of money and was more than happy to take the Germans' dough. The only catch was that the TV crew wanted the Embera' to look and act like they were before the arrival of the Spanish, 500-years before. John asked the women to take off their tops and paint themselves from head to toe. He asked the men of the tribe to all wear loincloths and carry spears, bows and arrows. The tribe only had a few spears left over from the pre-chicken and pig days. The Germans anticipated this so they had brought a few 'prop spears' of their own for the men to carry around.

With reservation, Luke introduced himself as Cristobál.

"Please do not get in our shots," the leader of the crew requested.

Luke was disgusted that the TV crew was presenting this false version of Embera´ society as fact.

Later that night, the TV crew invited Luke for a drink.

"Yes, I was in Iraq when Saddam fell. The USA looked like they might win the war at that point," said the pretentious tall, blond, middle-aged cameraman named Franz.

"Salud," said the Mexican soundman while toasting a shot of rum.

"Tomorrow, we go deep in the forest looking for petroglyphs," Klaus, the youngest of the crew, chimed in.

"Look, you guys really need to take some guns or a bodyguard," Luke said. "The FARC- the Colombian rebels, are here and if my guess is right, somehow they have already heard that you guys are on the scene. They are desperate and I am sure ransoming you and selling your gear is an attractive proposal."

The warning, however, fell on unreceptive ears.

"I was in Iraq," Franz said. "We are used to danger. You don't have to worry about us."

Luke lifted his glass in a mock toast.

"You guys will make beautiful corpses. Here is to you and your fake documentary."

"OK, American, you know everything. Now we go to bed."

Franz opened the door, motioning for Luke to leave the home they had rented for their stay.

The next morning the chickens woke Luke before the sun was up. He peeked out through the thatch to see the camera crew heading off into the bush guided by John Travolta. Luke knew nothing good would come of it.

Two days and a night passed. The crew was a full day overdue.

"Jimmy... Abuelo, what should we do?" Luke asked.

"Well, three dead foreigners is not good for anybody so we better go have a look," Jimmy replied. "Luke, you better stay here. If the FARC are out there they will leave us alone, but you, they might take you. So, please stay here."

Luke reluctantly obeyed Jimmy's command. He stayed behind with Abuelo while Jimmy and three other men, armed with archaic bolt-action .22 rifles, headed out to search for the TV crew.

Three hours later, Jimmy and his men returned. They were panting heavily, as they had been running for more than an hour. Jimmy held up Fronz's digital Camcorder. It was drenched with blood.

"Luke, come fast!" Jimmy yelled.

Jimmy thrust the camera into Luke's hands. Luke took it to Abuelo's home. He wiped some of the blood off and picked off bits of what looked skull fragments. Luke opened the viewing screen, scrolled back and pressed play. What he saw was nightmare material. Luke let the video play. Franz's voice could be heard yelling off screen, "Wait! Don't shoot, we are German! We have no problem with you!"

The camera panned towards the FARC guerrillas. The camera saw more than 15 of them, standing menacingly in the road. The moment the camera fixed onto the face of one of the FARCs, a shot rang out and the screen showed a crazily spiraling picture of the men, the trees, then the dirt as the camera plopped down onto the ground. A second later, a very dead Franz fell inches from the camera lens as the machine captured what remained of his obliterated face.

C.F. Goldblatt

Chapter Seventeen

IT WAS CLEAR THAT Luke could not stay in an area so full of FARC. Something was sure to go wrong. Plus, the press of the murdered TV crew was sure to bring retribution from the Panamánian defense force. A low-grade shooting war would ensue, bringing new faces to Povarondu and making it a less-than-attractive hiding place for a man on the run like Luke Dodge.

"Luke, I must stay here in case the FARC try to come to this village," Jimmy Carter said. "You can take my canoe and float to the mouth of the Sombu. You will find a small town called Puerto Indio. I have friends there who can take you to the only Embera´ village on the coast. It is called Playa de los Palos (beach of the sticks).

"God will be your co-pilot. Be sure to take some food. You can drink the river water. If you leave at dawn you should make it by dark. Halfway through the journey the Sombu merges with the Rio Venado, you will know it because Rio Venado is much clearer. Be sure to stay to the south side of the bank or you will be sucked towards the rapids. Stay in the dirty water and you will be okay."

"Here is some cash for the canoe," Luke said. He handed Jimmy the $200 that Dulup had paid him for lobster diving.

"No, you keep, they will bring my cayuco back to me, don't worry, be happy."

Jimmy, like Dulup, had surpised Luke with his honesty and lack of greed.

One of the village women had fashioned some traditional shoes for Luke. She handed them over shyly and disappeared. The children gathered around and pulled on his arms, asking that he come and play.

Luke woke as the sun warmed the eastern sky. He thanked Jimmy, Abuelo, Abuela and hugged the village children, grabbed his spear gun and his package of food that included cookcd chicken and rice. He took a leather *holsa* of medicinal herbs that Abuelo had given him, with instructions.

Luke stepped into the small tippy dugout canoe. With a single shove, he was in the flow of the river and started to float downhill at a brisk, six knots. The feeling of floating effortlessly through the virgin wilderness, with only the toucans and Harpia eagles as company was the definition of serenity. Luke stopped every hour to jump in and cool down his body. He covered his face with mud to protect it from sunburn.

Each time he stopped he held his breath, listening intently for any sign of the FARC. So far, he appeared to be alone. Luke waved as he passed each of the Embera´ villages. He stopped in one called Tigre. This village had a satellite pay phone and a mini store that sold Seco (sugar-cane alcohol) to the locals. A dozen or so men sat outside the store downing the cheap booze. Without an Embera´ guide, Luke was not greeted with open arms. The vibe was bad so, Luke returned to his canoe and continued downstream.

"Hmm, this water is clear," Luke observed as he floated along.

"Oh, crap! I missed the turn. This is gonna hurt!" Luke shouted.

Before Luke could react, the river turned into a washing machine. The canoe filled with water and he lost the the push pole. The rapids grew stronger and stronger. Luke held onto the rails of the canoe.

"Slam!"

The canoe hit a boulder, then smashed into another. Luke clutched his spear gun. The violent rapids tipped the canoe and propelled Luke into the churning water. The canoe went bouncing and banging down the river without him.

Indian children on the bank stood and watched as the gringo struggled to stay afloat. After a mile or so, the rapids calmed and the Rio Venado re-joined the Sambu, putting Luke back on track. Bruised but alive, Luke looked for his canoe. He floated for what felt like five miles before finding the battered craft caught in a jamb of fallen trees. Luke was glad to find that the canoe full of water but still afloat. He wrenched a stick off a limb to use as a new push pole and continued down the river.

"Stick to the dirty water, Luke," he instructed himself.

For the remainder of the day Luke sang out of tune Bob Dylan songs to keep himself company.

"How does it feel to be without a home, like a complete unknown, Like a rolling stone…"

And Kris Kristofferson's timeless words:

"Freedom's just another word for nothin' left to lose..."

As Jimmy had predicted, Luke arrived in Puerto Indio just before dark. He traded the canoe for a night's rest in a fleabag hostel across from the only cantina in town. Puerto Indio was a real frontier town where poachers walked the streets with rifles and dead monkeys, jaguars, caged toucans and iguanas.

The town was a mixture of black people of West Indian descent and Emberá. The government had exactly one soldier posted there whose only job was to report any FARC activity in the area. Other laws simply were not enforced. There were dengue/malaria quarantine warning signs posted on almost every home. The town received all its commodities via a weekly tramp-steamer hailing from Panamá City. The last shipment lacked a re-supply of beer and Seco, leaving the town dry for nearly a week. But, a new delivery had just arrived. The fresh supply of booze was cause for celebration.

"Musica Typica" blared at ear-bleeding decibels from the cantina's six massive speakers. This regional music was a pleasant Spanish-style acoustic guitar ballad that played for a few minutes, then the male singer would chime in with primitive screaming and yelling. It was basically scream-singing its worst. The speakers filled the town with noise, especially the cheap room Luke had rented. Unable to sleep, Luke decided to drink with the locals. Within an hour, and three beers later, Luke saw several fist fights, a knife fight and counted six people passed out at the street corners.

Clara, the "lady" of the town propositioned Luke. Clara was one of the town's few prostitutes. She was half Indian and half black. At more than 240 pounds, she sweated heavily from her chest, back and brow and was missing most of her front teeth. Her way of expressing her sexuality was to wear a pair of cut off sweat pants with no underwear that she pulled up much too tight.

"Hola, guapo," (Hello, handsome) Clara said to Luke as she ran her fingers through his sticky hair.

"You, me, we make magic, only five dolla," Clara said as she rubbed Luke with her breast, leaving a track of sweat.

"Gracias, pero yo tengo novia," (Thanks, but I have a girlfriend.) Luke replied politely.

Clara persisted.

"Take me back to Panamá with you. I cook clean, make love for you all day."

"I am not going there, going to Playa de los Palos."

Clara backed up and drew a serious face and said, "You not go there. Too dangerous, *peligroso*, maybe I give you boom boom for free as maybe you never come back."

"I appreciate that," Luke said. "Maybe next time."

Luke finished his beer and headed off to sleep. The bedbugs bit Luke half to death as he warded off nightmares of the FARC coming to kidnap, torture and kill him. Fearful thoughts of Caucuss and Gomez filled his head.

"We are hot on your trail, Dodge," An angry Caucuss told Luke in his dream.

Finally, around 3:00 a.m., the music stopped. Luke sent a goodnight kiss to Nici and fell fast asleep.

Chapter Eighteen

THE NEXT MORNING, with some effort and throwing Jimmy's name around, Luke managed to secure a boat ride to Playa de los Palos. He used the last of his cash for the five-hour boat ride. At $175, the boat ride was costly. Gasoline in these parts had to be imported by boat and cost $6.50 a gallon. The 22-foot panga he rented was driven by a handsome black man named Ariel, who looked like a young Denzel Washington. His crew member, Felipe, was a smiley-faced kid of Emberá descent.

Luke watched with trepidation as Ariel mounted two old engines on the boat -- first a 20-year-old, 15-horsepower Johnson outboard and then a slightly newer 9.9 horsepower Yamaha. Ariel primed the gas tank and tried to conceal his action when he shored up a gaping hole in the hull with an old sock.

"Listo," (Ready) Ariel announced.

Nursing his bruised body from the rough ride down the river, Luke climbed in.

They shoved off. Ariel pulled on the ripcord a dozen times as they picked up speed while floating down river. He removed the engine cover, unscrewed the spark plugs that were only hand tight, blew on them, wiped them clean with his shirt, replaced them, primed the gas ball again and gave the cord another tug. The old engine kicked to life and the panga chugged along.

Felipe smiled at Luke, showing off his pearly whites. If he did not know better Luke might think Felipe was judging what Luke's thighs would taste like in a stew. In fact, Felipe had never met a gringo and was simply curious.

"Enorme, tu harpoon," (Your gun is giant.) Felipe said, holding up Luke's spear gun.

Ariel spoke some English.

"Playa de los Palos, very dangerous, many FARC and other bad things, too close to Colombia. Why you go there?"

Luke searched for an explanation.

"I just want to spearfish and umm, spread the word of God."

Never a religious person, Luke knew that pretending to be a free-diving missionary might be a good cover for now.

"Palabra de dios," (Word of God) Felipe said.

"Sí, palabra de dios," Luke responded.

"Then God will be your co-pilot on your mission and he will protect you," Ariel said.

"Well, at this point, I think I'd like God on my side," Luke said as Ariel crossed himself and kissed his thumb.

They had run for an hour when the Sombu spilled into a shallow bay. A small fleet of homemade wooden boats plied the mouth of river. They fished with small gillnets for robalo, corvina and giant shrimps called langostino. Ariel and Felipe waved as they passed each boat as to say, "Hey I got a gringo here, everybody look at my cargo. I don't have to fish today!"

They ran though the muddy bay for another hour until they rounded Punta Patino. The ocean remained cloudy from the runoff of the Sombu. The hills to Luke's left were covered with virgin old growth hardwood trees and flowed with creeks that emptied into the sea. The land ended abruptly with cliffs jutting straight into the sea, indicating deep water close to land. They passed several exquisite black sand beaches that, Luke concluded, rarely had seen human footprints. A series of reefs broke the surface a mile off shore. The swell was up to about ten feet, causing serious white-water action and resulting foam near the wash rocks.

"Hay mucho pes aqui," (There are many fish here) Felipe said as he pointed at the rocks.

The outboard conked out.

Ariel went to work cleaning plugs and priming the gas. After half an hour of drifting, he gave up and pull-started his newer Yamaha. With less horsepower, they moved along at a scant 10 knots. Several more miles down the coast, the jungle grew richer and brighter green with the density of virgin, old growth trees increasing. The morning steam rolled from the treetops. They reached a line in the sea where the dirty river water no longer affected the ocean clarity. The sea turned from light greenish gray to deep clear green, even borderline blue.

The combination of such untouched waters, the remoteness of the location combined with the primeval forest abutting the sea and the Indian village destination created an atmosphere of adventure and discovery that Luke had known few times before. The jungle and sea seemed to be equally alive. Luke expected to see Godzilla or King Kong come charging through the forest. If the fabled Megalodon shark that stretched more than 60 feet from end to end could live anywhere on earth, this place would be it.

As the small lonely panga plugged away into the swells, Luke kept on eye on the water leaking in through the hole that Ariel had plugged up. Felipe continuously bailed water as it seeped through the hull. The mood of the men grew more and more serious as each passing mile brought them closer to the Colombian border. Felipe's job, aside from bailing water, was to keep a constant lookout for water bandits that were common in these waters.

"Cargue su arma," (load your gun) Felipe told Luke as he gestured to keep a sharp eye on the horizon. "Muchas piratas aqui." (Many pirates here.)

The sun shone directly overhead when the panga neared Playa de los Palos. Luke stood up to get a better view. He saw a dozen traditional open-sided, raised thatched roof Embera´ houses on a meadow abutting the mile-long, palm tree-dotted black sand beach that terminated with a flowing river on one side and a cascading 100-foot high waterfall on the other. Behind the village was virgin jungle. The children playing in the river were the first to sight the panga. They jumped up and yelled.

"Bote, bote, bote!!" (Boat…)

The men of the tribe, dressed in traditional loin cloths, came down to the water's edge and motioned for Ariel to bring the panga into the river. Ariel timed the crashing surf just right; gunning the motor he cleared the sand bar, putting the panga safely in the protected waters of the river.

With Ariel's help, Luke unloaded his meager provisions. A strong looking, well- built Emeberá man in his mid 30's approached with a smile on his face, "Estoy el jefe aquí. Mi nombre es Livardo…" (I am the chief here, my name is Livardo.)

Livardo shook Luke's hand then helped him from the panga. Luke took time to shake hands with all of the men, show him his spear gun (which they gazed at with mesmerizing expression, as if he had just landed a space craft in their village) and explained that he just wanted to shoot some fish. He decided to give up the missionary act.

"Todos los pescado para ti y tus familias, pero you neccisito aletas, solga, buoy y plomo." (All of the fish is for you and your families, but I need fins, rope, buoy and weights).

Ariel and Felipe stayed in the boat.

"Luke, we go now. We get back before dark. May God be with you." Ariel said as he rushed to turn the boat around. Ariel seemed nervous, timing the swells poorly and taking a green wave over the bow as he plowed back through the surf.

He really looks spooked, Luke thought.

The men led Luke to the home of the chief, where he would be staying. He was introduced to the chief's young wife and handsome sons. Livardo seemed to like the idea of the fresh fish that Luke promised to bring to his table. Luke would discover that he was the first gringo to come to the village in a year and the first to arrive with a spear gun.

Livardo showed Luke something that was not Embera´-- a fully fortified and manned military bunker. The bunker was built above and below ground with green sandbags and a hardwood roof covered by a camouflaged tarpaulin and was home to a garrison of four very thick, well-trained special forces men of the Panamá defense force. The soldiers picked up arms and trained them on Luke.

"Nosotros amigos, tranquilo," (Our friend, relax.) Livardo said.

The garrison, Luke learned, was established at the request of the tribe after the FARC raided Playa de los Palos a dozen times, stealing gasoline, candles, food and medicine.

Playa de los Palos was outside the reservation that the rest of the Embera´ villages enjoyed. This meant less government meddling, but also less protection against pillagers and pirates. As a show of good faith, the government had given the tribe a new panga with a 40 horse powered Yamaha, and a gasoline store of 200 gallons.

"Passaporte?" A camouflage-clad soldier asked Luke.

This was a problem.

Luke could not afford to be reported to the authorities in Panamá, but if he could not establish his identity the soldiers were sure to take him into custody. He strained for a solution while keeping his composure. Luke felt his packets and pretended to act shocked when he came up with no passport.

"Lo olvidó en el barco," (Forgot it in the boat) Luke said. He then grabbed the pen and wrote his name on the sign-in list as "Cristóbal Delgado, Canadian, Passport ou812344.

The man looked it over.

"Okay, Cristóbal, cuidado." (be careful)

"Gracias," replied Luke, submerging his relief by shaking hands with the soldier and looking him in the eye.

The defense forces were charged with fighting off the FARC, so they had other things to think about other than Luke's misplaced passport. From that point on, the people of the village and the military would call Luke by his given name of Cristóbal.

Chapter Nineteen

LUKE SPENT THE remainder of the day trying to piece together his missing bits of dive gear. As hospitable as the Emberá were, if Luke did not deliver on his promise to feed them plenty of fresh fish, he figured they might ask him to leave.

In lieu of a weight belt, Luke partially filled a burlap sack with river rocks. For a tow-line he spliced together several pieces of rope he found on the beach. He attached a round Chinese fishing float to the end of the line. The only fins the Indians could come up with were a rotten set of Churchill bodyboarding fins.

Luke took stock of his jerry-rigged gear.

"This should be interesting."

With his new gear by his side Luke settled in for the night. Livardo, who performed the role of medicine man for his village, was amazed when Luke was able to identify many of the herbs that lay around the small home and their uses. Livardo promised to teach him more, as the fauna of the coastal zone had an even richer variety of herbs than the inland river habitats.

Cackling chickens and barking dogs woke Luke before sunrise. Livardo and three of his men readied the panga. The men who would be diving with him had only plate glass rubber-skirted masks, no fins, no gloves – nothing; only the masks and the same short wooden spears that the river communities had. Luke concluded that the Embera´ Indians, although now living on the coast, had never learned to access the rich marine resources at their doorstep. They existed as if they were still a riverine people, fishing the river and spearing fresh water shrimps.

Luke held on as Livardo gunned the throttle. The panga sped out of the river mouth, through the breakers and into open water.

Livardo apparently wanted to see what Luke could do, so he burned much of their precious rare gasoline to take the visitor one hour north to the reefs near Pinãs Bay.

Pinãs was home to the Tropic Star Fishing lodge, a high-end American-owned fishing resort where the rich and famous would go to bag record Black marlin, Blue marlin, pargo, wahoo, tuna and many other species. The reef that supplied the lodge with an endless stream of enormous fish was named after Zane Gray, one of Luke's childhood icons. Gray, a writer of western novels, was the first man to rod and reel fish blue fin tuna in the Pacific and had had Pinãs bay as his own personal fishing lodge during the 1930s.

The two-mile-long reef sat on the edge of a precipice that dropped off into thousands of feet of blue water. The drop off and interface of cold and warm water attracted plankton that attracted bait fish that in turn, attracted large predatory species. Huge pelagic, blue water fish passed by the reef during their 2,000-mile journey that took them from the Galapagos Islands off of Equador to Coiba Islands off of Panamá, to the Zane Gray Reef to Isla Malpelo Island, off Colombia and back again.

Luke was sure that the American owners of Tropic Star must pay off the FARC not to bother them. Even so, shoot-outs erupted occasionally.

Too short on gas to deliver Luke to the best part of the famous reef, Livardo motioned for Luke and the other divers to get ready. They would be diving the wash rocks hugging the coast.

Luke studied the area before jumping in. The growing surge and crashing waves threw spray 30 feet into the air, the water offered a dirty 20-foot visibility and jellyfish floated by fast, indicating a strong current. The Indians removed their lion cloths and jumped in naked. Luke slid over the gunnels, loaded his gun and asked for the 15-pound bag of rocks. The 45-foot buoy line trailed behind. The round shape of the Chinese buoy was creating drag in the heavy current, making the swim forward tough.

The float was covered with Chinese characters. Playa de los Palos locals had found it on the beach along with a dozen others. The discovery indicated that the Chinese long line fleet was fishing their 40-mile long-lines directly offshore instead of outside the 200-mile limit of international waters and international convention. The curtain of long lines prevented many of the lager swordfish and tuna from completing their migration.

The shore's west-facing orientation gave Playa de los Palos its name. It acted like a big scoop, collecting many dead sticks. In recent years, the beach collected mountains of oceanic plastic trash including shoes, beach balls, plastic bags, golf balls and syringes. The clear plastic bags were a hazard, as the nesting sea turtles tended to mistake the plastic for their normal food of jellyfish. The turtles choked on the bags and sometimes died. Birds ate the small bits of plastic, filling their guts with indigestible particulate matter sometimes resulting in starvation.

Luke kicked into the current. He wore only his shorts. The rest of his flesh was exposed to the invisible jellyfish that the Indians called *agua mala*, meaning bad water.

"Zap, zappp!"

A jellyfish slid its mini poison-filled tentacle along Luke's upper lip.

"Oouch!" Luke screamed as the non-lethal but excruciatingly painful venom coursed along his lip. After several minutes, the pain abated but his lip swelled up, making snorkel breathing tough.

Luke screamed again through his snorkel as a larger, more visible purple jellyfish filled his lower abdomen with poisonous stings.

"Ouch, shit that hurts. Yeeeowww."

Luke rubbed the wound. Within minutes the small red marks left from the sting turned from pain to itching, similar to that produced by poison oak.

Luke rounded the corner of the point and found an eddy (still circulating water) in the current that created a spot of clear, jellyfish-free water. The Indian divers remained in a tight group, ten feet behind Luke. They watched intently as Luke calmed himself and prepared to dive. He had been out of the water and not diving for some time, so for the first few dives he felt like a novice. Holding the sack of rocks in his left hand added to the difficulty of calming down and focusing. The attentive, and expectant audience added to his discomfort.

Luke hit his stride on the third dive. He threw six kicks and let the sack of rocks take him the rest of the way down. As he glided down, a shadow at the edge of visibility caught his eye. Luke still had not become overly familiar with all the species in this part of the world. In California, a lumbering shadow generally meant a seal or sea lion, or great white shark. Luke assumed it could be either. Luke slowly glided over to the animal.

Wow, a big grouper, he thought.

The fish appeared to be more than 200 pounds. Luke felt a surge of excitement. He was thrilled at the idea of feeding the whole village and earning his keep. He envisioned a big Hawaiian-style buried pig festival with the Indians dancing around the bonfire singing Luke's praises.

He eased into position and took aim.

"Wow, that is not a grouper. It's the world's biggest pargo."

The huge dogtooth snapper was so big it looked fake. The five-foot-long dark red fish was not the slightest bit afraid of Luke. It turned and hovered, giving Luke a perfect side-shot at close range. This was sure to be a perfect stone shot. The fish locked eyes with Luke, his oversized snaggle teeth protruding from both its upper and lower jaw. The teeth were visible even with its mouth closed.

Luke had this fish in the bag. He aimed neatly at the horizontal line that indicated its spinal cord. He squeezed the trigger.

Nothing happened.

He squeezed harder.

Still nothing happened.

He inspected his gun frantically, fearing that through all the abuse of the past few weeks he had broken it. He discovered that Indians had taken the liberty of engaging Luke's spear gun safety mechanism, preventing the gun from firing. Luke normally never left the safety on when he dove. In fact, he usually removed the safeties from his guns to prevent just such a mishap.

His heart raced as he reached back to turn off the safety and watched the fish sinking toward the depths. After fumbling his gun around, Luke reacted, pulling off a poor shot. He missed the fish by feet, scaring it away.

With great sadness in his heart, Luke surfaced. He told the Indians what had happened. They indicated that it was better that he did not shoot the fish as the dogtooth snapper is known to turn on a diver, grabbing him by the wrist and even the throat.

Some new species, he thought. Luke considered that fish a challenge and hoped to meet up with his lost prize again. No wonder the critter was so nonchalant in the presence of a human.

The Indians continued to dive in the shallows, getting slammed around on the wash rocks with each swell. Leaving bits of flesh on the barnacles did not seem to bother them. Their legs and arms were covered with scars from such activity.

For the Indians, diving was a group activity. They hunted like a pod of sea otters, prying off delectable rock scallops called spondylus, whose shells make beautiful red jewelry.

They speared mirco-fish of less than a pound.

"Cristóbal, Cristóbal, venga!" the normally soft-spoken Indians were screaming bloody murder at the top of their lungs. Luke thought "shark attack." He powered over as fast as he could.

The three Indians closely guarded a crevice. They pointed and shouted.

"Pargo grande!"

Luke kicked down to the rock the Indians indicated and peered deep into the crevice. He saw a decent 15-pound red snapper. Luke aimed and shot. The fish flared open its gills, lodging its body in the cave. Luke pulled and pulled but the stubborn fish had planted itself like a redwood tree. The Indians proceeded to dive on the fish, two at a time for more than 45 minutes until they finally freed the snapper. They all screamed with joy as they removed the spear shaft and put the fish in the boat.

They moved the panga a few miles closer to the village, diving in a small islet. The bottom had no coral and was covered with naked boulders and was not pleasing to the eye. The lure of more gargantuan pargo kept Luke blazing along. The Indians continued to pry off scallops and spot fish that were holed up. Each time they called Luke and his gun to shoot the fish.

The fish were respectable-sized pargo and small groupers under 20 pounds, but Luke wanted his trophy fish. On occasion, spearfishing presents divers with a once-in-a-lifetime shot. An experienced diver recognizes these rare opportunities and Luke feared that he had just blown the pargo of a lifetime. He could not shake the image of that huge fish and the perfect shot that he had bungled. The feeling of miscalculating a shot on a big fish is deep and can really burn a diver up inside. It is nature's little way of punishing a hunter, as losing trophy fish back in caveman days could have led to starvation. Nature wants a hunter to seriously lament losing a trophy kill, and they do.

Luke dove hard for the rest of the day, but his bad vibe from losing the pargo kept any big fish from coming his way that day. With enough fish for dinner, the men headed in.

That night as he ate the smaller pargos, Luke promised, "Tomorrow, I will get your mother."

The Indians could not understand Luke's frustration, as he had killed plenty of fish for dinner. The need to kill really big fish did not compute for the Indians. To the Indians, big fish were dangerous and destroyed gear, so they stuck to fish less than 20 pounds. To them feeding themselves was the real trophy, not the size of the fish.

The Indians played melodic music with drums and flutes. Several of the women sat topless, painting each other with blue dye. Emberá custom dictates that each time a man hunts well and feeds his people, he receives a temporary tattoo. Livardo told the women to paint both of Luke biceps and forearms with hexagonal patterns that became snake-like forms. Luke turned the torch light on his new artwork as it dried. He liked the paintings. They gave him a sense of belonging. The markings made him feel primitive. Primitive was good.

Livardo made Luke some tea.

"Give you good dreams and good sleep," the head man promised.

That night he dreamt of Nici and hoped she was doing well. Hernan appeared also, showing Luke the incredible diving in Panamá in the 1950s, when the water was still full of trophy fish and sharks.

Luke heard Hernan's voice.

"Each time we pulled the trigger, a bull shark came in on our fish, slow- never fast. One time I was diving with the Kuna Indians and one of the lobster divers got hit by a big tiger shark. The bleeding, screaming man struggled to get in the canoe. Once he did, the shark attacked the canoe throwing it from side to side. The Indians took the bleeding man and threw him screaming back to the sea where the 17-foot tiger shark ate him to pieces."

Luke woke the next morning with renewed determination. He added more line and a second buoy to his gun.

"Vamanos!" (Let's go) Luke announced as he showed the other men that he was ready to go diving again.

"Hoy, tengo grande pescado!" (Today, I have big fish) Luke boasted.

Low on gasoline, they dove a point closer to home that day. The surge increased, sweeping 30 feet up and down the wash rocks. The waves, although smaller than ten feet, still had in them the unstoppable power of the nearby, deep sea. They tended to catch Luke off guard, throwing him violently from side to side. The Indians continued to find smaller fish holed up for Luke to plink.

He was getting used to the stinging jellyfish, the surge and the bag of rocks in his left hand.

Luke let the Indians work about 50 feet ahead of him, while he rested on the surface about 20 feet from the jagged wash rocks. He was doing his usual 15 deep breaths followed by three shallow ones combined with a mental meditation when a silver dollar-sized eye ball swam toward him. The eyeball grew larger and larger. The body of the first fish came into view. Luke's brain tried to connect the dots. His initial response was "nice sierra," which is a barracuda-like fish. Three fish swam in a slow mechanical way, straight toward Luke, veering left just four feet away. It finally came to him.

"Tuna!"

These were not yellow fin tuna. They were longer, with black anal and dorsal fins. Identification could come later. Luke took aim at the second fish in line. It looked to be more than 150 pounds. Again, nervous with his new surrounding and smaller than optimal gun Luke pulled off a poor shot, hitting the tuna in the belly.

"Oh, no!"

The fish bolted like a bat out of hell. In a single motion, Luke lurched forward. The shooting line had become wrapped around the muzzle, snapping off the end piece of his gun as the fish careened away. In the same moment, a powerful ground swell picked Luke up, throwing him into the middle of the barnacle-covered wash rocks. Luke let go of the bag of rocks and gun then kicked for his life before then next swell delivered a death blow. The surge pounded Luke into the rocks again and again. With his adrenaline pumping at a fight or flight rate, he felt no pain.

"Socorro!" (Help!) Luke shouted as he tried to fend off the next assault.

Livardo sped toward him, driving the panga as close as he could without ending up on the rocks himself. With a few lucky kicks, Luke managed to beat the next swell. He slid his battered body into the panga. Livardo grabbed the buoy and pulled up his broken gun. The spear shaft was bent and a large chunk of tuna belly hung on the tip.

"Mala suerte," (bad luck) Livardo said.

"Crap!" Was the only word that came from Luke's mouth. He realized the lost tuna was actually a dogtooth with razor-sharp snaggle teeth; it is more of mackerel on steroids than anything else. Luke knew that dogtooth tuna usually live on the other side of the planet in places like Australia and Bali. Knowing how rare the sighting was made the loss that much harder to bear.

With enough fish for dinner and a broken gun, the men headed back to Playa de los Palos.

The women, grateful for the fresh fish, covered Luke's back and chest with more painted designs. Luke wore just his tattered shorts, no shoes, no shirt, no hat. His hair was becoming more blond with each day in the sun and was getting long enough to sprout a few dreadlocks. Luke's beard was filling in, giving him a Grizzly Adams look.

Luke spent the rest of the day widdling on his gun and tweaking the spear shaft in attempt to make it straight again. Eventually he re-fashioned the muzzle and put the gun back into working order.

Livardo approached.

"Good," he said, surveying Luke's handiwork. "Come with me to find medicine."

The two men went on a foraging walk. Luke, still bruised and tender from having been thrown ass first on the wash rocks, limped gingerly and was careful not to bump into the underbrush. As they made their way slowly through the jungle, Luke pointed out the plants and herbs that he knew of. Livardo showed him new ones that only grew along the coast. They negotiated a winding foot path, refreshed themselves in a pool of cool, fresh water that soothed his aching body, and wound down to the beach.

At the beach, Livardo pointed out fresh jaguar tracks in the sand, the impressions of the soft pads and claw points gradually disappearing with each lapping wave. They followed the tracks to a large hole that had been fashioned by a green sea turtle to deposit her clutch of eggs. The jaguar had dug up and feasted on the eggs, leaving bits and pieces everywhere. Livardo showed disappointment that he would not be able to eat the eggs himself.

A few days passed before Luke was ready to dive again. He could not afford to damage his gear so, this time, he decided to stick to fish under 40-pounds. He studied the larger snappers. He watched them feasting on lobsters and the smaller of their own kind. He frequently saw sharks. On most dives, especially close to dawn or dusk, bull sharks, tiger sharks, reef sharks and duskies would steal a bite or two of fish dangling from Luke's stringer, which trailed 75-feet behind him on the end of the buoy line.

Each time Luke felt a strong tug on the line he knew the sharks were snacking on his fish and it was time to get out of the water. Luke fed at least 30 people of the village each day. When Livardo was busy, Luke acted as stand-in medicine man and he took this duty seriously. He carefully administered each treatment and felt great pride every time a patient recovered from an illness.

A man came to him one day, a bit embarrassed, and asked for the sundown powder.

"Sundown powder?"

"Ask Livardo."

A woman came in, indicated she had abdominal pain and asked for sundown powder.

"What IS this stuff?"

"Ask Livardo."

He asked Livardo.

"I will tell you, friend, because you are one of us. We call it sundown powder because it helps a man become strong at sundown, with his woman. It has other benefits. It protects us from the rotting disease and when our bodies ache."

Livardo shared the secret with Luke.

He showed Luke how to take a membrane from the gut lining of a conch, dry it in the sun for three days and make it into a tea. Luke drank it. Within several days, he could feel a surge of well-being in his body. Livardo showed him how to take some of the powder and rub it directly on the wounds of a villager who had suffered from cutting firewood in the forest. The cuts healed within a day.

The villagers shared with him their stories of healing and sexual prowess – the latter accompanied by strutting and satisfied references to children produced.

It was a miracle medicine. The material worked so well that Luke promised himself to go into business encapsulating it if he ever returned to his normal life again.

He decided to label the remedy simply "marine minerals." That would do for the technical name, but what about a catchy label?

"It's potent and from the sea. I will call it **PotentSea.** Eureka! I like the sound of that. PotentSea Marine Minerals…

With his activities feeding and healing the people of the Embera´ village, Luke had become a valuable asset and a precious commodity. After a big feast, Livardo performed a ceremony in front of the entire village, declaring Luke an official Embera´ and presenting him with a necklace made from boar's teeth. This symbolic accessory, bestowed upon him simply and graciously, completed Luke's transition into his primal self. Luke had gone native, and he loved it.

For the Emberá, daily life moved in a continuous, harmonious rhythm. If it were not for Nici, Luke would be tempted to forget his life back in the world and simply assimilate into the Indian's way of life and stay there for ever. He felt a deep sense of calm and purpose. His nerves were settled, his senses had become finely tuned, his belly tight and his arms strong.

His freediving skills, as a matter of survival, were honed sharper than a samurai sword. Happiness existed in Luke and in the Embera´ village that he had not known before. It was not a knee-slapping, burst-out-laughter-at-a-crude-joke type of happiness, but a true and deep contentment that his native United States seemed to lack. Perhaps, nature provides the feeling happiness as a payoff for living more closely to nature's design, as the Indians did. Luke began to feel that whole idea of material conquest and monetary gain or even private land ownership was out of balance with nature's design and was more of an affliction that anything else. As a budding healer, Luke developed a sense of ailment and its root cause. He could now see why so many people back in the U.S. were sick. He realized that living far from nature's master plan, living a lifestyle that was empty and synthetic, could only lead to illness.

The Panamánian military men kept a watchful yet distant eye on Luke. So long as Livardo allowed Luke to stay in the village, the military men really had no choice but to agree. Luke, generally, kept his distance from the bunker and simply nodded when he walked past any of the soldiers, who were rotated every two months to prevent any bribery or monkey business with the FARC rebels who were never far off.

To pass the time, the soldiers bench-pressed heavy weights made from cement blocks and fired shots far to sea at anything that happened to float by. From time to time, they would play soccer and baseball with the Embera´ on a large field behind the village.

As another month passed, Luke noticed an up-tick in their surveillance of his movements by the soldiers. On several occasions, Luke caught one of the men shadowing him. He figured the men were just bored.

Chapter Twenty

LUKE ASSISTED AS Livardo's wife labored to bring her fifth child into the world. The blood and thrashing made Luke queasy, but he helped anyway. After four hours of labor, a healthy baby girl was born. Livardo tapped the infant on the rear and she responded with a healthy wail. The mother cleaned the newborn girl and wrapped her in soft fabric, holding her close to her breast and staring into the baby's eyes.

"Please name her," Livardo said, giving Luke the great honor.

Luke was overwhelmed but quick with his answer. He stroked the child's cheek.

"Nici. That's her name. Nici."

Sleeping space in Livardo's small, humble home was limited. He politely asked Luke if he would be willing to sleep alone in a smaller home near the chicken coops. Luke obliged. Declining dinner, Luke took his leave and headed to his Indian style bachelor pad. He had only his dive gear, a toothbrush and a small block of wood for his head.

Now, that Luke was sleeping alone, several of the village mothers presented their daughters. None of the girls was older than 14. The Embera´ generally married at 15 and begin having children soon after. Luke politely turned down the offers.

One wet evening, the tropical rain and thunder pounded the village. The river overran its banks. Hundreds of blue and red lightning bolts struck the earth, followed by intense, loud explosions of thunder. Luke struggled to get to sleep. He would doze off and the thunder would wake him again. He lay on his back looking towards the entrance to his home. The lighting continued. Strike after strike, the lighting lit up Luke's dwelling. Luke saw someone standing over him. Thinking the lighting was playing tricks on him he rubbed his eyes. Another bright lighting strike flashed.

A stern woman's voice snapped in Spanish.

"Get his spear gun and gear."

In the wash of lighting, Luke caught a good glimpse of the person. She was a tall woman wearing army fatigues, combat boots and wore a red beret with a single gold star in front. She stood with her hands on her curvy hips.

"Tenemos todo comandante." (We have everything, Commander)

Another lightning strike and the woman was closer.

"No wait!" Luke shouted.

The last thing Luke saw was the butt of a rifle coming toward his face, then a loud crack. The sound was his nose breaking. Swearing profusely, Luke put his hand over his bleeding nose.

"Stop! What are you doing? Stop!" Luke shouted in anger and pain.

Another rifle butt to the head knocked him silly. He tried to stand up, but fell back and slipped in and out of consciousness as two men tied a gag around his mouth. They pulled a black hood over his head and carried his limp body down the ladder.

"Ouuh. Ou,…uugh…Uurrrggggg." Luke emitted incomprehensible sounds from under the hood.

The woman and her henchmen dragged Luke along for a full day, carrying him like a trussed-up ape. They hiked up and down footpaths and animal trails. Luke could hear crashing waves for most of the trip so he knew that wherever they were, it must be close to the sea.

The bandits stopped for water. Luke moaned through his blood-soaked gag.

"Agua, agua."

"Remove his hood," the female voice ordered.

The men removed the hood. The bright sunlight glared into Luke's eyes. Blood had caked over his eyes. The blood and trauma from his broken nose and concussion made his vision blurry. He made out the silhouettes of three men smoking cigarettes and the women who had struck him in the face.

The woman walked over to Luke and gingerly untied his gag. She opened a bottle of water and helped him take a few gulps. She stepped back, smiled and, "Drink this, American pig," she said and punctuated her words with a swift kick to Luke's head with the steel heel of her combat boot. Luke slumped over, unconscious. She kicked him twice more in the gut then spit on his limp body.

"Hey, we need him, don't kill him," yelled one of her companions in Spanish.

Luke existed in a semi-dream state for the next few days. The bandits put him in a bamboo cage and force fed him cold Spam and water. They kept his hands tied tightly to the supports of the cage. The ropes cut into Luke's wrists. After two days, his hands were without feeling and the wrist wounds had become infected. Flies buzzed around, freely landing on Luke, filling his ears, nose and eyes. In his delirious state, he could not think clearly. Every so often, he heard the woman's voice ordering her men around.

Luke still had not got a good look at this sadistic bitch, but when he had a chance, he would memorize every detail because he was going to kill her before this was over.

The woman came in and removed his gag. Luke mumbled a few words. "What do you want with me? How did you get past the guards at Playa de los Palos?"

Wrong thing to say, apparently. The she-devil grabbed Luke's hair and slammed his head against a rock. She tightened his wrist restraints. "I will ask the questions."

Luke spit out a piece of a tooth.

Luke remained in his cage for ten days. He figured he had been kidnapped by the FARC and the ransom request would come soon but it never did. Luke pieced the clues together. The soldiers back at Playa de los Palos must have been collaborating with the FARC. No doubt they had made some sort of deal with FARC. Perhaps, they'd traded Luke for a ceasefire agreement, money or maybe even drugs. Just the same, Luke was screwed and he knew it.

Infection and malnourishment set in. Luke's ribs protruded, his cheek bones became pronounced and his eyes grew blind and sank deep into his skull. Luke was too ill to be scared. He fully expected death at any moment. He welcomed it as a relief.

They kept him separated from the main FARC camp. He had no idea where he was and had not regained his vision. Each time his wounds showed signs of healing, the women with the red beret would pay him a visit, every time giving him a little aid and comfort followed by a brutal beating.

Is this where he would die?

Nici....

Chapter Twenty-One

NOTHING. THIS WAS the sum total of Luke's situation.

No hope, no prospects for escape, fading health, not even an idea of where he was. Anger and the desire to snap the neck of the woman who wore the red beret was all that kept Luke alive. One day, he figured his brain had really turned into pudding when he heard poorly sung Led Zeppelin lyrics followed by the world's worst electric guitar solo piercing the jungle foliage.

It was Stairway to Heaven.

"Yep, this is it. I am dying now. At least, God has a sense of humor. I will wait for you on the other side, Nici," he murmured.

Luke, mused "Maybe God is a Panamánian taxi driver; yeah that's it, generally he's happy and good-natured but he falls asleep too much. Wake up God, wake up!"

"There's a woman who thinks all that glitters is gold and she's buuuuuying a stairway to heaven…"

A man about Luke's age came strolling down the footpath leading to Luke's cage. He was playing a vintage electric guitar. Around his neck he wore a small amplifier that gave the notes a tinny sound. The Latino had long black hair, a wide, bulbous nose and stood about five-foot, six inches tall. On each arm was a skinny young woman. They wore camouflage spandex pants and tight white T-shirts with a knot tied in them above the naval. The girl on the left arm had dyed suicide blonde hair, the one on the right arm sported bright red hair with cropped bangs. Both had poorly done boob jobs and wore way too much lipstick and eyeliner.

The man approached Luke. He turned the volume up on the amp and bellowed that last verse of the Zeppelin ballad. He then reached into his left pocket, grabbed a hand full of white powder then shoved his face deep into the pile. He snorted deeply several times and gave some to the girls. They snorted away. All three had noses covered in the drug.

"Now, that's what I'm talking about!! Wanna hear Freebird, Mr. Gringo?"

As ill as Luke was, he managed to shake his head indicating NO. *Make that a please, NO*, he thought.

"Ok, then Mr. Gringo, let's untie you."

The girls opened the cage. Afraid of another beating, Luke crunched down and pressed himself against the back of the cage. The girls rubbed their breasts in Luke's face as they tenderly cut his hands free, removed his gag and helped him onto his feet. Once he was on his feet, the girls removed their supporting hands. Unable to support his own weight, Luke collapsed. They picked him up again.

"Hola. My name is Carlos, but you can call me Carlito."
Carlito grabbed Luke's limp hand and gave it a shake.
"Cigarette?"

"No, gracias," Luke answered.

"I am a going to be a famous singer, but until that happens I run this place. You look like shit. Take him to the tent, girls."

The women helped Luke walk about 300 yards to a large, well-camouflaged army tent. It was positioned under the tree canopy and was made with radar and thermal- sensing proof material. In front of the tent were about 25 men sitting around a small campfire, resting on their guns, telling stories. The girls helped Luke inside the tent and onto a cot.

Inside were more than dozen badly wounded or ill FARC soldiers. Moans of pain filled the air as a small medical staff tended to them. Medical equipment was limited to cleaning agents, gauze, catgut and sewing needles to sew up wounds. No IV's, syringes or operating equipment could be seen.

"Am I going to die?" one man asked the nurse.

"Si, pronto," (Yes, soon.) she replied

Luke figured she did not want the last words the man heard on earth to be a lie.

The man to Luke's left sat shivering and convulsing with some tropical illness. Another soldier limped through the tent door. His left forearm had been blown off and his right leg appeared to have been ripped by shrapnel.

Carlito sauntered over to Luke's bedside. He ordered one of the nurses to give Luke all available medical attention. She followed the order by cleaning Luke's wounds, wrapped them in gauze and giving him what she explained was some of their last antibiotics for his badly infected wrist lacerations.

Food consisted of more cold Spam and water.

Luke was allowed to convalesce and heal for more than a week. On his fifth day, an apologetic nurse came to him.

"No tenemos más comida o provisiones médicas, lamentables." (We have no more food or medical supplies, sorry).

Despite his hunger, Luke finally was able to get up on his feet and move around. He was in no condition to attempt an escape. Carlito allowed Luke to exit the tent and wander around the camp area.

Luke found and devoured some berries and mushrooms. Luke kept his food finds secret so as not to attract attention from the other soldiers who paced about and drank water to fend off hunger.

He learned that most of the soldiers were under 20- years-old and came from the impoverished coca farming area of the Colombian countryside. The FARC recruited them by coming to their homes and offering their parents protection and money in exchange for three year's service from one of their children. But, generally heavy-handed persuasion was not needed. Many of the new recruits came from areas of Colombia in the southern Amazonian region. Areas in the province of Caqueta like Monserrate and Pinãs Colorado.

These areas had essentially ceded from Colombia proper and had enjoyed autonomous self-rule under the FARC for many years. The FARC paved the roads, ran the schools, collected taxes and provided for the common defense. Ironically, in these places the FARC strictly forbade drug use, fist fighting and drinking during the week. The FARC were equal opportunity rebels, recruiting front line fighters of both sexes. The youngsters from FARC controlled Colombia and often joined the insurgency as a matter of allegiance to the only real government they had ever known.

In recent years, the FARC had wised up and started paying the tuition for their brightest to go to medical school in the US. The students would return after residency to repay their debts with up to seven years of service in state of the art, MASH tents the FARC maintained in Colombia, Panamá and Ecuador. The FARC extracted millions in hard currency from taxing, producing and running cocaine shipments from Colombia to the cash rich markets in the U.S. and Europe. Rumor had it that the FARC had even funded, in part, the political campaign of their current champion, Hugo Chavez, president of Venezuela.

Whether Chavez had a direct link to FARC or not, nobody knew for sure, but suffice it to say that he made life easy for them and enjoyed bolstering their ranks as true Anti-American and anti-Colombian government fighting forces. The FARC maintained permanent camps on the Panamánian side, Dairen rain forest; some better equipped than others. There they could seek refuge from the perusing, U.S.- backed Colombian troops. In the war on drugs, Darién was a no-man's land, much like that of Laos and Cambodia during the Vietnam era.

Luke never once saw Carlito eat. He simply would plow his face down into a small mountain of pure cocaine then proceed to play twenty songs on his guitar while singing loudly and out of tune. Carlito made sure that the best-looking women recruits were always made part of his private harem.

Although shell-shocked, Luke regained some of his composure. He sat down on a log in front of the ever-burning campfire. Before he could start up a conversation with the men, she appeared. The soldiers all stood up and saluted the women with the red beret. Luke shook like a wee dog. She had really put the fear of God into him. Luke stood up as she walked towards him. He waited for the inevitable boot to the gut or blow to the head.

"Just... just do what... what you're gonna do," Luke stuttered.

She came face to face with Luke, stared intently into his eyes and stepped back.

"Basta!!" (Leave) she ordered.

The soldiers left.

The she-devil removed her red beret and flung her long, black silky hair from side to side. For the first time, Luke got a good look at the women who had physically and mentally tortured him for the past two weeks.

"I bet you think I'm pretty evil," the women said as she offered Luke a candy bar.

Luke did not reply. He snatched the candy bar from her hand, unwrapped it and sucked it down in a breath.

"Isn't this the part where you beat me to within an inch if my life while calling me a capitalistic pig?"

"We kidnapped you for two reasons. A) Your Indian friend killed my cousin with an arrow to the neck, but I have taken my revenge on you already with the beatings for that, now we are even. And B) you have something that we need..."

"That was your cousin that Morgan killed?"

The woman made no reply and Luke recalled that the arrow had been swift, silent and deadly. The kid had never had a chance.

"So," he continued, "What do I have that you could possibly need?" Luke winced and felt his cracked tooth with his tongue.

"My name is Gabriella, my rank is comandante. I am the one in charge of the front-line battles we have with the capitalistic thieves called the Colombian army. They get almost all their weapons and training from the United States. We fight hard. Each week we cross the border into Colombia, kill as many of them as we can, then come back here to our place of safety, the Dairen jungle. We come here to hide and to heal. This is our only hospital for more than 300 FARC fighters. We are very far from re-supply. We often run short on food and medical supplies."

Gabriella removed her flack jacket. Underneath she wore a white tank-top and a necklace holding a locket.

"May I see?" Luke asked, gesturing at the locket.

She opened it to reveal a photo of her father with his arm around the iconic Cuban rebel leader Che Guevara, better known as El Che. In the picture, El Che sported the same red beret that Gabriella wore with such pride.

Gabriella was no more than 27-years old. Her hips were curvy and her full lips made up for a minor under-bite and a proud chin. Despite the tough living conditions, she managed to keep her hair long and silky black, draping down her back in soft curls. Her skin was a perfect olive tone and her eyes were hazel. Now that Luke got a good look at her, it was tough to imagine such a beautiful woman killing or hurting anybody.

Gabriella twisted her locket and gazed lovingly into the small photo of the two men.

Luke looked at a family of bullet wound scars on her arms.

"My Father, Aramis, was El Che's right-hand man. Together, they took back Cuba from Batista and his American masters. He raised me to believe firmly in the Communist way. When Castro fed El Che to the dogs in Bolivia, my father figured that the power had gone to Fidel's head. My papa so strongly believed in communism, he took a band of his best men, hired a cargo ship and came over to the Caribbean side of Panamá. The plan was to launch an amphibious invasion and take over Panamá, making it into a communist state. The ship foundered then broke in half. All of the men, including my father, were killed or captured."

That, Luke concluded, was the rusting cargo ship that Hernan had pointed out. His speculations about the crew were true.

"I was on that boat," Gabrilla said. "I was nine-years-old and alone in the jungle fending for my life. The FARC found me almost dead. They took me in, raised me and here I am. I owe them everything. The FARC factions are many, and they disagree. Some believe in Communism more than others. To remain alive and stay armed we traffic in drugs. You Americans have a huge appetite for the Columbian drugs. It is So huge, so much money. Sometimes the money makes our leaders crazy. I do my best to keep them on track and remind them we are fighting not for money or power, but to achieve a socialist state."

"But what do want with me?"

"You can see that we – our little band -- are hungry and have almost no medical aid. The soldiers on the beach in Playa de los Palos who sold you to us told us, they told us that you know how to catch many fish from the sea and know how to harvest the native plants and use them to heal people."

It all made sense now, but Luke wanted to know just one thing.

"How much did I cost you?"

Gabriella paused, "Three cartons of cigarettes."

"Is that the going price for a spearfishing, herbalist gringo?"

"We probably could have got you for two cartons."

"If I help you, what will do for me?"

"We might let you live."

Luke scratched his chin in thought, "Sounds pretty good to me."

Gabriella handed Luke back his spear gun, mask, snorkel and the rest of the gear the Indians had loaned him.

"We will take you to the sea tomorrow, but today get to work picking some herbs. We have five men with some sort of illness that we cannot identify and many more with infected wounds. I will be behind you every inch of the way, so don't try anything or you go back into the cage. Got it?"

"Yeah, I got it."

Luke cracked his neck, stretched and set off into the forest. Gabriella followed close behind as Luke filled a plastic bag with a selection of leaves, roots and berries.

He   stopped   several   times.

"What is the matter? Keep moving," Gabriella said.

"Look, I think you gave me bran manage... I mean brain damage with that rifle butt of yours, so bear with me. If I pick the wrong herbs they can kill your men or worse, it might make their juevos shrink up and fall off."

"Really. Okay, keep going." Gabriella softened her tone.

They returned to camp several hours later. It was nearly dark and Carlito was doing his usual mega coke-fest with his ladies. The other soldiers split a bottle of rum as they sat around the sputtering campfire cleaning their guns. Food and medical supplies may have been in short order at this FARC base, but guns and ammo were plentiful.

Luke reached for some sticks to freshen the fire.

"No," said Carlito, pushing his arm away. "We must keep the fire small so the choppers do not find us."

Luke sat down and reached into the plastic bag. He produced an odd-looking green fruit. He told the men to take just one bite each.

"It kills hunger and gives you energy."

The men obliged. Within minutes, they were up walking around and full of life. Carlito played a terrible version of Hotel California by the Eagles.

Luke entered the hospital tent. He started with the external wounds, rubbing large green leaves on the wounds. Luke instructed the nurses how to make a batch of boiled herbs, and he prescribed various doses of the elixir based on the severity of each wound. The men hated the foul-tasting concoction, but they drank it, nevertheless. They screamed and had to be restrained when Luke poured scalding hot potions directly onto their wounds. Luke worked through the night and treated more than 20 people. The next morning, the wounded soldiers felt less pain, the swelling had gone down and some of infections appeared to recede.

Each day, Luke did his best to teach Gabriella something he knew. He taught her how to make natural cat-gut for sewing up wounds from the same dried reeds that the Embera´ has used to weave their baskets.

Luke figured the more they knew the less they needed him.

The next morning, Gabriella woke Luke before dawn. He had been allowed to sleep on a cot in general barracks. However, he dreamt most nights that he was still in the bamboo cage and woke up sweating several times.

"Okay, gringo, time to get us some fish," Gabriella snapped.

"Now, you are calling me gringo, no more capitalistic pig? I must be moving up in the world."

Gabriella reminded Luke to grab his dive gear. They made their way down a long winding trail to the beachhead, Gabriella pounding Communist jargon into Luke's head the entire way.

The dense jungle gave way to crashing surf and sand. The black sand beach was stark, free of trash, strewn with seashells and strikingly beautiful. They might as well have been the only people on earth. There were several small wash rocks 50-yards offshore and a rocky point on one end of the beach. The north end of the beach was home to a near-perfect left-handed surf break. Luke wished for his surfboard as he watched the hollow six-foot waves peel for more than two minutes at a time.

Gabriella handed Luke his spear gun and flashed him a sassy smile.

"Don't come back empty-handed."

Luke's still badly aching body did not bode well in the water. He swam for ten minutes but was quickly winded. He tried to dive but his broken nose had not yet healed, making clearing his ears impossible. He would have to shoot from the surface.

He lay on his back and kicked hard, making it to the wash rock in half an hour. Dry season had kicked in. With little rain, the rivers muddied the ocean less than during the rainy months. Luke rolled over and was pleased to see that the water showed nearly 50-feet of visibility. A few jellyfish floated by, but they were the least of his concerns. He stayed near the eddy on the down-swell side of the wash rock.

He searched, floating on the surface, for over an hour, but only small aquarium-sized fish happened by. He could see Gabriella standing on the beach. She wore her red beret and rested her AK-47 on her hip and looked like she was posing for GI-Jane magazine.

A minor school of no more than five 15-pound sierras swam in on Luke, who delayed his shot until they were just a few feet away. He let the arrow fly, hitting his target in the forehead and killing it stone dead. He strung up the fish and waited for another.

The types of fish rotated. As the tide went slack, the Pargo came in. Luke shot and strung up nice 20-pound Pargos. After shooting each fish, he had to put the brakes on to keep them from holing up, as it would be impossible for him to dive down and free the fish with his plugged-up ears. Luke spent a full five hours in the water. His "wait and let the fish come to you" technique was reaping rewards with minimal risk to his person.

Little by little, Luke got his groove back. He dearly wanted to dive, but his ears were still as plugged up as a constipated sailor in a storm.

"Tiburon, tiburon!" (Shark, shark!) Gabriella screamed as she pointed at several dorsal fins heading toward Luke. At the edge of visibility, six bull sharks were closing ranks on him. In the middle, swam a healthy 40-pound bojala. After surviving the FARC, Luke figured he could handle the sharks; plus, he loved to eat raw bojala.

He pulled off. The fish briefly dragged him until a shark chomped off the fish's entire belly section. Luke pulled the speared fish toward him while making his way back to the beach. Each time a shark came in for a free snack he swatted it with the butt of his gun. The sharks backed off as the water became shallower. Getting a ride from the waves, Luke made better time than on his trip out. He gained the beach and exited the water, winded, and crept on his hands and knees.

"Hurry! Pull in the float before the sharks eat the rest of the fish!" Luke barked.

Gabriella hauled away until all the fish were high and dry.

"Oh, que lindo" (very nice.)

They each slung an equal amount of fish over their backs and headed back to camp.

"You can call me Gabby."

"OK, Gabby."

Chapter Twenty-Two

LUKE AND GABBY slogged back to camp, laden with fish, to find that Carlito had returned from a recruiting mission. He drilled the 40 fresh faces, making them do push-ups and jog in place while reciting the FARC credo. Then, Carlito saw the bounty of fish. He made the recruits stand at attention for more than twenty minutes while he inspected the fish, felt the firmness of the meat and looked at the of redness of the gills.

"Very well done, Luke and Comandante. Tonight, we eat well. Luke, you are needed in the medical tent. Grab your herbs."

Carlito returned to hazing the recruits. He asked them, one by one, why they were there. Their answers surprised Luke. Most of them were there because they wanted to be, because they supported the FARC and what they stood for. Carlito dismissed the recruits who soon huddled around a staticky TV, showing the anti-American tirades of the Venezuelan president Hugo Chavez. Each time, Chavez, (who was dressed head to toe in red) came to a point the recruits would raise their fists and yell, "Si, si, si juntos libertatamos!" (yes, together we are free)!

Chavez's fervor sent chills down Luke's spine. He thought of the impending terror attack on the Canal and the safety of Nici and his friends back in Panamá City. His conscience was creeping in. He had to get back, he had to act!

But, now was not the time to ponder his situation. The unknown illness of some of soldiers in the tent was spreading. Luke cooked up just about every recipe that Abuelo and Livardo had taught him. He tried the remedies for malaria, yellow fever, the foot worm, even influenza. Several of the soldiers showed improvement after a few hours. But despite Luke's efforts the majority of soldiers worsened.

The first one died.

Carlito entered the tent. He had cocaine speared all over his face and his eyes projected lunacy. "You better figure out what they are dying from or lay down next to them," said Carlito as he chambered a round in his .45 and pointed it at Luke's head.

Luke cringed and closed his eyes.

"Just kidding, my friend. You are the best goddamn spearfishermen here. I can't kill you. We need you."

"Carlito, did you see anything out of the ordinary out there?"

"We did see some low flying airplanes. They dropped orange powder."

Luke knew what that meant.

"They are using chemical warfare, Carlito. They are poisoning you like rats."

"Hijos de putas," (Sons of bitches)

Bang, bang, bang! Three holes appeared on the tent's ceiling and Carlito holstered his pistol.

A heated conversation between Carlito and Gabriella ensued. Using sticks in the dirt, they drew up hasty battle plans. The plan complete, they shook hands, saluted each other and hugged.

Around midnight, Luke finally got to eat some of the fish he had speared that day.

"What's going on?" Luke hesitantly asked Gabriella.

"We know where their main airbase is. We are going to destroy it. I am sure it's where they load the chemical that they have been using against us. It is guarded by more than 1,000-Colombian special forces soldiers and plenty of U.S. military hardware.

"But you are only 300 people, half of them wounded and sick. You would be committing suicide!"

"If we do not attack the airbase, they will poison us all. We have no choice. We attack at dawn and I will lead them."

Luke asked, "How far is it?"

Gabriella paused, threw Luke a look that said, mind his own business, then replied, "Just over the border, about a day's hike from here."

Luke could not believe his own emotions. He was fearful that Gabriella might get killed -- the woman who had kidnapped, brutally beaten, caged and tortured him. Luke recalled when he vowed to snap her neck. Now he hoped for her safe return.

Gabriella gave a long pep talk to her seasoned soldiers and the new recruits alike before retiring to her private tent. She fingered Luke to follow her. Luke obeyed.

Luke waited a few moments, took a deep breath and entered her tent. She had lit several candles, put on the Buena Vista Social Club CD, applied red lipstick and sat on her cot.

"Take off my boots."

He pulled off one boot then the other. Her feet were red and chaffed. She removed her flack vest. She put her .45 on the night stand and set her rifle on the ground.

"Tomorrow, we fight to the death. We expect to lose more than half our men and I will be leading the charge. I want to spend what might be my last night earth with you. You see, my father, God rest his soul, taught me how to survive and how to take what I want. Right now, I want you."

She grabbed Luke, unbuttoned his shorts and removed his sweat-soaked shirt. She caressed the bruises on his flanks that she had made with her rifle butt.

"That's your handy work," Luke said.

His flesh was leathery, tan and covered with the fading painted designs from the Embera´ village.

Gabriella stood up and put Luke's hands on her body, motioning for him to unbutton her pants.

Who was he to argue?

Gabriella exuded sexual energy. She kissed Luke's neck.

Luke sighed and thought of Nici.

Weighing the penalty for refusing Gabby's advances, he played along. Or at least that's how he justified it in his male head.

Luke's body was covered with goose bumps. She kissed his lips then forced him onto the cot. Gabriella's .45 was within easy reach. He knew it and she knew it, and she did nothing to push it out of reach.

Latin women are known to be fire crackers in bed. Gabriella was more like a nuclear explosion. She screamed inaudible Spanish phrases of ecstasy while she dug her nails into Luke's flesh.

The two made love through the night, finally falling asleep too close to dawn. At 4 a.m., Carlito barged in.

"Comandanate, the troops are ready."

Gabriella mustered, put all her gear back on, kissed Luke on the cheek and left him snoring on the cot.

Chapter Twenty-Three

LUKE WAS LEFT more or less alone in the camp. Even the pretty girls of Carlito's harem shouldered their guns and marched with the troops. The only people left behind were the nurses and those too sick or wounded to fight. He did his best to treat the very ill soldiers in the tent. Several of the soldiers suffering from gaping wounds asked to be stitched up and given a weapon so they could fight again.

Three long days and two nights went by.

On the third night, all hell broke loose. Wounded and hysterical soldiers trickled in. They all seemed shell-shocked.

"Where is Gabriella?" Luke asked

"We lost sight of her yesterday. Many were killed."

Luke's heart sank.

Did you destroy the airbase?

"Sí," a wary female voice said. It was Gabriella.

She limped over to Luke and collapsed in his arms. Her jugular had been punctured and her clothes were soaked in blood. Luke had no formal medical training, but he let his instincts guide him. He reached inside her neck and pinched the vein with his thumb and forefinger and dragged her into the medical tent. He caressed her blood-caked hair as the nurse readied the stitching material that Luke had made from the dried reed.

"Hold on, Gabriella, hold on."

She still wore the red beret. Luke went to work sewing her up. As she awoke from a stupor a half hour later, she gasped and lunged for a gun.

"Relax Gabby, you are safe now. What happened out there?"

She whispered. "We blew up all of their fucking planes, more then 15 of them. It was beautiful, now we are safe. But they unleashed hell on us -- mortars, helicopter rocket fire and even flame throwers. I am not sure who survived."

Luke nodded his head as he pretended to listen. "Gabriella, here, bite onto this." Luke said as he handed her a small stick. She bit down hard as Luke went work putting cleaning agents on her deep neck wound.

"Hang on, Gaby." Luke said as he readied his primitive suture kit. Luke poured more reddish sterilizing liquid over the cat gut and sycle-shaped needle. Luke first sewed a few internal stitches in her neck to stop the bleeding. Gabriella faded in an out of consciousness. Luke then washed off her blood-soaked neck area and neatly stitched up Gabriella's three-inch-long neck laceration. He then put into Gabriella's hand the last course of antibiotics he had access to. Gabriella lay passed out on the cot. Luke gingerly kissed her on the forehead and said. "I will be right over there if you need me."

Luke did his best to treat all the wounded but he was overwhelmed. More than 100 men and women did not return from the battle. The ragtag army had spent almost all their available ammunition to complete the mission. Without more arms and men, they were sitting ducks.

Luke spent the better part of three days mustering strength where he had none. He was forced to decide who would live and who would die, and giving medical help to those he thought would pull through; so far, Gabriella looked stable.

When she awoke, for his bravery, Gabriella tied the trade mark rebel red bandanna around Luke's forehead. Despite the fact the FARC stood for everything Luke was raised to despise-- terrorism, drug-trafficking and communism -- he felt that they needed him and he needed them. Politics; who was right and who was wrong, did not amount to hill of beans in that jungle. He was on the run from the U.S. and Panamánian governments. Right now, the FARC were the only allies he had. War makes strange bedfellows.

Luke took it upon himself to spearfish each day and bring back as much fresh meat as he could. The steady meals really sped up healing time for the wounded. He sat with Gabriella, told her stories of his old life and why he was on the run. He even told her about Nici.

"Maybe it's possible to love two women," Luke said as he carved a thick wood stick into a primitive spear gun. He routed out a slot for the shaft and constructed a basic trigger mechanism out of a wire hanger and a spring. The shaft was made from a random piece of a Jeep's undercarriage. He filed the tip to a sharp point. He powered the small gun with three pieces of surgical tubing. When he was finished, he gave the gun to Gabriella.

"Now you can shoot your own fish."

In time, Gabriella recovered and was busy planning her next step.

"Luke, before we fight again, I want to have a huge feast to reward everyone for their sacrifices. Plus, we need to rebuild morale and make some long-term food stocks.

"Carlito is expecting a shipment of product, coming in a week, that we need to move up to the Canal. We must move it to buy more arms. Right now, we have almost no ammunition and could all be slaughtered if they found this hideout. I want you to shoot a huge fish, something that we will all remember. That way our troops can feast and so can our brothers coming from Colombia with the product."

Luke knew better than to ask about Carlito's "product."

"What is the one with the long nose?" she asked.

"Uhm, a marlin?"

"Yeah, you are gonna shoot us one of those. We will eat it for a week, or if we smoke it maybe it will last for a year. Yes, mijo, you can do that for us."

"Gabby, look, to do that we have to go very far and my gun is too small and my fins are rotten."

"We can make a boat. And your gun, well, just get closer to the fish."

"Do you have a motor? Luke asked.

"No, we will make a sail."

Luke could not believe he was being asked to do this. He begged her to be happy with the fish he was providing.

"I will go with you, Luke." Gabriella said in her seductive firm manner.

I am gonna regret this, Luke said to himself.

Gabriella ordered her troops to start work on a makeshift raft with two sails. The sail material was made from old tent fabric. The raft was cut from balsa wood logs felled in the nearby forest. The stripped logs were pieced together via tongue and groove and secured with rope and dried reeds. The two masts stood ten and twelve feet tall. The small boat would be steered with a small rudder in the back.

The whole thing looked like a death wish to Luke.

It was 25-feet long by eight-feet wide. The balsa trees were freshly cut and had not had ample time to dry. As bouyant as balsa wood is, if it is not properly dried it can absorb water and sink in a hurry.

"The only place I know where we can find marlin for sure is Zane Gray reef off Pinãs Bay. How far is our beach from there?"

Luke was aghast when Gabriella drew a dirt map showing their location and the location of Zane Gray reef. The FARC camp was less than ten miles from the Tropic Star lodge and the famous reef. If the wind was just right they should be able to make the trip in less than two hours, each-way.

For a shake down, they assembled the entire raft in the middle of the camp. Luke decided that a double-masted design was too unwieldy. He asked that a single larger sail and boom be used. With little sailing experience, Luke felt funny giving instructions on what might and might not work for the wind-driven craft.

"Now build in a few storage containers for food and water," he said. "I don't imagine you have flair guns, life jackets and an EPIRB, do you?"

Gabriella gave Luke a blank stare.

"No mijo, just us and your gun."

Luke asked if the men could also carve one of the logs into a surfboard shape. When it was done, Gabriella stood over it.

"What is that supposed to be, mijo?"

"It's a life raft," Luke smiled.

The men did a decent job cutting the ten-foot log into a six-inch thick plank board. It narrowed on both end. Luke carved a deep notch into the hull of the plank where he planned to insert a fin for better handling.

"A life raft can come in very handy," Luke said, recalling the horror of his night at sea in a life raft with four other shivering friends. It had been three years since that fateful night when a petroleum barge split in two the sport fishing boat he was on. The fear from that accident haunted him still.

After a solid week of cutting, shaping and notching, the craft was ready for its one and only sea trial. A dozen of the soldiers each carried a piece of the craft to the water's edge. Luke and Gabriella and their soldier-crew worked hard to fasten all the sections together. The group ceremoniously lifted the raft up and gently placed it in the calm waters of the bay. Gabriella breathed a sigh of relief when the boat proved that it could float, and float well.

"Gabriella, I think we should let the boat float overnight. We need to be sure that it will not soak up water and sink on us," Luke said as he readied a large stone with a hole through it to be used as an anchor.

"If you are coming to sea with me, I need to know that you can both swim and shoot fish. Please go get the gun I made for you."

"No mijo, I don't need to do that..." Gabriella protested.

"If you don't you can go shoot your own marlin!" Luke barked.

Gabriella stomped her feet like a little girl as she walked up the trail. Luke figured she did not really like to swim, or worse, could not.

Go figure, a tough warrior like Gabriella afraid of swimming.

Popping into his consciousness was a visual of the boat that she had wrecked on as a young girl. Perhaps, she was traumatized in the water, he thought.

Gabriella returned in a pair of cut off shorts and her tank top.

"OK, mijo, where do you want me to swim?"

Luke gently assisted Gabriella. He helped her put on his fins and showed her how to use the mask and snorkel.

"The mask feels funny. I can't breathe through my nose," she said.

"You just need to get used to it."

Luke held Gabriella up by placing his hands on her firmly. As she kicked in place she made nervous sounds through the snorkel.

"OK, now go swim out to that wash rock and spear a fish, any fish." Luke said. "I will go with you."

He grasped her hand as she kicked the 50-yards out to the wash rock, holding the homemade spear gun in the other. Each time a small fish or sand shark came into view Gabriella gripped Luke's hand tighter. When they reached the wash rock, Luke handed her the spear gun and motioned for her to load it. She accidentally pointed the loaded gun at Luke.

"Please keep the sharp end pointed away from me," Luke said.

"Sorry, mijo."

Now, take a few deep breaths, then hold in your air and glide down towards the bottom. Gabriella followed Luke's instructions. She only made it three feet before the pressure created too much pain in her ears, sending her back up.

"Gabriella, grab your nose and put your tongue against the roof of your mouth. Blow gently to open your ears about every three feet and you will feel no more pain."

Gabriella followed the instruction. She made it a full, 15-feet down. Luke followed her each step of the way. He pointed out a small pargo a few feet in front of her. A natural with any type of gun, Gabriella aimed and shot the fish, hitting it near the tail. It zipped off.

"Pinga, where did it go?" she said with frustration.

"Fish look closer and larger underwater, plus they are moving, you are moving and the sea is moving. So, next time shoot for the head. That way you have more room to miss."

Gabriella took a deep breath and made it to a deeper, 20-feet this time. A larger Pargo, about 25-pounds, swirled near a boulder. Luke motioned not to shoot the fish, as it was too big for the small gun. She mistakenly thought he was telling her to pull the trigger. She fired, nailing the fish dead in the skull. It twitched and fluttered like a leaf in the breeze.

"That was fun, mijo, let's do it again!"

Gabriella was enjoying herself. She looked to Luke like a normal young woman with no cares in the world instead of a politically twisted, jungle guerrilla.

"We better go in. If you shoot too many fish in one spot the sharks will come."

They swam back in. Luke held the gun while Gabriella clutched her prized fish. She dragged it onto the beach and with immense pride she showed it to the soldiers.

"OK, you pass the swim-slash-spearfishing test. If the raft is still floating in the morning, we can leave then."

"No mijo, we must leave in the afternoon. The wind is better, but really there are many fishing boats from the Tropic Star lodge on the reef. By afternoon, they go home. We cannot afford to be sighted, by anybody for any reason." Gabriella grew serious and grabbed one of the men's rocket propelled grenades to demonstrate her point.

"Okay, okay, the afternoon it is, but if we get stuck out there, don't blame me."

Luke eyed the life raft. "I think I should test that too."

With some help, he launched the shaped plank, inserted the fin and tried to paddle. The big board was a slug.

Luke had to knee paddle to get it to move. It was so bulky, the only way to turn or change course was to physically get off the board and push the nose in the direction he wanted it to go. The surf break on the north end of the bay was still peeling perfect, hollow five-foot left-handers. Luke paddled to the break, aimed the board toward the beach and paddled for the first wave that came along. To his amazement, the wave picked up the board. Luke quickly stood up to pull into the wave, putting all his weight on the right rail. The board tucked into the curl. Luke walked back and forth on the board, finally ducking into the peeling, hollow tube. The curl covered him for a full six seconds. As the wave tapered off, he stood up and raised his hands, clenched his fist and let out a resoundingly loud "Yaaahoo!"

Gabriella and FARC soldiers observed the spectacle with amusement.

Luke paddled back out. He rode more than twenty waves all the way to the shore. With each wave, his control of the massive board increased, and so did his pleasure. He wished and dreamed that his childhood buddies back in Malibu could see him. After the twentieth ride, Gabriella insisted that he show her how to catch a wave. He paddled in to the beach then placed her on the board dead in front of him. He paddled on his knees while she flailed around. He took her out to the break and gave her a few instructions.

"OK, here we go. Paddle hard into the wave."

She swung her arms wildly. She screamed like a child as the wave picked up the board. The board scooted along for several seconds before Luke helped Gabriella stand up. He kept his hands on her waist as she struggled not to fall. When the wave ended, the two stood in three feet of water. By now the soldiers had returned to camp. Gabriella pushed the board out of the way.

"Mijo, now you owe me something... Triel me tu culo para aqui!" (bring your ass over here.)

Luke let Gabriella take the lead. After all, she was the comandante.

They kissed in the knee-deep water. She led Luke up onto dry sand.

Like Adam and Eve, the two collected sand on their, wet naked bodies as they rolled around on the empty beach. The world of pain and war and strife and terror drifted far away.

At the end of it, Gabriella dove into the water to rinse off, grabbed her trophy Pargo and headed back to camp, laughing.

Luke, reluctant to wash off the moment, watched her go as he waded into the water.

"Hey, woman. You better let me cook that fish. You haven't got a clue."

Chapter Twenty-Four

THAT NIGHT, LUKE dreamt that he was far out to sea on the raft and a fishing boat was coming to rescue him. He felt a momentary sense of relief followed by sadness and shock when Gabriella blew the boat to pieces with an RPG.

The morning came quickly. As he stretched and yawned he had a funny feeling that he was forgetting something. He took a mental inventory: "Nine liters of water, dried fish and Spam for food, diving equipment and a Huckleberry Finn hat that he had woven from dried reeds. What else... Oh shit, oars!"

Luke spent the remainder of the morning carving two small hand paddles out of hard wood.

"OK mijo, it's noon. Let's get a move on. The marlin are waiting."

All the able-bodied soldiers followed as Gabriella and Luke headed off to the beach. As they approached the beachhead they could see the raft floating in the bay.

"She still floats!" Gabriella said with joy.

"Yes, but she looks lower in the water," Luke said. "I am sure she is absorbing water. But I am not sure how much and how fast."

Luke knew canceling or delaying was not an option. Carlito would be back soon, bringing with him the "product" Gabriella had spoken of and most likely some new recruits and even some FARC brass from the Colombian side of the border.

Luke slid the surfboard /life raft into the water and tied it with a ten-foot line behind the main craft.

Luke and Gabriella stood on the beach, glancing briefly and chuckling at the disturbed sand from their escapades the previous afternoon. They beheld the raft with a shared sense of pride and accomplishment.

"Gabby, it's bad luck to have a boat with no name. This is your idea, so you pick the name."

"Aramis, for my father, God rest his soul."

Luke waded out to the raft, carved ARAMIS into the port and starboard bow logs. He raised the sail and helped Gabriella aboard. He handed her a paddle, weighed anchor and started to row.

Gabriella slung her AK-47 around onto her back.

"Paddle in time with me, one and two and three..." Luke said.

The soldiers on the beach applauded loudly and fired off a few   shots.

"Buena suerte!" (Good luck) they cheered.

Luke and Gabriella paddled hard. Water covered the deck as they took their first wave near the wash rock, but the Aramis remained afloat. They stopped rowing after passing through the breakers.

"OK, Gabby, I'll work the tiller. You manage the tension on the boom line." Luke had rigged a piece of rope from the leading end of the boom back down through a simple block and pulley attached to the deck. To prevent water from shooting up through the hull, they had covered the deck with two layers of woven mats.

The strong afternoon north wind freshened and filled the sail which was made from pieces of tent canvas. Gabriella cinched the boom tightly and the Aramis was off and sailing at a swift three knots. The sea state in a normal vessel would have been tolerable, even pleasurable. But in the bogged down, clunky raft, even the two-foot wind waves on top of a three-foot ground swell managed to keep the deck continuously covered with water and pitched the raft back and forth. Gabriella grew queasy. After an hour of fighting off what she considered to be weakness, she lost her lunch.

"Gabriella, if this is too tough we can turn back. Now, is the time."

"No mijo, we keep going. I will be okay. Just keep going."

"Are you sure? I can see more wind up ahead."

"Good. The boat will sail faster."

Gabriella pulled the sail even tighter.

By early afternoon, they were more than three miles offshore. Gabriella gripped her gun, scanning the horizon for any sign of other boats.

"Looks good. I think we are alone out here," Gabriella said.

"That's good for them," Luke joked.

The light of the afternoon sun reflected off the swells, giving the sea a solemn mood. Luke recalled his many earlier voyages on boats he had owned and worked on, the Giant, the Endurance and the Mistoes. But none was quite like this. Luke kept an eye on the balsa logs. He watched for any sign of water logging. So far, things appeared to be okay. But he had heard stories of balsa rafts hitting a critical mass where they slowly absorbed water. When the water content reached a certain point the logs and the rafts would sink in seconds like a lead weight.

Luke steered 45-degrees into the wind. He was careful not to put too much torque on the rudder. He did not want to snap it off, as he did not have a spare. Pretty much any failure from any part of the craft at this point would spell- stranded at sea and eventual death.

The pair pressed on.

"Look Gabby, the water is getting blue. We are getting close to the reef. Keep your eyes out for fins sticking out of the water. The black marlin often hang near the surface next to the edges of deep reefs and seamounts. You can tell they are marlin because you will see a sharp tail and dorsal fin."

The black marlin, one of the world's largest game fish. The Blacks can reach 1,200 pounds with the largest on record closer to a ton. They are fierce fighters and have been known to turn on their pursuers, harpooning boats with their sharp, five-foot long bills. Often battling for six hours or more, anglers have died of heart failure struggling with monster, black marlin.

"Look Gabby, up there about 200 yards, a marlin bird."

Luke did his best to steer the raft in the direction of the small white bird which earned their name from following sunning marling around the sea. The Aramis was in hot pursuit. At a whopping four knots, they struggled to catch up with the slowly swimming fish.

"Let out the sail." Luke said as they approached the marlin.

"Good luck, mijo."

Luke tied his 60-foot float line onto the life raft. He checked his gear, put on a camouflage cotton jacket that he brought along and slid into the water. He hoped the jacket would protect him from the plentiful jellyfish. He had not been in deep blue water for some time. With land barely visible, the sun setting and the bottomless ocean below Luke felt like a needle in a field of hay. Luke held onto the raft while he collected his courage.

"Go mijo, go get me the fish."

With that, Luke pushed off the raft and took a few fin strokes. Towing the log life raft against the strong current was futile. After five minutes, he climbed back into the raft.

"We have to sail up current from the fish. I will drift down to it."

They tacked back and forth until they were ahead of the fish. Again, Luke slid into the water, drifting along as he loaded his gun. By the time he had prepared the gun, he was nearly on top of the fish. He rolled over and allowed his eyes to adjust the limitless crystal blue visibility.

Bait-fish were everywhere. The dry season had kicked off the sardiná run. The Panamánian sardiná supports a vast fishery. Round, haul-boats wrapped up millions of tons of the fish each year and turned them into fish meal and oil. The sardiná were the basis for the entire run of game fish along the Panamánian coastline. Fish of every variety schooled up to gorge on the shiny little fish. Fifty feet below him, Luke could see the small bonito tuna that ran in schools of a thousand or more.

Although, he could not see the bottom, Luke knew that he was near the reef when a small grouper glided in on him to investigate. Luke loved the lobster-like texture of the Grouper flesh. He would have been happy to spear the 50-pound fish and go home, where ever home was.

The reef was bubbling with fish. When one type of bait fish school swam out of sight, another one came in, taking its place. A school of a dozen medium-size yellow fin tuna caught Luke's eye. The 100-pound fish swam slowly along side several dolphins and were not the least bit afraid of Luke. He loved to spear a tuna, any tuna.

But the order was for a marlin.

The current carried Luke closer to the unsuspecting, meandering billfish. Luke glided silently. He planned to approach the fish from underneath. He stuck his head out of the water to see how close he was to the tail fin. It was sticking nearly a foot out of the water, less than 20-feet away. Luke took a deep breath, dove and hovered at 20 feet. This way he could float to the surface and get the best profile shot on the fish.

This was no time to be sporting. Only a perfect head or spine shot would subdue the fish. If Luke hit the fish in any non-vital part of the body, it would rip off or destroy his gear in the blink of an eye. Luke could see the shiny white underbelly of the fish and the tail sweeping from side to side. Smaller baitfish schooled under the belly of the marlin, finding protection from predators.

Luke closed in, taking a moment to enjoy being a hunter. The sight of such a magnificent fish was the stuff of dreams.

The fish looked to be more than 12- feet end to end. Judging the weight of such a creature seemed silly, but its thick mid-section and many scars indicated that it was old. The fish could have been 500 pounds, it could have been 1,200. The jet-black upper body, hand-sized eye balls, erect dorsal fin and the glimmering white belly made the fish seem surreal. It was the type of fish you fillet and expect to find a whole family of Filipino fishermen in its stomach. Luke figured that Hemingway must have based *Old Man and the Sea* on a fish just like this one.

The fish then did something Luke was not accustomed to. It turned in his direction, pointed its bill at Luke and swam toward him. The fish did not swim fast or take a threatening posture. It just swam up to Luke in the way baby harbor seals do when they poked at his mask in play. This change was not random. It was premeditated and meant something. This fish had seen battle before. Perhaps rod and reel anglers had hooked it. Perhaps it had challenged sharks for their dinner or maybe it had fought during mating. Whaever the fish's history, it exuded the vibe of a convict, in prison for life, who wanted nothing more than for you to take a swing at him so he could kill you with a plastic fork.

Nonetheless, Luke knew that the only ticket back to the beach was a dead marlin. He drifted along at the same speed as the fish. The fish's head would be the best choice for a shot. The only problem was that it looked like it was made from a two-by-four lumber plank. His shaft would never go deep enough to kill it. The next best choice was a perfect Stone Shot, which would snap the spine, causing paralysis. Luke only had one problem. If he killed the fish straight away, the 1,000-plus pound marlin would be dead weight, snapping his shooting line like peanut brittle. A dead fish of such magnitude tied to the Aramis would simply sink the homemade raft. No, Luke would have to paralyze it, thus making it alive but easier to handle.

That's how Luke calculated his options. he swam to within three-feet of the marlin that he had named, *"Viejo."* (old man).

"Viejo, if I am gonna die, it would be an honor to have it happen out here with you."

Snap!

Luke let the shaft fly. He was sure he had taken the best shot. With just three-feet of water between him and the fish, he was sure to knick the three-inch diameter spine. When the shaft impacted the marlin, it made a thud and sent reverberations through the water. Luke felt the impact in his chest, like he had shot a brick wall. The fish was solid muscle. At first, the old fish did not react. Luke figured he had hit his mark and prepared to swim the fish back to the raft.

Then, he gave the shaft a firm tug. He saw the fish literally turn its eyeball, locking his sights onto Luke. Luke could tell something was coming. The marlin arched around while swinging its tail violently from side to side. Viejo shot toward Luke like a missile, moving so it fast its motion was barely discernable by the human eye. In an instant, Luke found himself on the losing end of a sword fight. The fish speared him though his jacket in the area just under the armpit. Viejo's bill missed the meat of Luke's body but the hunter was none-the-less, close-pinned to a ragingly angry, black marlin longer than the raft and wider than Gabriella and Luke combined. The fish shot ten feet out of the water and shook his head, throwing Luke from side to side.

Gabriella watched with horror as Like flew through the air, attached to the marlin's bill. Gabriella aimed at the fish with her gun, but she knew that any shot she made might hit Luke. Behind the marlin trailed Luke's spear gun, which was tied to the life raft. Pulled by the raging marlin, the life raft sped along at a fast clip. The whole scene would have been funny if Luke's life was not on the line.

The fish sounded into the deep, taking Luke with him. When it hit the end of the 60-foot towline, the angry fish kicked and thrashed, sucking the log life raft halfway under water. It kicked until the spear tip pulled free. The life raft popped back up.

Gabriella screamed.

"Mijo! Mijo! Don't go, mijo!"

She fired rounds into the air.

Luke had been thrown free of the fish when the shaft dislodged. He treaded water, out of Gabriella's sight on the back side of the life raft. He could hear her crying and wailing. Luke took perverse delight in the fact that the women, Gabriella, who early on had tried to kill him, was in utter grief over his death. Her anguish touched his heart.

"Hey, I am over here!" Luke shouted as he swam back to the raft.

Gabriella composed herself. "I knew you were not dead. Where did my marlin go?"

"I think that fish is not a fish at all. I named him Viejo. It is some sort black magic animal sent from Haiti. Maybe when I was there I pissed somebody off, so a witch sent it to kill me. Or maybe it's just a really old, really fucking, strong fish. My shaft did not even make a scratch in that fish and it certainly did not slow it down any."

Luke climbed back onto the Aramis. He pulled in his spear gun, inspecting the shaft for bends. Luckily, his gear had made it through the episode undamaged. The same could not be said for his nerves. As the adrenaline left his body he turned to Gabriella.

"Gabriella, look, let me shoot a small tuna. You guys will be happy with that. No, marlin. I got lucky that time. Those things are just too powerful. They can kill you and me both."

"Mijo, look, next time tie the line directly to the Aramis. That way we can stop the fish better and you will be safer."

Luke could see that his argument was falling on deaf ears. "Okay, but I need to get my nerve back. Let's sail a while. I need to relax, otherwise I cannot hold my breath. We still have just enough daylight left."

"Well, don't take too long. If the wind dies, we could get stuck out here for the night and that would be bad," Gabriella replied.

Luke steered as Gabriella worked the sail. He let the tropical wind dry his hair and warm his face. Luke knew better than to let reality creep in. He stopped any rational thoughts from going through his head. He recalled a time, long ago in another lifetime, when he went night diving for lobster with his buddy, Josh.

They had been teenagers, biting their nails, waiting for lobster season to open. The season always opened on midnight, the second Wednesday of October. That year, the winter storms had arrived early. The west swell was up to fifteen feet. The swell pounded the local breakwater that they planned to dive. Red lights flashed at the launch ramp, indicating a small-craft advisory. The testosterone-filled boys headed out, anyway, in their 14-foot Avon raft. They rounded the break water and listened to the thundering surf smashing the rocks

20-yards inside where they had planned to make the dive. With hesitation Josh suited up and slung his tank over his back.

Luke had asked Josh, "Hey, are you a man or a mouse?"

Josh replied, "I am mouse. A man would not be this stupid."

Luke thought now; *That is just what I am- a mouse. No man is so foolhardy to attempt what I'm trying to do.*

"Okay Gabby, let the sail back out, I see a break in the current up ahead. I will float around there for a while and see what shakes."

Luke pulled his mask over his face, cracked his neck and gave Gabriella a wave. He splashed into the water. The water was clear, but it had a funny, greasy look to it – a phenomenon that appears when bodies of water with two different temperatures collide.

Luke swam for ten minutes. The sun had passed its zenith, reducing the ambient light. Luke breathed up for two minutes, turned and dove. He kicked for the first twenty feet, and after that, he became negatively buoyant and allowed his mass to carry him deeper. He glided and glided until he reached what felt like 60 feet.

The surrounding water was devoid of fish. Something was up. Luke learned long ago that when the small fish split, something that wants to eat them is near. Luke looked hard into the depths, which seemed to have no limit. He thought his eyes were playing tricks on him when a grayish-white object appeared at the lower edge of visibility. Luke's mind struggled to make sense of the growing bulbous object. It gained speed and grew as it closed in on Luke. Luke stayed down past his usual two-minute bottom time. His curiosity pulled at him to stay down until he could identify the object that was coming near him. He struggled to suppress his urge to surface.

"It's a whale! It's a sperm whale!"

The rare sperm whale eased toward Luke. Its elongated bulb-shaped head was covered with scars. Luke locked eyes with the whale as it passed, distracting him from the real sight. A dozen 20-foot long suction cup-covered tentacles hung out of the whale's mouth, rippling in the current. The whale must have been diving to great depths of more than 1,000-feet, where it fed on its main quarry of *Architeuthis*, the world's largest squid.

The sperm whale's mouth, full of six-inch long, ivory teeth was designed to do battle with the giant squid, which can reach lengths of sixty-feet or more. The squid had a beak like a parrot but much larger. Squid were responsible for the scars covering the whale's head and could easily cut off a man's arm or head in one bite. Keeping 15-feet from the whale, Luke kicked towards the surface. He ascended toward the surface at the same speed as the whale. The whale chomped away at the struggling squid. Luke and the whale broke the surface at the same moment. Luke took a deep breath.

"Hey Gabriella, look at the whale eating a squid!"

The whale breached. He jumped three times, each time clearing most of its 60-foot long body from the water. As it landed, it slammed its head on the water's surface in an attempt to knock out the fighting squid.

"Be careful mijo, it's jumping!"

"Thanks for the tip, Gabriella."

Luke swam back to the Aramis and climbed it. They watched as the battle of the titans ensued. The whale spat out the squid several times. The squid threw a massive ink cloud and the whale chomped back down on the fleeing animal. On the last round, the whale made an extra-large splash and disappeared into the depths.

"Guess Moby Dick won that time," Luke said.

Luke rested and drank water. Ten minutes later, the whale flew from the water, executed a back flip and came down with a massive splash, soaking Gabriella. The whale stayed on the surface, riding the water aimlessly.

"I think it's sick," Gabriella said.

The whale started to convulse. It twisted and twitched. Luke had never seen anything like it. The beast vomited up a mass of grayish-yellow matter. It shook its head and sank out of sight. The grayish yellow stuff floated on the surface.

"Let's go see what that is," Luke said.

"I need my marlin. There is no time for whale barf," Gabriella protested.

"No. I think I know what it is."

They paddled over to the floating hard, sponge-like material. Luke reached down and grabbed a piece. He broke it open and smelled it. The stuff smelled like burning hair.

"Yep, it's ambergris. Pull it in," Luke ordered.

They loaded nearly 100-kilograms of the ambergris into the boat, broke it into pieces and jammed it into the baskets with the food.

"This stuff better be important, mijo," Gabriella said, making a lemon face.

"Ambergis is used for perfume. The French have fought wars over it. It is the most powerful natural base for fragrance in existence. It is the only natural element on earth that never loses it fragrance."

Gabriella expressed interest.

"Is it valuable?"

"I'd say so. Buyers pay more than $4,000 a kilogram for it."

"Wow," Gabriella said, inspecting a piece with renewed respect.

"The Muslims need it, as the Koran forbids them to use perfume with alcohol, so they must pay the price and use this stuff. When it's diluted it smells like musk or Sandalwood. My friend, Raja, in India used to ask me to get it for him all the time when I was sending him seashells. Sometimes it washes up on the beach making fishermen and beachcombers rich."

"What is it, actually?" Gabriella asked.

"The sperm whale eats the squid, but it can't digest the beak, which is made of the same material as your fingernails, keratin. So, its stomach makes like an ulcer, producing this waxy blob of cholesterol. That is the ambergris."

"Great. You made me stuff stinky whale ulcer into my food basket."

"Yes, but a really, really valuable whale ulcer."

"Look, mijo, over there! Another marlin!"

With the light fading quickly, Luke really did not want to hear those words. He hoped Gabriella had had enough and would cash it in, giving the order to head for home.

No such luck.

This marlin cruised on the surface just like the first one. Its dorsal and tail fins protruded from the surface, cutting through the wind chop. Luke readied himself to be humbled or worse. It was getting late. Short of a miracle, there was no feasible way to shoot even a small marlin, subdue it and sail back to shore before dark. If they were going to make it back they needed to get going, now.

Per Gabriella's advice, Luke fastened the buoy line to the main raft. Luke hoped against hope as he rolled back into the water that was lit with nothing more than the shadow of a setting sun. The ocean at dusk is alive. It is the time when everything feeds. After all, critters of the sea need to eat dinner too. Sharks eat, marlin eat, bonito eat, even sardiná eat at dusk. To prevent Luke from having to pull the raft, Gabriella had positioned it just ahead of the finning marlin. By the time Luke had loaded his gun and started to kick, he was already a heartbeat away from the fish. As he did before, Luke dove and let his buoyancy slowly take him back to the surface. As he ascended, he got his first glimpse of the marlin. Something seemed strangely familiar.

Is that a mark from spear shaft? Luke questioned.

No, my mind is playing tricks on me.

Luke swam toward the fish. He saw scars on its hulking head. Its stout, thick bill told stories of fights won and lost in the blue water. The dim light made focusing on the details of the fish's black, blue and purple color patterns difficult. Luke saw a small open wound on the fish's shoulder.

My God, it's Viejo.

He shuddered at the thought of taking a second stab at such an unstoppable, already pissed-off monster fish. It was nearly dark and even a well-placed shot would mean hours of fighting and pulling -- hours they did not have.

The odds of seeing the same marlin, especially one of this size, twice in the same day was unheard of. Perhaps the fish was being territorial. It had reached such a mammoth size that it feared nothing else in the sea. It had found fertile hunting ground and it was going to stay there.

Luke swam alongside the fish. Viejo seemed more annoyed than scared. It snapped at ten-and twelve-pound bonito crossing its path. The old marlin simply wanted to be left alone so it could gorge its belly for the long night ahead. Luke lifted his head from the water and looked back at the raft, where he could see Gabriella watching, the sail furling in the wind and the radioactive orange sunset on the horizon.

He had nothing to lose. Every day since his great escape in Panamá City was essentially borrowed time, time that he would not have traded for anything. He had lived life to the fullest while on the run. From Hernan, to his trek through the jungle with Morgan and then Jimmy, to his time with the Embera´ and now his love-hate relationship with Gabriella and the FARC. He thought of Nici. He aimed lower this time.

He pulled the trigger. Again, the thud of hitting something solid vibrated through the water. Viejo went reeling. The line went tight and pulled Aramis at a right angle.

"All right, mijo, you got him!"

Luke held on to the shooting line. It was as tight as a guitar string. Viejo jumped, clearing the water by ten feet. It jumped again while throwing its head violently side to side. It jumped a third time and slowed its pace. Luke took the opportunity to get in the raft. To help him up, Gabriella grabbed Luke by his shorts. Once he was back in the raft he tested the tension on the buoy line.

"Man, that's tight! We can't pull on it. Our only hope it to wait Viejo out and hope that he tires," Luke said.

Gabby put her faith into Luke, hoping he knew how to deal with the fish. Viejo was wounded, but not vitally. Viejo swam at a steady pace. Like a small tugboat, the fish pulled the raft along at three knots.

"Gabby, we need to cut this fish loose. It is pulling us to sea and we have to get back to land."

"I have not won twenty battles with the Colombians by quitting. We will stay and fight until we win. If it takes a week we will own that fish!"

The sun disappeared at the horizon. Thirty minutes later, land sank out of sight and the sky turned black.

Chapter Twenty-Five

Let the sail go free, secure the boom so it does not hit me in the head," Luke said." I will steer. You keep your hands on the line. Viejo is swimming steady. He is alive as long as you feel heartbeat in the line from the tail kicks."

"Where do think Viejo is taking us, mijo?"

"Maybe Hawaii," Luke suggested. "No. Not there. It's in the U.S, I am wanted in the states. Tell him to steer towards Tahiti or Fiji. Good diving there and we can open up a bed and breakfast." The two shared a chuckle.

As the sun disappeared under the horizon the wind stopped. The sea went flat, taking on a plate-glass look. The swells rolled by in sets of two and three. Flying fish could be heard zipping from the water. Every so often, a flying fish landed on the deck and Gabriella helped them quickly back into the water until one of them flew right smack into her head.

"Pinga! That hurt."

It spooked her. From then on, she let them suffer and wiggle until the next swell washed them back into the sea.

Viejo pulled and pulled. The marlin never slowed or sped up, he just plowed on, almost unaware that he was towing a raft and two really, spun-up humans. The Aramis now was far from any manmade lights. The night was clear and the sky chock-full of stars of every color and size. Satellites and shooting stars could be seen every few minutes.

"I hope none of those satellites is looking for me," Luke said.

"Look, mijo!" Gabriella shouted as she pointed skyward. A massive star-like ball streaked across the sky. The fiery ball glowed yellow in the center and red on the edges. It had a long pinkish trail. The ball did not burn out like normal shooting stars. Instead, it burned brighter and brighter until it appeared to strike the ocean just over the horizon.

"Wow!" Luke exclaimed. "That was a meteor! I've never seen one of those. A real piece of outer space just splashed down."

As the meteor impacted the water, Viejo jolted. He detoured, pulling the raft around in circles.

"I think he is dying," Luke said.

"What do we do if he dies?" Gabriella asked.

"I have not really figured that part out yet, but I am willing to entertain suggestions."

Viejo corrected his course and once again towed the Aramis at the same steady three knots.

The raft felt sluggish. Luke stuck his hand in the water and knocked on the balsa logs.

"Gabby, I think the logs are absorbing too much water. If they take on too much, we are finished."

Gabriella reached into the storage baskets, muddling around. Under the layers of stinky ambergris she found a tin of Spam. She opened the tin. She used her fingers as a spoon while sucking down the outdated meat product. She opened a second tin and handed it to Luke.

"Mijo, eat up, you need some protein."

Luke had grown accustomed to the processed pork. He followed suit, sucking down the Spam. He even licked the can when it was empty.

"That was good. I'll take a cold beer now, please."

Shortly before midnight, the full moon crept up over the horizon. Oversized and orange at first, the moon gave a new mood, even hope to the situation. It grew brighter as it rose. After two hours, Luke and Gabriella could see for miles in either direction. Luke put on his mask and stuck his head over the side. He could see the outline of Viejo. Each wag of his tail lit up purple phosphorescence in the water.

"What about sharks, mijo, won't they eat the fish?"

"Yes, that could happen. But Viejo is not bleeding and is swimming strong. Sharks usually only eat bleeding, wounded dying   things."

The constant submersion in the warm sea water was starting to cause blistering and swelling on Gabriella and Luke's skin.

"We need to drink more water," Luke insisted.

"But we only have a few liters left."

"Drink it down. It's the only way to neutralize the salts in our bodies. If this thing keeps pulling us to sea, water will be the last of our concerns."

Luke and Gabby looked up. Off in the distance the outline of a large ship could be seen. As it neared, they could see that it was a full-size cruise ship. With thousands of lights showing, it looked like a floating city. The 900-foot vessel motored past the Aramis at the distance of about a mile. Luke could hear the sound of music being played in the ship's dance hall. He fantasized about the warm meals, booze, comfortable beds and buffets onboard the ship. Even if he had the means to hail the vessel, a FARC outlaw and wanted terror suspect would be shown directly to the brig and handed over to authorities on arrival at the next port. The waves created by the wake of the ship lapped over the Aramis. Gabriella pretended not to have such earthly desires, but Luke could tell she was getting tired and – what was it he detected? – envious.

Luke knew that the cruise ships dumped their biodegradable trash off the lower poop deck. This created a mile-long line of sharks that followed the ships across the seas waiting for a free lunch to fall from the decks. Apparently, however, one of the sharks decided that it had had enough of stale french fries. It wanted a bite out of Viejo.

"Mijo, the line feels funny. Come here."

Luke grabbed the line. The heartbeat rhythm slowed. He stuck his head in the water. He could see a ten-foot oceanic white tip shark stalking Viejo. The oceanic white tip is a cunning shark. It was the shark responsible for killing most of the 1,200 sailors on the infamous USS Indianapolis that was torpedoed by a Japanese submarine while returning from Midway Island after it had delivered the A-bomb, ending WW II.

The dark water made it tough to see exactly what was happening, but it looked like the shark was trying for a piece of Viejo's belly. Viejo stopped its forward motion. This allowed him to better ward off the shark with its bill. Viejo's swinging bill persuaded the shark to give up on its marlin snack and return to eating T-bone steak leftovers from the cruise ship.

The coldest hours of the night had arrived. Luke and Gabriella huddled to prevent hypothermia from setting in. Even in the tropics, a cold wet chest when exposed to the elements can cause intense shivering and even loss of motor function or consciousness. Luke stared at the horizon. He counted the seconds until the first sign of daybreak could be seen. The bright moon made seeing the first light difficult. The phrase "it's always darkest before the dawn," is most noticeable when you are at sea. Just when the night seems to have no end and the cold no limit, nature grants you a last-minute reprieve. The sunsets and sunrises on the equator happen faster than in other latitudes. It is more like a light switch than a dimmer.

Gabriella fell asleep in Luke's arms.

Gabby, wake up. The sun, there it is, there it is!" Luke said softly.

Luke had not seen such a beautiful sunrise since the morning after the barge collision three years earlier. It had been the longest night of his life as he floated in a life raft with four friends, their boat at the bottom of the San Diego shipping channel.

The two rejoiced that they were not dead. The warmth of the sun gave them new life. Luke looked at the sun rising in the east. It was easy enough to tell that if he followed it, land would have to appear sooner or later. The question was how. Luke took a moment to think.

"Gabby, if you want Viejo, I am going to give an order. If you don't want to follow it, then fine, we can cut the line and sail back to camp while we still have our lives."

"What is it, mijo?"

"Take the small spear gun, put on my mask, fins and snorkel. Grab the line attached to Viejo, work your way down to the fish. My spear is lodged well in its left shoulder. I want you to place your shaft in the same place, just in its right shoulder."

"I don't know if I can do that."

"I need to stay here and steer the boat. You can do it, just like I showed you back at the beach. You are a natural. Now, go while there is still time."

With that, Gabriella attached a second line to the back of the smaller gun and tied it off to the Aramis. She loaded the small spear gun, slid into the water and worked her way down to the marlin.

She swam as fast as she could to keep pace with Viejo. She lined up a good shot to the right shoulder and pulled the trigger. She scored a perfect hit. Afraid of the bottomless blue water, she hustled back to the boat. She surfaced to find Luke on the bow of the Aramis holding both the buoy lines in his hands. Luke gave the left line a delicate tug, and Viejo veered left. Luke then gave the right one a tug, the old fish veered right.

"Get on, Gabby, we are going home!"

Like Santa Claus steering his reindeer Luke drove the marlin in the direction of the rising sun.

"Lemmie try, mijo!"

Luke handed Gabriella the reins. She copied Luke's motions.

"Steer toward the sun. I have no idea how far we are from shore, but let's do this until Viejo dies or figures out the program and stops being our free sleigh ride."

Luke and Gabriella took turns steering the mighty fish. Viejo occasionally slowed, then sped up. But he never quit. Each time Viejo turned off course, Gabriella or Luke would tug on the opposite rein. The old fish pulled and pulled for more than five hours.

"Look, over there, I think I see the bay!" Luke yelped.

"Sí, it is our bay. We made it."

The Aramis was still more than three miles offshore, but the sight of land was enough to fill their weathered, hungry bodies with renewed spirit. Out of excitement Gabriella stuck her hands in the water and started to paddle.

"I really don't think that helps," Luke said.

The lines connected to Viejo went slack. The lines creaked with tightness as they went from 45 degrees to vertical.

"I think he's dead. Cut the lines, Gabby. He will pull us under for sure," Luke ordered.

The dead weight of the fish started to pull the bow under. Gabriella reluctantly unsheathed her jungle knife.

"We almost had you, old man."

Just before she cut the line attached to Luke's gun, the line rose back to a 45- degree angle and the heartbeat rhythm began again.

"Guess he just needed to take five," Luke said.

Viejo slowed to less than half a knot. The end was near. Luke could see the white water created from the wash rock in the bay. They had less than a mile to go.

"Come on, old boy, don't quit now," Luke pleaded with the fish.

It was clear that the raft could not support the dead weight of the 1,000-pound marlin. The only chance they had of landing the great fish would be to coax it into water shallower than the lengths of the shooting and buoy lines, about 100-feet. As the water shallowed, Viejo acted erratic. He zig-zagged, sped up and stopped several times. Marlin are a deep, blue water species. Viejo could tell that the water was unnaturally shallow for him. The wash rock was now just a stone's throw away.

"Okay, Gabby, game time. I am going to slowly pull Viejo up by the lines. When his dorsal fin breaks the water, I want you to empty your clip into him. Aim for his head."

Luke hauled away. He pulled the huge fish up, inch by inch. Viejo continued to tow the Aramis until they were less than 20-yards offshore.

Luke managed to maneuver the struggling fish under the raft. The bill protruded past the front of the bow, and the four-foot long fork-shaped tail stuck out past the stern.

"One more pull!" Luke's hands bled from the lines.

The dorsal fin broke the surface.

"Now, Gabby, now, shoot!"

Both Gabriella and Luke had grown fond of the fish. They respected his fighting spirit.

"He saved our lives, Luke, let him be free."

"He is too far gone. If we let him go now he will surely die."

"I am sorry for this." Gabriella aimed her AK-47.

"Crack, crack, crack, crack…"

More than 30 shots rang out. Mighty Viejo twitched and then fluttered to the bottom.

While Viejo acted as the anchor, Luke and Gabriella slipped onto the surfboard- life raft and paddled ashore. They scrounged up some old rope on the beach. Gabriella strung one end around a tree trunk and waited on the beach while Luke swam back to the Aramis. Luke tied the line around the water-logged timbers of the raft and returned to the beach.

"Pull, pull!" Gabriella sang as they struggled to heave the raft and fish beach-wards. A half hour passed with only several feet of progress. Luke's line cuts grew deeper with each tug on the ropes.

"You better go back to camp and get some help," Luke said.

Gabriella returned shortly with twenty men in tow. They hauled away on the rope. Within fifteen minutes, the Aramis sat floating in knee-deep water. Luke swam the short distance to Viejo. He caressed the fish's head as he removed the spears. Luke then strung another, thicker line through Viejo's gills and mouth. The men were then able to leverage the fish up onto dry land.

The soldiers cheered in disbelief. Luke and Gabriella looked on with somber expressions. They were happy to be alive, happy to have caught such a great, once-in-a- life time fish, but at the same time lamented his death.

Chapter Twenty-Six

LUKE CARVED UP the great marlin right away. Any ceremony would have to wait. The midday tropical sun was beating down, threatening to spoil the meat. Luke fletched off 50-pound chunks, handing them one by one to the soldiers. He asked Gabby to go back to camp and start as many small bonfires as she felt comfortable with. There were no Filipino fishermen in Viejo's belly, just a dozen partially digested bonito and a few small squid. When he was finished, Luke sawed off the bill and carried it back to camp along with his dive gear.

"Ahorra!" (*Now!*) Gabby ordered as Luke entered the main part of the camp.

Everybody, including the injured, Carlito, the new recruits and several highranking members of the FARC who had returned with Carlito all stood up and saluted Luke.

"Thank you," he responded simply.

Viejo was going to feed the entire camp for weeks. Most of the meat would be smoked Indian style by pinning it to tall stakes facing a low burning fire for 48 hours. The sweet flavor of smoked marlin flesh is a delicacy and can be stored and eaten for more than year with no refrigeration.

Luke carved the word 'Viejo' into the bill and hung it over the entrance to the hospital tent.

"Mijo, come here," Gabby said. "I want you to meet General Ortega. He supplies us with product from the other side of the border. It is our job to move it to the Canal. Once there, we hand it off to a Mexican cartel who, in turn, provides us with fresh ammunition and arms. We badly need to be re-supplied."

General Ortega, a mild mannered, tall thin man with gray hair of about fifty years, gave Luke a firm hand shake.

"If the comandante trusts you, then I trust you," Ortega said as he lifted a tarpaulin. Underneath were more than 500, one-kilogram cellophane packages. They told him that half were filled with cocaine, the other with black-tar heroin.

"Oh shit," were the only words Luke uttered.

"Mijo, General Ortega has arranged a Baja Boat to come and pick this product up. You have healed us, you have fed us and you have not judged us. I want you to go, return to your life, return to Nici, clear your name and be free. Mijo, I love you and this is my gift to you. This is not your fight. If you stay here I am sure you will die."

Luke was shocked to hear Gabriella proclaim her love in front of the general.

Luke was too tired to protest. He was uncomfortable hitching a ride back to Panamá City with a couple of FARC operatives, and a thousand pounds of cocaine and heroin.

"When do we leave? And what is a Baja Boat?"

"You leave at first light, and the boat…well, you will see," the general said.

Luke spent his last night with Gabriella and the rest of the FARC eating copious amounts of the marlin and singing and dancing around the campfire to the offbeat tunes emitting from Carlito's guitar.

Early the next morning, Gabriella walked Luke and two FARCs, Paco and Juevo, to the beachhead. Paco and Juevo helped Luke carry the 100 kilograms of ambergris.

Gabriella was not much for goodbyes. She simply gave Luke the longest wettest kiss of his life. "See you later," she said.

"Here, take this, use it to feed your people." Luke handed Gabriella the only possession he had in the world, the one thing that had been his provider and companion through his whole ordeal, the beloved spear gun that Hernan had loaned him. Gabriella accepted the gift with humility, did an abrupt about face and returned to camp.

Luke collected himself then walked over to Paco and Juevo. They were new to the FARC and had been chosen for this mission as way to prove their loyalty.

"There… there it is," Paco yelled, pointing at something in the water.

All Luke could see was a pipe sticking out of the water.

Then it surfaced, and Luke stared in disbelief.

"A submarine?"

I think I am pushing my luck here, he concluded. *Oh, I get it. BAJA Boat." (baja means below)*.

The men beached the bow of the 30- foot-long blue, fiberglass sub. A man opened the top hatch and stuck his head out   of   the   conning   tower.

"Hola, compadres!" The man said with exuberance. His name was Julio. At 6 feet, two inches, he was a tight fit for the tiny sub. He had jet black skin, lanky arms and a glimmering, white smile.

He climbed out of the sub to help Paco and Juevo load the drugs into the vessel. It took an hour to stow all the narcotics.

"OK, vamanos,"

Julio was a little too excited. He appeared to be using his own product.

"Hey guys, I need to load my ambergris," Luke said.

They threw him blank faces. Luke grabbed the ambergris which he had wrapped in banana leaves then packed carefully into plastic trash bags. The crew knew Luke was Gabriella's special hitchhiker, so they did not protest and allowed Luke to pack the extra weight.

Luke was the last one to board the small submarine. He was shuffled to the back of the boat. He squashed himself between the diesel motor and the kilos of drugs. He cringed as Julio   sealed   the   hatch.

"Dive, dive, dive."

Julio laughed. Big joke.

"No, just kidding," he said. "Here, you gonna need this. Put it on."

Julio handed gas masks to Luke and his other crew members. The reason was soon made clear. Luke donned the mask as Julio fired up the old Ford engine.

"Rrrr, Rrrrr, cahugh, grumple pop, pop, pop...." The engine kicked to life. The gaskets on the engine leaked badly, filling the submarine with thick diesel fumes that would have been deadly without the masks. The engine powered two small, overhead light bulbs. The quarters were so cramped that Luke's legs fell asleep in their contorted position. His legs tingled with pins and needles.

"Okay, here we go," Julio yelled. Everything he said was at top volume.

"Why is he yelling?" Luke asked Paco.

"Bastante mucho guerra." (Too much war) Paco replied.

Luke figured Julio had taken one too many mortar explosions and lost most of his hearing.

Julio put the engine into reverse, backed up into 20 feet of water and again opened the hatch. He poked his head out of the tiny conning tower. He could not reach the steering while standing so he yelled steering orders below for Paco to follow.

"Derecha, izquierierdo, adelante lento… (right, left, go ahead, slowly) After they cleared the wash rock, Julio closed the hatch. He pulled the steering wheel toward his body. Luke could hear the lapping water against the outer hull. After submersion, the only sound was the loud clunky diesel engine.

"How deep can we go?" Luke asked.

"No more than 100 feet, and only for an hour at a time. We just need to get 40 miles up the coast, past the heavy aerial surveillance area. Many gringo DEA fly birds 'round dees parts. Then we transfer the cargo to a fast, surface boat."

"Gabby said nothing about transferring the drugs."

Julio leveled off at 50 feet. The fiberglass walls creaked, water dripped in several spots. The gas mask constricted Luke's airflow, making him dizzy. Never a fan of tight quarters, Luke did his best to stay calm. He put his ear against the submarine wall. He swore he could hear humpback whale songs.

Julio's only means of navigation was a handheld GPS and compass. Each swell picked up the sub and moved it in a circular motion. Paco dozed off. He had affixed a bayonet to his AK-47. As he slumbered he leaned on his rifle. The pressure pushed the bayonet and punctured one of the kilograms of heroin. Several teaspoons of the black sticky substance spilled onto the smoking hot engine block. A flash fire ignited.

"Holy shit, surface!" Luke yelled.

If the fire spread to the rest of the drugs, the submarine would go up like a small nuclear bomb. Julio pressed the wheel in. The sub made an emergency, uncontrolled ascent. The sub shot up and out of the water like a breaching whale. It slammed down with a splash, throwing water a hundred feet in every direction.

Juevo was quick to open the hatch. He removed his gas mask and used it to collect seawater to throw on the flames. After the flames were doused, Juevo looked up to see two 32-foot Bertram Sport fishers close by. The Baja Boat had surfaced on the Zane Gray Reef smack in the middle of a Tropic Star Lodge, marlin fishing tournament. The confused anglers looked on. The skippers of the Bertrams could see the smoke plume emitting from the sub. They powered up and put some distance between themselves and the flailing sub. They went on about their business and did not report the incident to the authorities. The Tropic Star enjoyed an uneasy peace with the FARC. The resort could not afford to ignite any trouble. It would be bad for business.

"That was a close one," Luke said as he re-arranged his cramped legs.

Julio barked a few insults at Juevo, sealed the hatch and pulled the wheel back. He submerged to a shallow 25 feet, then planed off.

They motored along at eight knots. Julio stared intently at his GPS and compass. His face indicated confusion as he shook the GPS, then put it against his ear, listening for loose parts. Luke could feel the power of the ten-foot ground swells as they moved the sub around in larger and larger circles.

To pass the time Paco took his gun apart, then re-assembled it as fast has he could. He handed the gun to Luke asked if he wanted to give it a try.

"No thanks, I don't care for guns."

"Guns are your friends. They protect you, give you food and make you look tough for the women…" Paco replied in Spanish.

Julio handed the wheel over to Juevo while he checked the engine fluids. Julio added three quarts of oil.

"Every hour she burns this much," Julio said.

The weak overhead lights flickered on and off. Two hours into the trip the lights simply shut off. The only thing lighting the cabin was the green glare from Julio's GPS.

"Who made this boat anyway?" Luke asked Julio.

"I did, in my back yard, in Colombia. Pretty good, huh?"

"Oh, great! A homemade submarine. Does it come with a screen door?"

"This is her maiden voyage, too!" Julio said with pride.

Luke did not need to hear this. The engine and the rest of the materials were hand-me-downs, leftovers and junk.

"How do you know how to make and drive a submarine?" Luke asked.

"I read a book and I checked on the internet," Julio replied.

"Oh good, for a moment there, I was worried."

The lights came back on, but it did not make Luke feel much easier.

"Listen, you can hear a ship," Julio said.

Luke could not hear anything over the popping diesel. Julio made a cone with his hand then placed against the hull.

"Yes, ship coming."

They had no idea how far off the ship was. Knowing that the largest ships can draft up to 35 feet, Julio pulled the wheel back to avoid getting run over. The sub descended.

"OK, forty-five feet. That should be fine."

Luke watched the simple needle dial depth gauge go to 50… 55…60…65 feet.

"Uh, Julio I think we are still sinking," Luke said calmly.

Julio pushed and pushed on the wheel but they continued to sink...70… 80…85 feet, the gauge read.

"I can't stop her!"

Julio put all his weight onto the wheel.

Snap!

The wheel broke off, leaving an exposed piece of black pipe.

"A hundred feet," Luke yelled.

The sub sank deeper, and at 125 feet the fiberglass slowly began to implode. Unlike steel, fiberglass can flex. Luke could feel the walls encroaching in on him. One of the drips turned into a high-pressure hose down that shot into Luke's face.

"Hand me the vice grips," Julio barked.

Julio secured the large vice grips onto the wheel column and pressed. Juevo and Paco joined in. Again, the lights shut

C.F. Goldblatt

off. At 140-feet, the sub leveled off, hovered for a moment, and began to slowly rise. Julio managed to plane off at 25- feet.

"Gracias a dios," (Thank God) the three men said as they crossed themselves.

"How much longer?" Luke impatiently asked.

"If we are on course. I think another hour," Julio yelled back.

To ward off panic, Luke closed his eyes and visualized shooting white sea bass and Pargo. A long hour crept by. Luke sucked in air through the gas mask and did his best to keep his legs from falling asleep. The GPS's arrival alarm sounded. *Beep, beep, beep.*

"I think we here," Julio said happily. He pressed on the steering column and the sub worked its way to the surface. As soon as the sub broke the surface, Luke plowed his way over Paco. He unscrewed the hatch, ripped off his gas mask and stuck his head out into the fresh air. He drank in the clean air for several minutes before letting Julio have a look around. Julio and Luke exchanged places.

"The other boat should be here. The coordinates are right," Julio said. "We just have to wait."

No land or islands could be seen, just limitless ocean in every direction. The sub was at least 25-miles offshore, floating around like cork. Julio insisted that Luke retreat into the cabin while he scanned the horizon for the pick-up boat. Hours went by. Luke's confidence sank. He was not sure if he could tolerate a return trip on the death-trap submarine. He figured he would stand a better chance by jumping ship and swimming for it. As Luke counted his limited options, through the hull he could hear a high-pitched whine.

"I think I hear your boat," Luke told Julio.

Julio squinted his eyes. A black speck could be seen a mile away. The boat jumped from wave to wave while approaching at lightning speed. In less than a minute the boat throttled back and then came alongside the sub. Luke squeezed his way past Julio to have a look.

"Wow, nice boat!" Luke exclaimed.

The pick-up boat was perhaps the sleekest offshore racing boat Luke had ever seen. It was a 40-foot Midnight Express. A boat like that could be used as a high-speed offshore fishing craft, but with its aftermarket, souped up triple 300 horsepower Mercury outboards, this $700,000 boat was built with just one purpose in mind: To run drugs. Able to scream over ocean waves at 90 miles an hour, the jet-black Midnight Express could outrun any of the standard Coast Guard and military boats.

The FARC had built the boat to state-of-the-art evasion standards. It had a bow-mounted tripod with a 50-caliber machine gun mounted to it. It had custom-built holds for the drugs. With a push of a button the illegal cargo could be dumped. The holds would eject water-tight containers outfitted with GPS tracking devices. The containers were designed to sink to a depth of 50 feet. When the heat was off, the boat could return to the dump site, push a second button and the cargo containers would rise to the surface for collection.

Two Colombian men in their 20s manned the speedy craft. They looked to be twins. But it was tough to tell, as both had severe facial scarring.

Luke's presence disturbed them greatly.

"¿Quién es el gringo?" (Who is the gringo?) the angrier of two asked.

Julio explained that he was sent with the authority of the comandante. The Columbians reluctantly allowed Luke to board. When Luke introduced himself, and stuck out his hand the men simply ignored him and started to load the drugs. Luke never learned the names of the two men, but their serious expressions and scars told plenty about their histories. They were heavily armed, each with an AK-47, a pistol, several grenades and an RPG launcher never more than an arm's length away.

Luke helped load the cargo. Ignoring the scowls the two Columbians were sending his way, he took a moment to marvel at the electronics panel. The boat was equipped with a radar and GPS jamming unit, two ten-inch chart plotter/radars, five different types of radios, a bottom sounder, an expensive side-scanning sonar unit and a radio directional finder. Luke ran his hand over the black paint on the gunnels. It had a tacky feel to. Luke assumed it was some sort of special paint intended to create a low radar signature.

After the narco cargo was loaded, Luke proceeded to transfer his ambergris. Again, the men protested but permitted it when told it was organic material for remedies he was preparing for the FARC. The two men threw off dangerous vibes. They had little reason to keep Luke alive after Julio left.

Julio saluted the men and told them to hurry back with the new ammunition and arms as the FARC camp was nakedly exposed to attack from the Colombian military.

"Wop, wop, wop, wop."

A gray, silent, low flying helicopter appeared to rise out of the sea.

"On the guns, now!" one man yelled in Spanish.

Luke heard Julio yell, "Dive, dive, dive" and watched as the rickety submarine disappeared under the waves.

An aggravated voice blasted from the helicopter in Spanish.

"This is the United Stated Drug Enforcement Agency. Lower your weapons and surrender or be killed."

Luke recalled the FARC talking one evening about the fact that the U.S. DEA often flew drug intercepts in this part of the world and they were dangerous.

The chopper fired a dozen warning shots ten yards off the bow of the boat.

Luke's heart raced as he saw one of the scar-faced men ready his RPG while the other loaded the first round of belt-fed ammunition into the 50-caliber. All hell broke loose. The man on the bow fired a stream of bullets at the chopper.

"Rat, tat, tat." The 50-caliber was deafening. The spent rounds filled the air with the smell of burnt gunpowder. Several rounds hit the tail section of chopper. Luke reacted by slamming the boat into gear and laid into the triple throttles. The boat flew out of its hole, hitting 60 miles-an-hour in less than ten seconds. The chopper gave chase, firing several hundred rounds from the turret-mounted machine gun near the nose cone of the aircraft.

Luke saw the chopper hold steady, then launch a missile. It made a bee-line toward the boat. Luke pushed on the throttles harder while spinning the wheel around, arcing a hard right, then a hard left. The two men held on to the railing. The boat hit maximum speed. The rounds missed the boat by a few feet, and the impact threw up a hug splash covering Luke and the FARC soldiers with sea water. Luke's lips flapped in the wind. He looked back and saw another missile coming at them.

"Hold on!" Luke yelled. He threw the boat into reverse. The force threw both the men onto the deck. The missile impacted the water just ahead of them. The one man got back on the 50-caliber and fired wildly at the approaching helicopter. The chopper continued pumping machine gun fire at the boat. Two rounds hit the man on the 50 cal, one in the chest, the other in the head. The sight was grizzly. The surviving man did not skip a beat. He held steady as he grabbed his RPG launcher, slung it over his shoulder then took careful aim at the approaching helicopter. The chopper turned to make another pass. He held his fire until the aircraft was clearly in the cross hairs. The man fired, in the same instant Luke zagged the boat to throw off the shot. The RPG made a whizzing sound as it flew through air. It hit the chopper near the tail section blowing it apart. A piece of the tail rotor rocketed back toward the boat. Before anybody could react, it ripped into the remaining FARC soldier, killing him instantly. Luke appeared to be the only one on the boat still breathing.

The front end of the chopper remained intact. Luke watched as the wounded aircraft spun wildly out of control. He could see the pilot struggling to regain control as smoke plumed from the wounded chopper. The chopper spun around and around like a child's top until it splashed down several hundred yards from the boat. Luke collected himself and instinctively began to motor towards where he thought the chopper had splashed down. He soon reached a debris field. Luke slowed down as he entered a large fuel slick dotted with life vests, and smaller floating matter from the chopper.

He somberly leant over the rail to collect a blood covered, pilot's helmet. He idled back the throttles and turned off the engines. Luke heard a faint voice coming from beyond the next swell, "Help over here…" It was one of the airmen. Luke started the engines and headed towards the man. Then he saw two other men floating near buy, one of them clutching an escape pod (self-deploying inflatable raft). For some reason, the escape pod had failed to inflate upon impact.

Luke was in a serious pickle. He could not leave the airmen to the sharks, but putting them in his boat would ensure his capture. Luke pulled alongside the man holding onto the escape pod. "Please help me; I have a wife and family." The man pleaded as blood dripped down his face from a head wound.

"Let go of the escape pod." Luke ordered. Luke grabbed the escape pod and with a strong yank on the tether, the pod burst open and inflated to form a sort of red floating igloo. Luke helped the man into the pod. "Thank you," the wounded airmen said to Luke. Luke motored over to the next nearest airmen, but he appeared to be too late. The man was floating face down in the water. Luke grabbed him by the armpits and drug him over the gunnels onto the go-fast boat. Luke started CPR, cleared water from the man's throat, then started in; three breaths followed by twelve pumps to the man's sternum using the palms of his hands. "Breathe, dammit breathe!" Luke shouted at the man.

Luke continued on for a full ten minutes. As Luke resigned himself to give up, the man choked, spitting up vomit and sea water. He managed a few breaths then sat up. The airmen had no idea where he was. Resorting to instinct, the airmen grabbed his leg holstered 45-caliber pistol and took aim at Luke.

"What the hell are you doing? I just saved you life." An exhausted Luke snapped at the man.

The man, whose embroidered name tag read Fisher, attempted to regain his faculties and asked, "Who are you and why are you shooting at us. I should kill you right now."

"My name is Luke Dodge, and my story is a long one. I am pretty sure I am a wanted terrorist… they think I want to blow up the Canal. No time to explain. I have been held captive by the FARC. I am not really sure for how long."

Fisher could apparently see that if Luke was a terrorist he would never have saved his life, something did not add up, and he re-holstered his gun.

"You better get into the raft and tend to your friend, he's bleeding pretty bad." Fisher climbed into the raft. Luke motored towards the third man who was still treading water. On the way, Luke could see the floating emergency locating beacon (EPIRB). He leaned over the rail and picked it out of the water. The switch had not been fully turned on, thus no rescue signal had yet been deployed. Luke helped the third airmen, who was the pilot, into the boat. The man, although in severe shock, thanked Luke and asked to join his comrades in the raft. After helping the last airmen into the raft Luke activated the locating beacon and handed it to the pilot. This would ensure their rescue within a few hours. Luke made sure they had plenty of water, food and a first aid kit.

"You guys need to get to a man named Caucuss at homeland security in Panamá. Tell them who I am and tell them I have nothing to do with the terror threat, nothing."

The pilot extended his hand. He shook Luke's hand saying a simple, "Thanks."

With the clock ticking, Luke wasted no time. He lit up the engines and laid into the throttles.

Explosive Crossroads

Chapter Twenty-Seven

BACK AT HOMELAND SECURITY headquarters, situated next to the shining new 300 million dollar U.S. Embassy on the outskirts of Panamá City, Luke's old pal Caucuss paced back and forth inside interrogation room number 33. Caucuss took a seat. Across from him sat Luke's Kuna Indian guide, Morgan. Homeland Security had managed to stay on Luke's trail and through whatever means found out that Luke had transected the Dairen with Morgan as his guide. The intelligence was gathered from other Kunas in exchange for money. Morgan, however, sat calmly, resolute not to give Caucuss any information.

"Why are you protecting him, he is a terrorist and the fact that you helped him makes you a terrorist."

Morgan replied defiantly in Kuna and broken English saying, "Luke good man, you wrong, he not hurt nobody, he help feed our people, you bad people, you mistake."

Caucuss then held up a picture of Morgan's family. Morgan got the message and offered Caucuss only vague misleading details where Luke might be, "Luke near waterfall, four days walk, he probably dead from disease or FARC, anyhow."

Caucuss motioned for the guards to take Morgan away. Caucuss then met with his superior. The two men examined charts of the Darién and plotted Luke's probable transect pathways. As they traced Luke's estimated route, the line intersected several areas highlighted in red. Caucuss pointed to the red areas, tapped his fingers and said to his boss, the red areas are known FARC rebel camps, if he is really so close to them, he is as good as dead.

His boss spoke up, "Let's not take any chances, go ahead and deploy two SEAL teams to trace this route. Send one in starting from the Caribbean and the other starting from the Pacific. We'll get this guy."

Chapter Twenty-Eight

THE FAST BOAT, the drugs, Luke and the ambergris zoomed away, cutting through choppy seas at more than 80 miles an hour. To steady himself, using both hands, Luke tightly gripped the steering wheel. The wind swept past his face so fast, breathing was difficult.

Now what?

Luke had no idea what to do. He figured the chopper must have reported its position. If not, the EPIRB would have done it for them, so putting some distance between him and the crash site would be a good idea. The boat charged along. Luke looked at the two dead FARC soldiers lying on the deck, then at the cargo holds full of narcotics. The soldier who had been working the 50-caliber was a mangled corpse. The three direct hits left nothing more than dental records to identify him with.

Think, Luke, think!

Luke tried to collect himself but the drama of the situation overwhelmed him. Luke pointed the bow towards at what looked like offshore. His first instinct was to run, just keep running.

OK, get a grip Luke, you are already a wanted a terror suspect, so a drug charge will not make much of a difference.

Luke recalled a TV news piece he had seen in Panamá City. The Panamánian DEA had arrested five Columbia drug runners. The news showed footage of three of the five men shot to death, lying on the deck of a boat while the agents rifle butted the remaining two. The only complaint from the Panamánian public was that they wanted to know why all five had not been shot. One could say that the Panamánian DEA had special license to essentially eliminate drug traffickers on sight. So, he wanted to steer clear of them.

The sun loomed low as the afternoon breeze turned into a strong north wind. The swell increased to ten feet. This allowed Luke to launch the boat from swell to swell. With each jump the propellers cleared the water and the decreased drag allowed the props to spin at eight or nine thousand RPM's, giving the engines a temporary high-pitched dragster sound.

After running for an hour, Luke calmed down and decided it was time take some action.

Ok, deal with this one step at a time.

Luke pulled the throttles back. He first grabbed the man closest to him. Luke looked away so he did not have to see the tail rotor sticking out from the man's head. Luke slid his hand under the man's armpits, lifted him a few inches and dragged the limp body over to the rail. Luke closed his eyes as he rolled the man into the sea.

Luke figured he needed to say a few words. He tried but they came out fragmented.

"Ashes to ashes, dust to dust, amazing grace, once I was lost, now I am found, I now commit the body to the deep, Amen, okay, good bye".

Luke paused to capture his courage to deal with the second corpse, and he made his way to the bow. What was left of the man looked like an insect that had hit a windshield.

Luke quickly reached down, scooped up the man plus several of the body parts lying near him, and then dumped them over the side.

Luke was covered in blood. He motored the boat 100 yards, put it in neutral and jumped into the sea. He washed himself thoroughly, then climbed back aboard.

Now for the cargo.

Luke entertained the idea of keeping the drugs. Perhaps he could use them to barter his way out of any situation that might arise. Luke opened the hatches. He looked at the glistening white mountain of cocaine, then at the pitch-black tar heroin. He held up a kilogram of each.

I am holding more than $100, 000.00 in my hands. Enough to buy a small house, enough to get out of the mess I am in. Then he thought about all the work Nici had done around the world. So often the wars that sent dying orphans into Nici's Red Cross tents were fought over drugs, the right to traffic drugs or the right to grow the raw material for the drugs. From Afghanistan to Colombia to Mexico the drug trade had ripped families apart, killed millions, destroyed lives and brought down governments.

No. He could not profit from them. But his Ambergris was legal tender, maybe worth as much as $400,000. Luke figured that would be enough to hire the best lawyers and explain his way out of this terrible mess he was in.

Luke spoke out loud, "Raja, India. That is the only place I can sell the Ambergris, get the cash, get free."

But Raja and India were 7000 miles away, Luke had no idea how he was going to make it there. Luke's thoughts skipped back to the explosives in front of the Canal, he was sure that, even as hostile as Cuacuss had been to him, for sure he had sent divers to remove the explosives and foil the terror plot.

Caucuss had submitted a request to close the Canal for a week. After President Jimmy Carter brokered the hand-over of the Canal in 2000, The ACP (Canal Authority) was an independent Panamánian run agency who had the final word on anything that happened in, near, or on the Canal.

So far, they had drug their feet and passed Caucuss's request up a very bureaucratic food chain. In the end, nobody at the ACP was willing to accept the $100 million in losses that would occur by shutting down the Canal for a week of search and recovery instigated by what they saw as a hyper-paranoid, U.S. Homeland Security agent acting on weak intelligence.

One by one, Luke lifted each packet, made a deep slice in the middle and tossed it over the side. The slices allowed the seawater to seep in, sinking each package. Luke did not want to leave a breadcrumb trail of floating drug packages leading to his position. He wondered if the fish would get high.

When he was finished, he drank some water and settled in at the captain's seat. He turned on the all the electronics. Setting the radar on the 32-mile setting, he watched as it made back and forth sweeps. The screen remained blank.

Good. Nobody is coming yet, but they will.

Luke flipped on the chart plotter. The screen showed his position on a perfect, multi color interactive map of the Panamánian coast line, from Costa Rica down to the Colombian border. Using the track ball mouse, he enlarged the map. The Las Perlas island chain dotted the screen. Luke used the track ball to place the cursor over several of the islands. As he did so the range and bearing plus the name of each island appeared. He placed the track ball over a familiar looking island in the middle of the archipelago. The screen read "Isla Pedro Gonzales, 003 degrees magnetic, 67 miles."

Pascal.

Luke lined up the compass heading to 003 and laid into the throttles, quickly reaching top speed. Despite the circumstances, Luke managed to enjoy the power and speed of the lighting-fast boat. Luke watched as the cursor on the screen closed in on the island. A blip indicating an approaching vessel appeared on the radar, then another, confirming that the chopper had managed to get off a distress call when they started taking fire. The DEA had launched a marine search and destroy mission to find the Midnight Express. The boats were not yet visible to the naked eye. Luke only hoped that the special radar-deflecting paint on his boat had prevented his detection.

Luke veered off course. He was going to have to take the long way, hiding behind smaller islands until the coast was clear. Luke pulled up to the first small island. He then waited for thirty minutes until he figured the boats had passed. Taking a chance, he gunned the throttles, making it to the next island five miles to the east in only ten minutes. He did this several more times until he could see the town and bay on the lee side of Pedro Gonzales. He had no choice but to beach the boat and pray that Pascal and the villagers would come to his aid.

Luke aimed toward the center of the bay. With 100-yards headway he maxed the throttles, trimmed up the motors and braced for impact as the boat neared the beach. The boat jolted as it felt bottom. It skidded all the way up the beach, past all the sand and into the tree line. Luke was lucky that the two policemen stationed on the island had gone back to Panamá City to visit their families. The officers were supposed to work two-week rotations but the new shift was late to arrive.

The boat slid to a stop under a palm tree. Thud, thud! Two coconuts plopped down on the boat. Luke took a deep breath and jumped out of the boat. He went to work cutting up palm fronds to cover the boat. The camouflage was crude, but combined with the tree cover would prevent detection from the air. After all, who would be looking for the boat high and dry in the forest?

Luke plotted his next step. He recalled the house where Fofoo, the deck hand who allowed Pascal's Mako to grind away on the reef, could be found. Luke did his best to remain hidden behind hedges as he made his way over to the house. He could see Fofoo drinking rum, swinging in a hammock on the front stoop.

"Psst, psst, Fofoo esta Luke, necesito su ayuda." (It's Luke, I need your help)

Fofoo lifted his head and looked around. When he did not see anybody, he figured the booze was making him hear voices. He took a swig of some rotgut then went back to swinging in his hammock. Luke could see he was not getting through. This time, Luke stood directly in front of Fofoo.

Fofoo opened his eyes to focus on Luke. He nearly fell out of the hammock.

"Fantasma!" (Ghost) Fofoo yelled as he lurched back.

Luke spoke to him in Spanish.

"Shhhh, Fofoo, it's me, Luke, remember? The friend of Pascal's."

Luke had not looked into a mirror in months. His dreadlocks were down to his shoulders, he smelled like Tarzan and his skin was practically as dark as Fofoo's. By Fofoo's reaction, Luke realized that he looked like a crazy person.

"Luke, we thought you were dead. You are alive. Gracias a dios. Pascal, he his in the camp up on the hill. But he does not let me work for him anymore since I blew up the fuel depot one month ago," Fofoo replied in Spanish.

"Please Fofoo, I need you to go to him. Tell him I am here. Tell him I need his help."

"Sí, senior Luke, pronto."

Fofo then led Luke up a foot path towards the highest point on the island. When they approached the fish camp, Luke asked to wait behind while Fofoo went inside to fetch Pascal. Foofo hesitated.

"I don't think the Frenchman wants me here. He says I am too clumsy," Fofoo said in Spanish.

"Please, just go."

Luke watched as Fofoo entered the main entertainment area of the fish camp. Pascal had built a fishermen's paradise. The facility was built out of bamboo with a thatched roof. Its strategic location received both south and north breezes, keeping the bird-size mosquitoes to a minimum. Luke could see a half dozen French men sitting at a long table enjoying grilled fish and smoking cigars. They toasted and drank cognac as they took turns telling their version of that day's fishing. One man with a long beard stood up and then opened his arms wide to show the size of the fish he had caught. The rest of the men nodded and cheered him on.

***

"The fish pulled so fucking hard, I nearly put my back out," he shouted in drunken French.

The men listened to Edith Piaf on the CD player. Behind the fully-stocked bar stood a handsome Venezuelan man who went by the nickname Chammo. He had chiseled features and took pride in his ability to spin and juggle the alcohol containers as he whipped off his custom version of Sex on the Beach, and Mudslides. Two well-endowed Colombian girls sat at the bar chatting with Chammo. As a side business, Chammo made sure that the fishermen had plenty of top notch Columbian tail to choose from every evening. He would bring different ones in each week. The gig paid so well that the working girls in Panamá City were known to get into cat-claw, fist fights over the right to work at Pascal's fish camp. Mounted trophy marlin, dorado and amberjack hung on the walls.

Pascal entered the room. The stress of starting a new fish camp had left him with several more gray hairs than the last time Luke had seen him.

"Fofoo, I told you never to come here," Pascal snapped.

"It's señor Luke, Pascal," Fofoo whispered. "He is here and needs your help."

"He is alive?"

Pascal followed Fofoo to Luke.

"Luke, is that you?"

"Yes, I know I look like shit, but it is me."

"I am so happy you are alive! What can do for you?" Pascal said.

"Well, better for you to see for yourself. Follow me."

Luke led Pascal and Fofoo to the hidden Midnight Express. Luke spent the better part of an hour telling Pascal his entire adventure.

"...and you see, that's why I need your help."

When the story was over, Pascal stood stunned, with his jaw wide open.

"I think I can help. My guests return tomorrow. If you pretend to be one of them, maybe you can evade detection. But, after that, what will you do?"

"I really don't know. I have to sleep on it. Have you seen Nici?"

"Yes. I visit her when I can, she is a strong woman. She works every day to keep her mind off you. I can tell she is hurting inside, but she does not show it."

Luke's jealous streak came out. "What do you do when you visit?"

"Come on Luke, I am French, but please..."

Luke retreated.

"I know what I am asking comes at some risk to, so you can keep the Midnight Express as compensation. But sell it fast as some really pissed-off people are looking for that boat."

"Thank you, Luke, I would have done it for free. Now let's get you looking like a Frenchman."

Pascal trimmed Luke's hair, set him up with some fresh clothes, including a black beret and tight pink turtle neck shirt. He made him shower off three times and sprayed him with copious amounts of cologne. Pascal made Luke light a cigarette and repeat a few French phrases.

"Où est le marché de poisson?" (Where is the fish market?)

"You are missing something. Yes, you need a mustache."

Using Luke's snipped-off dread locks, Pascal formed a dignified looking mustache and glued it to Luke's upper lip.

"Yes, you are now more French than Napoleon."

Luke felt like an idiot.

"Pascal introduced Luke to the rest of the fishermen. Luke enjoyed his first round of drinks in more than three months.

Luke knew that even if he managed to make it past the port authorities in Panamá City, he would really need to kick it into gear and he needed a good plan if he was ever to enjoy the taste of freedom again.

"Luke, what about the explosives you found in the Canal? You know they are going to use them at some point. You said you saw radioactive signs on the barrels! Well, what about Nici and Panamá City? If they light those things off we are all fucked. What are you going to do?"

"I guess I assumed that Homeland Security must have sent divers to diffuse the bombs by now. Have you heard anything?" Luke asked.

"So far, not a single word in the press." Pascal replied.

Luke calculated his position. All this time he had banked on Caucuss finding and diffusing the bombs. But, apparently, this was not the case, and again the clock was ticking. The Canal, the city, his darling Nici, all were at risk.

"Pascal, the only way I will ever be off the hook is to show the government proof of the terror plot and even more proof that I am not involved. Sounds like that is the only way to get them to send divers and diffuse the explosives and clear my name. A pretty tall order."

"Sounds like you have to engage the enemy… go into the lion's den. But you have no money, no passport. Plus, you are a wanted man." Pascal added.

Luke pondered and then a light bulb went off in his head.

"OK, I know what I am going to do."

Clarity had come with a plan. Luke sat up straight.

"I need you to contact Nici. Be sure to use a hand-written letter only, with instructions to flush it when she is done reading it. Tell her to contact my friend John. He flies for Global-Fast Airlines. He goes to the Middle East all the time, flying for the CIA. He flies coffins to Baghdad, empty coffins through Germany and India.

"Why do you want to go there?" Pascal asked.

"I don't, but if I am going to ever be free again and live my life, I need to sell my Ambergris for cash and from there, hire a good lawyer. Maybe the lawyer can make those idiots stop chasing me and go look in front of the Canal for the bombs.

I have a friend in India, named Raja… I used to sell him seashells for his Hindu temples. He often asked me for ambergris. I think I can sell my 100 kilograms to him or his contacts. When I used to ask him who he sold the ambergris to, he would reply, 'The bad guys'. Not sure what he meant by that, but I know more now.

Really, he sells the ambergris to a traditional Arab operated perfume factory in India. These guys pay a huge amount of money for perfume ingredients. They follow the letter of the Koran, and are very fundamental in their beliefs. I know it's a long shot but I think I can sell them my ambergris."

"Luke, you are nuts."

"Yeah, I know."

Pascal dispatched one of his three fully-equipped 25-foot super-pangas. The well-outfitted fishing boats ran at a top speed of 25- knots. The skipper running the boat delivered the letter to Nici in less than three hours. She was elated that Luke was alive and went right to work following his instructions. She clandestinely used an internet café to contact John, who could be anywhere in the world at any time.

John was in Turkey when he received the message. His reply simply read; "Tocumen Airport, cargo depot, 12:00 Wednesday, stay low."

That night, for the first time in months, Luke enjoyed a nice long slumber in a real bed. The French men woke early and hit the water for their last day's fishing. Luke rolled out of bed around noon. He filled his belly with leftover soufflé and conversed with the Columbian girls. The fishermen returned with more stories of trophy fish caught and released. They gathered their things, thanked Pascal for the trip of a lifetime, then boarded the panga for the trip back to Panamá City. Sporting his laughable Frenchman disguise, Luke grabbed his ambergris, thanked Pascal and boarded the boat.

At dusk, they reached the port. Luke did his best to blend in as the guards met the boat. He grew nervous as they randomly asked each man for their passports. When they got to Luke he blurted out the French he had been rehearsing.

"Où est le marché de poisson?"

The guard spoke up louder "Passaporte señor!"

"Où est le marché de poisson?"

The guard quickly tired of the game and waved Luke on.

"Luke, do you want to join us for drinks tonight?" one of the fishermen asked.

"No thanks. I need to see about a lady. But I will take you up on your earlier offer for a ride to the airport tomorrow."

"OK, see you then. *Bonne chance, Luke.*"

Luke used the petty cash that Pascal had given him to hire a taxi.

"Casco Viejo, por favor."

Luke ordered the driver to stop three blocks short of his flat. Luke hid his ambergris in a bush and made his way down the street. He was relieved to see that nobody, so far, had ID'd him. Luke did his best to stay in the shadows of the streetlights. He reached the corner leading to his street. Luke longed to see and hold Nici. He practiced what he would say and contemplated apologizing for his fling with Gabby. The thought of seeing Nici was the only thing that had kept him alive through his epic journey of survival.

I can't go to her. They might be watching. It would put her at risk.

Luke entered an abandoned building across the street from his flat. Cockroaches scampered while Luke plugged his nose to avoid the thick urine stench. A homeless man sat in one corner. He worked his way over to the staircase.

"Desculpe," (Pardon me) Luke said as he passed him.

Luke found an open door on the second floor. He walked into the room and over to the wood shutters on the windows facing his flat. Luke spied through the cracks. He could see Nici standing on their terrace smoking a cigarette.

"Hi, babe," Luke said quietly.

To improve his view, he gently cracked open the shudder. The street light showed in her direction. She had grown her hair longer and kept it in braids. Nici had quit smoking years ago, but the stress of missing Luke must have driven her to light up again.

Luke tried to send loving thoughts to her as she looked up at the stars.

Luke heard the laughing of children coming down the street. They stopped and rang the buzzer to Luke's flat. Nici let them in. The kids soon appeared on the terrace. Luke watched as she picked them up one by one and asked them how they were doing. She pointed out a few stars to each one. Nici retreated to cook them all a fish dinner. Luke stayed up past midnight, hoping for one last glimpse of the woman he planned to marry as soon as this mess was all over.

Luke spent the remainder of the night in the building. He watched as Nici left for work the next morning.

Luke took a cab back into the city, ate a big breakfast then met the French group for a ride to the airport. They dropped him near the cargo terminal and wished him God's speed.

Luke counted the minutes. He did his best to stay out of view. He could see the giant late model Global-Fast 747-cargo freighter standing vigil on the tarmac. At exactly 12:00 noon Luke watched as John walked down the gangplank. He wore aviator glasses and a neatly pressed captain's uniform.

"Luke, is that you?"

"Yes, I know I look ridiculous."

"Let's walk."

"Okay, here is how it is gonna work," John said. "You know, I could get fired and court marshaled for this, right? That's okay, I'm burnt out anyway. If I get busted you better bail me outta prison."

"So long as the judge accepts Ambergris for your bail, no problem," Luke replied.

"By the way, John, have you heard anything about Homeland Security foiling a terror plot to blow up the Canal? I know you hear these things from the inside." Luke asked.

"I did hear something about that, turns out the Canal Authority overrode D.H.S. and won't let them dig for bombs in front of the Canal gates. Said it'd cost too much money. That is the story D.H.S is putting out there, anyway."

Luke stammered, "But they have to stop it! It's going to happen, people are going to die."

Luke suddenly had an epiphany. He realized that he was up against competing forces of lunacy. Homeland Security wanted him as a terror suspect, but Canal authority refused to do anything about the actual impending terror attack. To Luke, it seemed as if catching a terror suspect trumped stopping an actual attack.

John changed the subject, "Okay, inside the jet are 40 empty flag-draped coffins. And lots of very big bombs. Do not touch the bombs. It's gonna be a very long trip. We will fly directly to Ramstein Air Base in Germany to take on fuel and a few troops returning to battle. Then we will fly another nine hours direct to Chennai, India to pick up more fuel and the Indian Ambassador to Iraq.

The crew will be here in one hour. Here is a liter of water, a sandwich, six Xanax and a .45 pistol. Trust me, the Xanax (mild tranquilizer) will come in handy and the gun… well, better safe than sorry It is locked and loaded. You just need to flip the safety off. It is 14 hours to Germany and the only time you will have chance to use the bathroom is a ten-minute window when we change over the co-pilot and engineer.

I will knock on your coffin when that time comes. Until then, do not make any noise whatsoever and, under no circumstances, get out of the coffin. When we land in India, I will knock on the coffin again to signal the all clear.

"Any questions?"

"What are you doing in Panamá anyway?"

"Some asshole Columbian rebels, I think you call them FARC blew up all the aircraft that we gave to the Colombian military. We are running in replacement parts for the new ones."

"You mean the ones that were dumping chemicals on the FARCS?"

"How did know that? It's classified?"

"Uhm, lucky guess."

"OK, empty your bladder. Then, let's get you loaded up."

Luke followed John up the gangplank, used the bathroom and headed back to the cargo hold. John stowed the ambergris in one coffin. He opened a second coffin for Luke.

"Rest in peace," John said as he closed the coffin lid.

It went pitch black. Luke placed is arms over his chest and tried to get comfortable. He slowed his breathing to fend off the claustrophobia.

This is gonna be tough.

Chapter Twenty-Nine

THE RHYTHM OF THE crew making the pre-flight check reassured Luke who, against all logic, was feeling relaxed and drowsy. When the engines finally came to life, Luke had been in the coffin for two hours. Luke's body was heating up the interior of the closed, satin-lined box. He heard the engineer close and seal the aircraft door.

Luke's first panic attack kicked in as soon as the plane left the ground. He reached into the small bag that contained the Xanax. He put one under his tongue and let it dissolve. He took shallow breaths. Once each hour, the flight engineer walked back to cargo hold to perform checks on the cargo. Luke held his breath as he heard the man approach. Two, fully-armed U.S. marines remained in the aft section with the ordnance. Luke did his best not to drink water that would fill his bladder but the dry hot air in the coffin forced him to take a sip. He nibbled on small pieces of the sandwich John had given him.

Ever since his sadistic step-brother had smothered his face with a pillow when he was seven, Luke had a tough time tolerating tight spaces.

About hour five, Luke's legs and arms cramped up and he had the urge to pee. He clenched his fist and squinted his eyes. When his panic became intolerable he downed another Xanax and opened his mouth wide to let out a silent scream. By hour ten, Luke's bladder pain reached unbearable levels. Making it worse, the plane hit heavy turbulence over the mid Atlantic, throwing him around in the coffin.

Luke's compulsive thoughts of the terror plot did not help the situation. He envisioned the Canal exploding and a wave of radioactive material blanketing nearby Panamá City. He felt so helpless, he had to do something, but what?

By the time they arrived in Germany, Luke was ready to open the coffin and turn himself into the Marines who were sitting 20-feet away from him. Luke thanked God when he heard the wheels skid on the runway. He waited patiently for the knock on the coffin. There was a delay, then nothing for two more hours. Then, a barely audible, knock, knock. Luke jumped out of the coffin and ran straight into the bathroom.

"Ahh, that's better," Luke said, feeling like a peeing, naked, Roman statue. He peed for nearly three minutes straight, filled his water bottle, moistened his face and climbed back into his box. Luke heard the fuel truck connect with the aircraft followed by some German being spoken and the sounds of the Indian Ambassador and his entourage boarding the aircraft.

Then he heard John say, "Welcome aboard, Mr. Ambassador, it is an honor to have you with us."

Twenty minutes later, the engines fired up again. Luke took a deep breath as they took off. The smell of jet fuel lingered in the coffin, giving him a headache. Three hours into the transit, Luke took his last Xanax. His system was overloaded with the anti-anxiety drug, causing him to drool. He tried not fall asleep, as snoring would attract attention.

As they flew along, Luke thought about the purpose of the coffin he was in. On its trip back to the U.S.A. it would be carrying the dead body of a fallen U.S. soldier who did only what their country and the President asked of them.

The war in Iraq was in its late stages and had grown unpopular back home. Luke recalled a young man he knew in the states. He had enlisted in the Marines just as the war broke out. He was proud to be serving his country and really wanted to get some pay back for 9-11. Six months into it, Joe was killed by a roadside bomb near Fallujah. Joe's body was sent back to his family in Santa Cruz, California in a coffin just like the one Luke was stowing away in.

For some reason being in that box really brought Luke closer to the sacrifices so many of his countryman were making. They were fighting the same people, in a way, that Luke was entangled with… the same people who had planted the bombs in the Canal, the same people disrupting the world everywhere. It seemed like when it came to contributions to the world, the terrorists added only misery, bloodshed, bombs and upheaval.

Luke had every reason to be bitter about his home country. They had kicked out his wife-to-be, and had branded him as terror suspect. However, he realized that his country was forced into taking harsh measures against the insane, violent actions taken by the Islamo-facists. He recalled his mother telling him, often, about the sacrifices his ancestors had made to build up the U.S. and make it into a great country. "Freedom isn't free. You have to fight for it," she'd said.

If Luke wanted to be free, that was just what he had to do. He would need to follow the example of his distant relative, Joseph Warren, who had been a good friend of Paul Revere and was the first officer to die in the Revolutionary War at Bunker Hill in Boston. Had Warren lived, he certainly would have been a signatory of the Declaration of Independence and the Constitution.

Luke tried not to dwell on the irony that his family had laid the foundation of Unites States and now he was not even allowed to bring his own wife into the country. His loyalty to the U.S. was a little more than confused.

To Luke's great relief, the plane landed in Chennai and came to a stop. This time the knocks on the coffin came quickly. Like count Dracula, Luke opened the lid and sat up. John was standing over him.

"Hurry, put these on," John said, handing him a flight uniform and an ID badge. Grab your ambergris, or whatever that crap is and get a move on. Walk like you belong here. Go past the guard gate, get a taxi and get the hell out of here."

"John, I really owe you one."

Luke followed John's instructions. Luke gave the gate guard a salute as he walked by and the man let him pass without checking his ID badge.

The air in India smelled different from the air in Panamá. It was mustier and heavier, with layers of warmth and spice. It was good to be back in the world, no matter what it smelled like.

As soon as Luke reached the main street in front of the air base, a dozen, three- wheel, motor powered rickshaw taxi drivers vied for his business.

"Taxi, taxi, I give you the best price, go with me. No, me!" they clamored

Luke got into the newest looking vehicle. He struggled to recall where exactly Raja's business was.

"In Tamilnadu, near the temples, Ramworm or Ramswwwerm," Luke said.

"You mean Ramasawaram?" The driver said as if it were an easy word to pronounce.

"Yes, that's it."

"Oh, very far from here, you should take an airplane. More than seven- hour drive." Luke had no passport or travel documents. Air travel was not an option.

"How much?"

The driver rubbed his chin and bobbled his head side to side.

"I am needing to stay in a hotel for the night if I take you there, so that will cost you an extra hundred rupees. That's about $4 U.S. So, I think I can do it for $20 U.S.

It seemed like a good price. Luke agreed and the three-wheeler took off. After being cooped up in the coffin for nearly 30 hours, the 20-mile open-air rickshaw was a pleasant relief. An endless stream of speeding trucks zoomed around Luke. The roads were narrow, forcing cars to brake and veer off the road when they passed each other. As populous as India was, much of the countryside was barren bushy fields with hawks and vultures patrolling the sky. Luke watched as a five-mile-long cargo and passenger train passed, leaving a thick black smoke trail for ten miles. It was overloaded with people hanging out of the windows and sitting elbow to elbow on the roof. The train must have been the last coal-fired locomotive on the planet.

The driver, whose name was Seker, asked Luke if he was hungry.

He was.

They stopped at some sort of industrial town and ate at the local cantina. The menu was simple, chicken or beef served with curry on a banana leaf. The workers filling the joint were a rough bunch who all spoke at the top of their lungs, giving an impression that the whole room was vibrating.

"Can I have some utensils?" Luke asked.

"We eat with our right hand," Seker explained. "The food tastes better that way and nothing to wash."

It did make sense. No plates or forks to wash.

Luke slurped up the food in minutes and they were back on the road. Luke waited for food poisoning to set in, but to his delight he tolerated the food just fine.

As the sun went away they passed the mid-sized town of Madurai. Seker pointed out the gates of the U.S. consulate and Luke made a mental note of its location. Three bumpy hours later, they reached the outskirts of the small town of Ramaswaram. It was already dark. The lack of street lighting made it tough to avoid the many wondering cows that strolled everywhere, unmolested.

Luke grabbed his ambergris, paid Seker and shook his hand.

"I am good from here. Have a safe drive back, and remember, life is like ice cream. You must enjoy it before it melts."

Seker smiled and drove off.

Finding Raja's seashell plant was not difficult. He asked a few of the townspeople where he could find Mr. Gandhi, Raja's Father. They all pointed in the same direction. Luke could tell he was getting close to the plant by the thickening smell of rotting mollusk meat and hydrochloric acid used to clean seashells.

Luke found Raja's facility. The blinking neon seashell on the door was hard to miss. Despite the late hour the front door was open. Luke entered. He could hear Raja speaking loudly on the phone in the back room.

"No, I told you, I must have the shells for the festival... festival! I have paid you one *lock* dollars [an old British term for a hundred thousand]. Please to be sending me my product soon. Bye bye, now"

Luke plopped the ambergis down on Raja's desk.

"How much will you give me for this?"

The ambergris had changed from yellow to brown and had lost most of its moisture. Raja, stunned, fell out of his chair.

"Luke, what, why, how did you get here?"

Ramaswaram was an out-of-the-way place. At the very southern tip of India, it was full of 2,000- year-old temples and devout Hindus. It was the last stop before Sri Lanka and did not see many foreigners. Raja knew that Luke must have a good reason for showing up unannounced.

He looked at Luke. "I don't owe you money, do I?"

Luke explained most the mess he was in.

"Luke, I am very happy to see you. Tomorrow, we must go to the temple to pray and give our hair, then the Gods will show us the right path. Plus, I must speak with my Father. For now, come with me to my home. You will stay with me."

Luke removed the remains of the mustache that Pascal had glued to his lip. Raja laughed.

Raja introduced Luke to his entire family and extended family. There were more than fifteen in all, and they all lived under the same roof. Raja's mother, who wore a colorful traditional Indian sari and had a third eye painted red between her brows, prepared dinner while Mr. Gandhi spoke to Raja in rapid, excited Hindi.

Mr. Gandhi, although he did not speak English, was a one-man army who had started out working for one dollar a day. Twenty years later, he ran the largest seashell business in India, grossing more than $3 million a year. He kept three hundred people employed. Mr. Ghandi was a Hindu. Most of his competitors were Muslims, making his domestic his dealings with them difficult.

Ghandi Seashell Mart dealt in every type of shell conceivable. From the rarest to the most abundant, domestic and imported -- they had it all. Business was tough since the massive Christmas tsunami of 2003 had covered their town with water, killing hundreds. Their most cherished shell, the left-handed Chankus, came from Sri Lanka.

The killer tsunami had all but destroyed the Sri Lankan fishing fleet, putting that supply offline. Mr. Gandhi compensated by sending his fishermen over the border to harvest the shells in the Sri Lankan waters. The rebel group called the Tamil Tigers of Sri Lanka had a previous monopoly on the valuable shells that brought in badly needed income for their fight against the government. Although their boats were destroyed, they aggressively protected their fishing grounds and would shoot at the Indian boats for entering their waters. Many of Gandhi's fishermen bore bullet wound scars as a result.

The prized, left-handed Chankus was a heavy shell. About one out of a million, through genetic chance, was born with the opening to the left instead of the right. This left-handed shell was precious to a Hindu, and to own one was a great honor. Families would save their entire lives just to buy a single shell, which could cost as much as $10,000. Once acquired, they would place the shell on their prayer alter and light incense. Entire stores in Ramasawaram were solely dedicated to trading this one species of shell, which can be seen on ancient statues of the Hindu God, Vishnu. The pearly white shell generally has a lotus flower carved into the top. The very tip is cut off so it can be used as horn that is used to announce the start of Hindu festivals.

"My father says we will help you," Raja said with a smile. "I think we can sell your ambergis for more than $4,000 a kilogram. But as you know, as I have told you, the buyers are very bad people, up to bad things. I would report them, but we need their business right now to stay alive. When we sell your ambergris, we will need a 20% broker fee. Is it okay?"

"I will give you half, but we need to do this fast" Luke said.

"Deal," Raja said. They shook hands.

" I need you to go the buyers ahead of time, okay? Be sure to hammer them on the price. Don't sell cheap." Luke knew that he would not stand a chance at getting a decent price if he cut the deal alone.

Not sure what to make of Luke's strange request, Raja turned to normal discussions about life and family.

"When is your wedding, man?"

Raja asked this same question every time he spoke to Luke.

"As soon I get out of this mess," Luke replied.

"Okay, if it means you will finally marry Mrs. Nici, we must try very hard to help you."

To the Indians, weddings are the most important events of their lives. They are worth traveling across the globe to attend, to pay thousands in dowries and, if need be, face potential terrorists to help get a friend off the hook so he can go home and get married.

Raja removed a picture from his wallet. It was a photo of a beautiful young Indian woman.

The smile ran away from his face as he said, "We want very badly to marry, but her family forbids it. She is of a higher caste than me."

"You mean she has more money than you?"

"No, we have much more money than her family. In fact, she needs an operation, and I am going to pay. In India, it is forbidden to marry under your class, regardless of how much education or money the person may have."

Luke was sad for Raja. At least Luke was free to marry the woman he loved, even if he couldn't bring her home to Mama.

Luke enjoyed a hearty home-cooked Indian meal with fantastically colored herbs and spices. He shared a room with three of Raja's youngest cousins. The room was humble, but he was glad to have a safe place to rest.

The next morning Raja woke early.

"This is Mutu. He will be your man while you are my guest."

"Nice to meet you," Luke said.

Mutu wore traditional garb and a turban. He was older than fifty and had been with Mr. Gandhi since the beginning. Mutu was exceedingly loyal. He followed Luke around and did not let him do anything for himself, whether it was opening a jar, closing a door, carrying a bag or making his bed. Mutu anticipated every need that might arise and did it ahead of time for Luke.

Luke, Raja and Mutu strolled through the seashell plant. It was a five-acre fenced-in yard. The ground was dotted with mountains of seashells and about a hundred workers wearing only loin cloths were hunkered down, scrubbing and cleaning the shells. One man hand painted small shells with funny designs of footballs, lady bugs and snakes to be used as hermit crab homes. The workers were happy to be employed and worked along in harmony while singing songs and rocking back and forth.

They exited through the showroom where the most valuable shells were displayed. Luke marveled at the huge pink conches, nautilus shells, murexes, tritons and a man-eating sized clam shell. Raja held up a single left- handed Chankus.

"I paid $12,000 for this," he said. "Listen."

He blew through the cut-off end of the spiral, making a loud horn sound like a Jewish shofar.

$12,000 for a horn?

"Now, we go to the temples to pray for good luck," Raja said.

They piled into a Range Rover. Mutu drove a short distance to a massive, glistening white temple. It was situated beach side. More than 1,000 worshippers bathed in the waters. Some did their laundry and dishes too.

Raja led Luke to an outside shaded area.

"What is that?" Luke pointed to a ten-foot high mountain of black hair.

"We shave our heads, giving our hair as a gift to our Gods."

"Oh, so that's what you meant by giving our hair away."

Raja sat inside the booth then paid the man 50 rupees. The barber shaved Raja bald in less then ten seconds.

"Now your turn, Luke. It's okay. I pray to more than fifty Gods, they all appreciate this gift to them."

"I think I would like your Gods on my side at this point, but they will have to settle for money instead of hair."

"No, it must be your hair."

The man gladly honored Luke's request to leave his hair at least two inches long.   Luke looked at the pile of hair. It looked like a paradise for lice but he was too polite to say so.

They waited in line to enter the temple, paying a few pennies entrance fee. A young boy sold them red and yellow die to be painted on their foreheads and they entered the main hallway.

This was different than any place Luke had ever been. A series of exotic, larger than life sized Hindu statues sat countersunk into the walls. Luke could see one elegant statue of a God with an elephant head who was making a sign with his left hand while holding a left-handed Chankus in the other. Natural light seeped through a few small windows and cracks to provide the only light in the hall. A thousand sticks of mixed fragrance incense burned in front of each statue. Smoke filled the entire temple down to the tiled floor. Two dozen worshipers knelt in front of each statue, chanting in unison. The whole thing had a narcotic effect. For a short while, Luke felt completely at peace with himself and his current situation. Just being in the temple made him feel that he was doing the right thing and that everything would work out. It was sanguine.

"Come Luke, I want to show you something," Raja said.

Raja took Luke through a series of tight tunnel corridors. Raja said the pathways had been cut through the 2000-year old temple around the time of Christ. The tunnels were made for smaller people. Luke had to arch his back to get through. The candlelit tunnels terminated in a large cubby hole. Raja knelt, folded his hands and began to pray in front of the world's largest left-handed Chankus. Raja said the shell was more than 40 inches long and weighed 25-pounds. He said the shell, which would sell for a million dollars on the open market; was brought to the temple by a holy man more than a century ago.

"The shell is the heart of the temple. Kneel, Luke. Pray and you will have your answer to any questions you seek."

"Who do I pray to? Not the shell?"

"No, the shell is only a symbol, a gateway to the many Gods. I like to talk to Vishna, he is the destroyer. He destroys obstacles that are the in way of achieving your goals."

Luke knelt, closed his eyes and tried to connect with the Hindu God. He saw himself walking down a road that was floating in the clouds. The road was slick and covered with engine grease. In the middle of the road sat a big black rock. Luke approached the rock. He could not get around or over it. He pushed and pushed but could not budge the stone. Luke had to be careful not to lose his footing on the slippery surface. Luke prayed more. A small man, painted purple and riding a giant elephant, approached from the other side of the rock. The man gave a command to the elephant, who lowered its head and pushed the rock off the pathway, sending it plummeting out of sight.

Luke opened his eyes.

What the hell did that mean? he wondered.

Luke explained his prayer dream to Raja as they made their way back through the maze of tunnels.

"Luke, you are very lucky. That was the God talking to you. He was trying to tell you that he will assist you in your mission and remove any obstacles in your way. You will be safe. You do not have to worry. I told you giving up your hair was a good offering."

"Oh, good. Now, let's go finally do some business," Luke said as he felt his short hair.

"I will go ahead. You can stay and bathe here in the sea, but do not let the water go in your mouth, too dirty," Raja said.

Raja left Luke in front of the temple with Mutu, as he drove off with the ambergris samples to cut the deal.

Luke swam in the warm waters. He looked off into the distance, squinting to see Sri Lanka, whose territorial waters started twelve miles offshore. The island was just out of sight. In times past, one could take a ferry to Colombo, the capital of Sri Lanka. Current tensions between India and Sri Lanka now required travelers to get a visa and take an airplane from a large city, hours away just to fly to a country 25-miles away. Raja often told Luke of the beautiful blue coral reefs and the abundant fish near Sri Lanka. Luke promised himself to one day visit and dive around the island.

Luke expressed a desire to walk around the small town. Mutu obliged as a guide. He showed Luke more than twenty smaller temples. Along the way, they stopped to eat more curry chicken. The young children gathered and followed Luke around everywhere. A few came close to him. They touched his skin and pulled on his hairy legs. They simply wanted to see what a white person's skin and hair felt like. Men with long beards and faces painted white roamed the street, while a few snake charmers played flutes as their cobras danced.

Meanwhile, Raja drove to meet the men from the perfume factory. Raja called ahead and asked if they could meet up at a roadside café at the halfway mark. The men agreed, which shaved fifty miles off Raja's trip.

They met in a no-name, overcrowded to bursting café. Raja had to yell to be heard. He then showed the men the sample, and they seemed pleased and willing to do business. The two men wore traditional Saudi Muslim attire and sported full grown, well-trimmed beards.

"Well, my little Hindi friend, seems you have finally found a decent cache of ambergris. I am sure Saeed and the rest back at the plant will be most pleased. What are you asking?"

Raja replied, "I am only negotiating for an American friend of mine who has brought the goods here from South America. Panamá, to be exact. He is asking $5000 per kilo."

The men skipped over the price, "Panamá… American? What is his name and can he be trusted?"

"He is Luke, Luke Dodge and I have known and traded with him for many years. He as honest as the day is long, he sent me the gold-lipped conch and many other fine things from the sea."

"My Hindu friend, it seems a little odd for this Dodge guy to just show up with such a valuable asset to sell. What is he hiding?"

Raja had no choice but to come clean, or the men would surely grow cagey and cut the deal off in its tracks.

"Well, to be honest, his soon to be wife, a real beauty name Doctor Nici said the wrong thing at the U.S. /Canadian border and Homeland Security arrested her and banished her for five years or maybe for life, it is not clear. Luke decided to start over in Panamá to be with Nici and once there… I am not sure what happened, but I get the feeling he is on the run from something."

The men paused, took out a pen and pencil, then started to write down the facts that Raja was so freely providing. Raja could see the man to his left circling the words, *American*, *on the run* and *Panamá*.

"$5,000 is too high, but if your man, Dodge comes by the perfume plant tomorrow, we can discuss the real price with him. But he must come alone, only alone."

"Please be good to him, Luke is my friend."

With that, the men shook hands and took their leave.

Luke, Mutu and Raja rendezvoused with Raja's family home around dinner.

"Luke, I have made the deal. I left a 500-gram sample with the buyers. They want to meet you tomorrow. I did as you asked. For some reason, when I said Panamá and that you were an American, the man I was talking to really focused in on what I was saying. They asked more questions about you and about the merchandise. Very odd men…"

"Well done, Raja. With any luck tomorrow we will be $400,000 richer. That's good because that's $400,000 more than I have." Luke laughed.

"They insisted that you come alone."

Chapter Thirty

THE NEXT DAY, Raja stayed behind to work with his father while Mutu drove Luke to the perfume factory. The Arabs were waiting for Luke to arrive with the balance of the ambergris. Luke looked out the window as they drove. For a hundred miles, the scenery was basically the same: shanty towns, blue tarp-covered huts, cows wandering the streets and garbage lining the roads. As they neared their destination, a town called Kayalpattinam, the scenery drastically changed. Suddenly, it seemed they were in the wealthiest part of Saudi Arabia. The streets were wide and clean and lined with brilliant white, sturdy-looking bulbous architecture with high, arched doorways.

Women wearing full black veils walked ten steps behind their men who had long black beards, black turbans and baggy pants. The men all wore daggers on their left hips and long scimitar swords on their right. The swords had elegant gold handles and fancy sheaths embossed with Arabic writing. The swords were long and curved, almost like a sickle, with the widest portion at end.

The normally quiet Mutu spoke up.

"This town, it sits on Indian soil, but really, it is in Saudia Arabia. The money comes from Saudi, the schools only teach the fundamental version the Koran and the teachers come from Saudi. They have their own law. Even Indian police cannot come here. They are very strict Muslims. The women cannot go outside without a man to accompany them. If you steal, they cut your hand off and things like that."

They pulled up in front of the perfume factory.

"I will wait for you. Be careful, Mr. Luke."

Luke grabbed the rest of the ambergris, took a deep breaths and drug the heavy baskets towards the door. He banged on the heavy door knocker, *knock, knock, knock.* The door slowly opened. Two large men appeared wearing western suits, dark sunglasses and badly concealed listening pieces in their ears. The men said nothing to Luke and gestured for him to follow.

Luke entered the main perfume production area. There were 50 wood-fired distillers boiling off 1,000-gallon caldrons containing centuries-old formulas of rare woods, ambergris, herbs, flowers and even parts of marine mollusks. The smell soaked into Luke's clothes and stained the inside of his nose, leaving the trace smell long after he'd left the facility. The caldrons boiled the raw materials until the oils rose into bleed-off pipes and settled into vats. After the oils from the raw material had been fully extracted, the remaining materials were reduced and used further to make incense.

More than 200, traditionally dressed Muslims labored to keep the place going. At high noon, the call to prayer came.

Everybody put down whatever they were working on, knelt, faced east and prayed. Luke passed one room full of boys' younger than ten who were reading and reciting verses from holy texts. Each time Luke paused to look at the fascinating perfume operation, the two guards, who looked like they had been hired from a European security firm, ushered him along.

Luke reached a door at the end of the production area. He was told to wait. Luke waited and waited for nearly an hour. The intense fragrances filled every pore of Luke's body and made his eyes water. The door opened.

"Hello, you must be Mr. Luke. Please come in. You guys can go. Go!"

The man shooed away the bodyguards.

"I am Sheikh Mohamed Saeed. Your friend Raja came to us yesterday. He told me about your ambergris. That stuff is getting hard to find. The Japanese used to kill the whales just for that material. Now, we have to hunt the globe to find it."

Luke was startled to hear the man speak perfect English with a Bronx accent.

"I grew up in the United States and studied there until I was twenty-five. After that I wanted my life to mean something so I got involved with some people who showed me a better way to be. Maybe you will meet them, soon." Saeed was vague.

"Would you like some tea?" he asked.

"Yes, thank you."

The Sheikh poured the tea, smiled at Luke and sat down.

"Please, Mr. Luke, have a seat and let's test your ambergris."

Luke broke off a chunk. Saeed grabbed it, weighed it, removed his dagger and cut off a smaller piece. He put the piece up to his nose. Touching it to his nostrils, he inhaled deeply. He nodded, then took the same piece and lit a match. He burned the piece then wafted the smoked in his direction. The smell was cross between burning hair, musk and the body odor of someone who eats too much red meat. Saeed's face read satisfaction.

"Mr. Luke, I think we can help you. How much do you want?"

It was the opening of what would likely be a challenging, Middle Eastern haggle.

Luke began the negotiations by asking $5,000 a kilogram.

"What! Are you trying to kill me?"

"Okay", Luke said, "if you can't afford it, I have buyers in Dubai."

Luke stood up and headed for the door.

"Wait, wait sit down, please, sit down. I have never paid such a high price, but I am willing to offer you $2,000 a kilo.

"FIVE THOUSAND." Luke returned.

"Please, I have three children in college and one getting ready to go, no more than $3,000."

"Saeed, don't twist my nipples, I know what this stuff is worth. $4,500 and no less."

Luke had haggled with everybody around the globe for all sorts of goods, Saeed's flee market tactics were lost on Luke.

"$4,000, cash money, final offer!" Saeed said with a lump in his throat."

Luke paused.

"Well, only because it's you, Sheikh."

Luke stuck out his hand and threw a cheesy smile. The Sheikh hesitated, then said politely, "Forgive me." He shook

Luke's hand with a limp, insincere handshake. It sent chills of distrust through Luke's spine.

"So, Mr. Luke, business is based on trust. Can I trust you?"

"I have the goods. I think that's enough."

"You see, my friends, the ones who showed me a better way to live – they are the ones who took me from the corrupt, vulgar ways of America -- they want to meet you. These men have the cash for the ambergris anyway, so you need to meet them. But they are not what you call, uhm let's say, 'public' people."

"Go on," Luke said.

"Raja said you have been living in Panamá. He said that the U.S.A. expelled your fiancée from their soil and banned her from entry for five years."

"Yep."

"That must have made you very angry."

"Like you cannot imagine."

The Sheikh produced a color computer printout. He slid it across the desk to Luke. The piece of paper was taken from a classified Homeland Security database. It had a picture of Luke and five more images of what he might look like in various disguises. The alert read:

Wanted, dead or alive. Luke Dodge is suspected of collaborating with terror cells, possibly Al Queda. Dodge is considered armed and dangerous. Due to his non-Muslim appearance, he is considered an especially dangerous security risk.

Reward: $10 million, USD

International ranking on wanted terror suspects list: 23

Luke's jaw dropped. His suspicions were confirmed.

"Mr. Luke, I do not know what you did to piss these guys off, but they really want you. I guess you could say that we have that in common, like it or not, we are on the same side now."

Luke could see where this was leading.

"Come back tomorrow. Meet my special friends and we will have your money. Say, 9:00 a.m.?"

"See you then," Luke said.

Luke exited the building, again dragging his cargo of Ambergris. Mutu drove him back to Raja's.

"Raja, I am going to be paid tomorrow. I need you to drive me. Is that okay?"

"Yes Luke, but my father needs the car so Mutu will drop us off and bring the car back here."

"Well, that's not quite perfect, but it will have to do. I will tell you more on the way."

"So, tell me did you make a good deal?" Raja asked.

"Raja, my friend, we did really good, but when you said these guys do bad things, you were more correct than you know. They are up to something, I just don't know exactly what."

Luke did not have all the facts and did not want to alarm Raja or his family so he kept the details of his meeting confidential. But deep down inside, Luke knew the day to come would change his life, one way or another. He had no idea what to expect. He had to get his cash, so skipping out now was not an option. That night, Luke had an iconic dream.

He was Luke Skywalker and Saeed was Darth Vader but with a turban and a beard. He kept hearing Vader repeating, "Luke, I am your father, come over to the Dark side, there is power and safety here, the Dark side, Luke, it's where you belong."

The next morning, Raja found Luke praying in front of their family Hindu altar.

"I did not know you were Hindu."

"I need all the support I can get right now. Let's go." Luke prepared himself to do business with the devil, not the first time.

Luke grabbed the ambergris and headed out the door.

"Be careful," Raja's mother said, sounding just like Luke's mother. She said it in Hindi but the meaning was clear.

Mutu drove while Luke and Raja sat in the back.

"So, tell me," Raja said.

"It's like this. You were right, these guys are bad and I think they want me to help them with something very terrible. I think these guys can lead me to whoever is planning a terror attack back in Panamá."

"What will you do, Luke?"

Luke skirted the question.

"I can promise you we will get the money. I saw the U.S. consulate in Madurai on the way to your home when I drove here from Chennai."

"Yes, I know that place."

Luke had learned the hard way to trust his gut, he knew the perfume dealers would try something, he just did not know what.

"When Mutu goes back with the car, I need you to find another one. A very fast one. Also, I do not want to put you or your family in jeopardy, so it is best that you wear some sort of disguise. They cannot know that we are leaving together."

Raja was uneasy. He spilled the fears that had been building inside.

"Luke, listen to me. Do not mess with these guys beyond selling them your ambergris. They are a thousand-pound hornet's nest. If you hurt them, they will come for you, for Nici for the rest of your life until you and everybody you love and care about are dead or very badly hurt.

I am asking you to think before you act or even speak, keep it just to the business of the day, ambergris. I think their connections go deep into governments, maybe even the United States and, for sure, the Indian government. You would never again know a peaceful day if you upset them."

Raja's accented, excited words hung heavy in the air.

"Please just have a fast car ready. I am not planning anything bad, but it helps to have plan B."

"OK, man. I am with you no matter what. After all, it is about your wedding, right?"

"Yes... and much more," Luke replied.

An hour later, they neared the perfume factory. Luke asked to be dropped in front.

"The Gods are with you. I am with you," Raja told Luke.

Luke got out of the car, shook Mutu's hand and watched them drive off. He lugged the heavy baskets of ambergris down the street towards the entrance. He passed traditional-looking Muslims who stared daggers into his western eyes. Several of the men went out of their way to cross the street just so they did not have to share a sidewalk with an infidel.

Luke knocked at the large, arched doorway. The two somber security guards answered the door.

"Hey, guys, how 'bout them Lakers?"

"The Father will see you now.

The Father?

Luke was led down a different route this time, bypassing the bubbling cauldrons. He passed the vats full of boiled-off essential oils. He entered a clean room with a dozen men wearing white lab coats. They were mixing and testing samples of the oils. His mute guards led him through a series of locking gates and doors that looked like they had been inspired by the comical beginning of the television series Get Smart.

The trio came to a final doorway. A guard posted there motioned for Luke to go in and his pals left.

"You guys have a nice day then."

Luke dragged his load of ambergris through the door.

"Welcome, Luke, welcome," Sheikh Saeed said with a smile. "Sit down, please. They will be coming in a moment. You will soon be part of a small brotherhood that will show you a better way of life, an offer to paradise. We are God's warriors and seek to balance all the evil brought into the world by the unclean west and the Jews."

A buzzer rang.

"The Father is calling us."

They passed into a second room. It had earthen walls and was lit only by candlelight. On one wall was a large portrait of Osama bin Laden, on the other a framed image of the first airplane crashing into the Twin Towers on Sept. 11, 2001. The message was anything but subtle. Behind the large oak desk sat a man who faced the wall. He remained facing away from Luke as he spoke.

"Welcome, Mr. Luke. Forgive the theatrics, but we have many enemies, so we must be careful. Saeed has told me that you have been living in Panamá and that your country, the

United States of America, has banished you and your fiancée. And now you run as a man suspected of terrorist acts."

The man turned and faced Luke.

"On the watch-list you are number 23 … I am number 4," he said, establishing bragging rights and alpha order. "Saeed sent me an encrypted e-mail about you. I flew straight away from Pakistan to meet with you."

Luke studied the man. He was in his late forties and wore a long black beard and a turban. He was comfortably stout and spoke with a calm, relaxed, even tone. The dim light made it difficult to discern any real facial distinctions.

Luke spoke. "If you don't mind, let's do business. I do not have much time."

No. 4 snapped his fingers, and Saeed produced two satchels.

"Two hundred thousand in each," No. 4 said.

"Luke picked up the bundles and smelled the newly printed money. He pulled out a few bills and held them to the light to check for counterfeiting.

"Consider that a down payment," No. 4 said.

"I do not like to do business with people whom I do not know their names," Luke said as he held onto the bags of cash.

"People here, they call me the *Father*."

"A down payment for what?" Luke asked.

"Do you want to live a better life, Mr. Dodge? Do you want to get some revenge on the U.S.A. for the crimes they have committed against you? Make the world a better place?"

Luke egged him on.

"Yes. The United States is a criminal state, and I would love to hurt them any way I can. What do you have in mind?"

"If you do this one thing that we ask, then we will pay you one million dollars. But the real benefit for you will be a new identity. We have connections across the globe. You and your fiancée' will become new people and you will be protected by the brotherhood that is Al Queda."

Luke's heart raced as he heard the words- Al Queda.

"Keep talking," Luke said.

"We have plans to disrupt global shipping, supply chains. We have plans to blow up both the Pacific and Atlantic entrance to the Panamá Canal. We have already laid the explosive at the entrances to the Canal, plus it was Saeed's brilliant idea to add 50 barrels of radioactive waste that we collected from hospital radiology departments. The explosives ensure that the Canal is offline for a long time and the radioactive waste will ensure that it takes years to repair. The cost of consumer goods will skyrocket. The evil traitors in Saudi and Dubai who sell their oil to the west, who are in bed with the west, will be crippled. Chaos will ensue making the world a better place and easier place to convert more warriors to our cause."

"Tell him the good part!" Saeed said with childish glee.

"As an added benefit, with the help of certain people inside the U.S. government, we will detonate the bombs on the 10th anniversary of the handing back of the canal."

"Isn't that when the president will be transiting the canal for the celebration?"

"Yes, we had not even dreamed of such a wonderful coincidence but the same people who provided us with the intel about you, insisted that we wait to set off the bombs. Happy 4th of July, America!"

Luke had no way to know if the Father was telling the truth or not about working with agents inside the government. *Why would the US want the Canal and, for that matter, the president to be vaporized? Who could do such a thing and for what end? Such a connection would explain why the bombs had not already been found and disarmed though. Such a thing would have to be buried very deep and start at the highest levels of government.*

Luke was not much for politics, but he recalled that the newly-elected, President Obama had pledged to rein in many of the unchallenged powers given to Homeland Security after 9-11. After his first 90 days in office, President Obama held frequent debates about abolishing the Patriot Act and Homeland security, altogether. The president felt that Home Land security was out of control and becoming too much like the old KGB in the now defunct USSR.

Luke hid his mixed feeling of glee and fear, he could not believe that he had stumbled into the terror cell that had gotten him in this mess to begin with. He refrained from quoting Casa Blanca, 'Of all the bars, of all the gin joins in all the world'.

He said, instead, "What exactly do you want me to do?"

The Father put on his reading glasses and handed Luke a set of blueprints. They showed in detail the complete layout of the Panamá Canal and its depths, average tides and transit times for the ships. The Father smiled as he pointed out the areas marked with red Xs where the SEMTEX and radioactive waste had been dumped.

Luke pretended to act impressed and surprised at the terror plot.

"How did you manage that? Do you mean that stuff is already on the sea floor?"

"The bombs are in place but, so far, we have no way no to detonate them. That is where you come in. All you have to do is fly back to Panamá under a new identity. Once there, you will simply buy a cell phone and call this number-64977927. You simply call the bombs, setting them off. When you and your fiancée are far away, you dial the number from the cell phone and goodbye, Panamá.

"Why don't you call the bombs yourself?"

"I would, but the detonation device only works if it is called from a local Panama number." The Father replied. "Also, there is a chance that we may have damaged the remote detonator when we dumped the barrels in front of the canal. We need you to go SCUBA diving and check to make sure it is still operational."

"I can do that and I don't even need SCUBA gear," Luke said without hesitation. "I need to keep these blueprints so I know where the barrels are laid."

"That is satisfactory. You will be paid upon completion, memorize the plans and then burn them."

Luke gripped the blue-prints. The paper and what it represented felt powerful in his hands.

"I am taking a big risk here. I need more good-faith money. $200,000 more should do it. You can pay me the $800K when the Canal no longer exists."

"What you ask is reasonable. Saeed, please get Mr. Luke another $200,000 from the safe."

Saeed exited the room. He returned in less than five minutes and handed Luke the cash. Luke put half into each satchel.

Saeed and the Father looked at each other with satisfaction. After all, the world was on high alert for terrorists fitting the profile of Arab extremists. But to have a young, white, half-Jewish American in their pocket could serve them well.

Saeed took a phone call, then whispered into the Father's ear.

"OK, now we must go upstairs. The children are waiting," the Father said with a half-baked smile.

Luke followed the men through several doors until they reached a large underground, miniature golf course. A door on the opposite side of the room opened and in ran 20 boys and girls, all under ten. They ran up, taking turns hugging the Father and Saeed. The Father asked them to welcome Mr. Luke- the newest member of their family.

The children were orphans from the war in Iraq, mixed Sunni and Shia who had lost their parents to U.S. bombing raids and arrests. A few of the children were missing limbs. The Father and Saeed helped them along. One young boy came to the Father with a special gift, it was a small basket that he had made with verses of the Koran written on the sides. The boy hugged the Father and said in Arabic, "Thank you, Father, for saving us, thank you."

Suddenly, the idea of being a terrorist seemed one-sided to Luke. *One man's terrorist is another man's freedom fighter,* Luke thought.

Luke, the Father and two of the oldest boys, teed off. This was no ordinary miniature golf course. Each hole had a special anti-American theme to it. When the first hole was sunk, a bobble head of G.W. Bush popped up and was pounded into the ground by foam mallets. The third hole was an effigy of the Statue of Liberty. When the ball sunk, a speaker sounded that said in English, "I'm a whore, I'm a whore."

The effects grew in meaning and showiness culminating with the final hole. As the ball sunk it set off an elaborate three-dimensional display of the twin towers being struck by model airplanes and setting the buildings aflame. The message was anything but subtle and it burned clearly into the minds of the young one's looking on.

"One last thing before we let you go. We have a little ritual that we do when we bring a new member into our organization."

"Please tell me it's a round of vodka."

"Even better."

The Father motioned for the children to leave the room. The three men walked back to the first room that they had met in.

The Father unsheathed his scimitar sword from its holder. It made a slicing sound as the long, shiny, sharp metal blade slipped out.

"My grandfather gave me this scimitar. He killed five men with it. He was a Bedouin chief. He roamed the dunes of Arabia with his family and our tribe until the Americans and British came to our soil. They scoured our land, digging for oil. They corrupted our leaders with their money and our way of life was lost forever."

The Father grabbed Luke's right hand tightly and turned it over to expose the veins on his wrist.

"We seal these deals in blood. After this, you are no longer an American, no longer a westerner, no longer Luke Dodge. You will be given a new name, a proper Muslim name.

With that, the Father sliced into Luke's wrist, missing the main artery but releasing a steady flow of blood. Luke scrunched his face. Saeed smiled.

"Saeed, please roll up your right sleeve."

"Yes, Father."

The Father did the same. He made shallow slices in his and Saeed's wrists.

The three men stood there with blood dripping from their forearms. The Father set his scimitar down on the desk.

"Now, we will mix blood and you will forever be one of us. We will be brothers until death, sworn to bring down the Americans and the corrupt West."

The Father pulled Luke's wrist toward his own. As the men were about to mix blood, Luke looked up at the wall. He saw the burning Trade Towers. He looked at the image of Osama bin Laden. By mixing blood with these men, he would become part of Osama's organization and subject to his will.

Luke's thoughts skipped around on fast forward. He thought of his mother telling him to love his country even when it does not love him back, Nici, his ancestors who fought to make America great, Hernan and his friends back in Panamá and 9-11.

Luke dove for the scimitar.

The surprised men lurched back. Saeed went for his dagger but was not fast enough to counter the scimitar that Luke plunged into his heart.

The Father reached under the table for a pistol. As he swung the gun around to fire, Luke cocked the sword back like a baseball bat, closing his eyes just as he had always done before shooting a big fish. With all his might, throwing his entire body into the blow, he brought the sword down on the Father.

It connected, a perfect stone shot.

One second, the Father was a frightening presence, creating havoc and despair. The next second, his head was rolling on his desk, bumping against the computer keyboard, his blood spattering all over the images of his hero, Bin Laden and their hollow triumph of the Twin Towers.

"Fuck you, and the horse you rode in on!" Luke screamed.

Shaking from his pumping adrenalin, he consciously forced himself to think clearly. He laid the sword on the desk, turned his jacket inside out to conceal the blood stains, wiped his hands on the sofa and picked up the blueprints of the Canal, folding them so they would fit into one of the money satchels. He grabbed the Father's head and stuffed it in the other satchel.

The encounter had been swift and quiet and the guards remained outside the door. Luke took a moment to cover his eyes and breathe deeply. He had never taken a human life. It was not as difficult as he imagined it would be. He felt oddly detached.

Shouldering the money bags with their contraband, Luke calmly walked out the door, waving at the corpses as if he were bidding them farewell. The security guards stood vigil.

"Hey, you guys have a nice day, now. Be sure to write."

Unimpressed and still dour, they escorted him past the maze of gates, elevators and secret doors. The guards took their jobs seriously. Any wrong moves and Luke would give himself away. To remain in control, Luke conjured up a daydream of walking in the park with Nici and their dog Chewy. He thought of her standing on their terrace looking at the night sky. Luke walked down the last hallway leading to the arched doorway exit. The guard eye-balled Luke, paused and typed in a security code and opened the door.

All righty then, say hi to the Mrs."

"The man nodded uncomprehendingly.

Luke crossed the threshold to freedom and looked around for Raja. Coming out of the cave-like environment to the open street made the sunlight hurt his eyes. His bloody deed would be discovered soon. Maybe it already had, and he was a dead man.

He saw a beautiful brand new black Mercedes Maybach approaching.

Raja really listened to my instruction about getting a fast car.

"Raja, Raja, over here!" Luke walked toward the car. As it pulled up, a tinted window smoothly descended to reveal a liveried chauffer behind the wheel. A wealthy-looking Arab couple could be seen in the passenger cabin.

"Sorry, sir. I thought you were somebody else."

Beep, beep, beep.

"Over here, Luke, get in."

Luke looked up to see a red, three-wheel rickshaw driven by an Arab woman covered in full black veil. The woman had a familiar voice.

"Get in, Luke, get in, hurry!"

Raja?

Luke ran to the rickshaw, threw his bags in and they sped off.

Raja removed the head covering.

"You like my disguise, Luke?"

"I asked you to get a fast car!"

"Hey, Luke, this is the best I could do on short notice."

"Raja, listen carefully. In about five minutes a lot of angry, very well-armed terrorists are gonna come out of that building gunning for us."

316

"Did you get the money?"

"Just drive!"

Raja gunned the hand throttle. The rickshaw backfired as Raja shifted from second to third gear.

"I put super unleaded in. I think we can get up to 40 miles per hour. Hold on."

Luke shook his head and opened one of the bags.

"Three hundred thousand, just for you, my friend. But if you are going to live to spend it, you need to get us to the U.S. consulate in Madurai in a hurry."

"Three hundred thousand? For me?"

"Oh, and I kept a little souvenir."

He opened the other satchel. The cash was washed red with the blood of the Father's head. Luke moved the cash around until Raja could see the head.

"Oh my!" Raja exclaimed.

Luke pulled out the chart of the Panamá Canal showing the planned terror attack.

"What is that, Luke?"

"This is my Get Out of Jail Free card."

"Luke, I really hope the Gods are with us."

Two shiny black Mercedes appeared in the rearview mirror.

"Luke, get in the back and cover up with the towels back there."

Raja slid the veil back over his face. The Mercedes pulled along side the rickshaw. The tinted passenger side window rolled down. Inside sat one of the security guards from the perfume factory. He turned his head in a robotic fashion and looked at Raja, then at the ricksaw.

Raja waved. The man held a powerful German-made machine gun that looked like it could sink the Titanic in a single shot. The ruse worked and the men sped off. Raja arced a right.

"I think we lost them," Raja said with glee.

Luke climbed back into the front seat.

"Now take off your veil, so next time they come around, it might trick them again. They are sure to figure out that Arab women generally don't drive. They will figure it out and come back.

"I am running low on fuel," Raja said.

"I thought you said you filled it up!"

I did. It only holds three gallons."

They stopped to fill up the three-gallon fuel tank. As Raja paid the gas station attendant, bullets ripped through the air. Bullets spun the attendant around and punched holes in the gas pump.

"Let's go!" Luke yelled.

Raja jumped into the rickshaw.

"Oh, this very exciting, Luke."

"Go, go go, go!"

More shots followed them. Raja pulled onto the road, stopping to look both ways and put on his turn signal before proceeding. Luke reached over and maxed out the hand throttle.

So far it was not clear where the shots were coming from.

Luke looked back.

Kaboom!

The entire gas station exploded into a brilliant fireball.

Again, the two Mercedes' appeared, this time supported by a Toyota pickup truck accessorized with a small missle launcher and a .30 caliber machine gun mounted on a tripod.

"This does not look good, Luke. Vishnu, help us now," Raja sang.

Raja and Luke had a quarter-mile lead on their pursuers.

"There, turn left down that alley, Raja."

Raja swung the little three- wheeler around and floored it down the narrow alley, knocking over fruit and fish stands. He honked his horn.

"Out of the way, please, sorry, sorry," he yelled politely.

The bad guys could not squeeze their cars down the alley.

"I think we lost them," said Luke, lulled into a false sense of security.

They made their way out of the area of Arab influence, pulled into a garage in an Indian neighborhood and paid the owner $20 to hide them. They hid in the dark garage for almost two hours, giving them plenty of time to contemplate their situation.

"Let's wait until after dark, get a real car and we can go the rest of the way," Luke said.

"That sounds like a good idea. We have $600,000. I think we can buy a real car for that price."

"Maybe we can get a deal for $500,000."

They laughed.

"I want you to know that whatever happens, Luke, the Gods will help us and I do not regret helping you," Raja said.

"You are my good friend, Raja, and I will never forget your kindness. Shhhh. I think I hear voices."

Harsh voices broke through the darkness.

"Where are they?"

Crack, crack, crack!

More gunshots.

Luke and Raja peered through a crack in the garage door. A woman was shaking as she protected her little girl from a belligerent man speaking with a thick South African accent.

"They must have come down this alley," he shouted at her. "Let's see if this helps you remember."

The man picked up the terrified young girl by the shirt collar and pointed his machine gun at her head.

That was enough for Luke.

"Okay, you asshole. Here I am."

He raised his hands and left the garage. The man dropped the girl and took aim at Luke.

Smash!

The girl's mother, a fierce protector and angry as hell, had snuck up behind the gunman and clobbered him with a steel oil drum. He fell unconscious.

Luke and Raja were taken aback.

"Cool," said Luke.

"Thanks," said Raja in Hindi.

"Come on. More will come soon," Luke said, helping himself to the man's gun and his radio.

Like and Raja gave the woman $20,000 by way of thanks – enough to take care of her and her family for the rest of her life -- and headed off in the rickshaw. They remained on the narrow side streets until they reached a section of town that forced them to return to the main highway for the last ten miles of the trip. Luke stood lookout, clutching the gun he had taken from the guard.

"Here we go!"

Rat tat tat!

The pickup truck had found them and was hot on their trail. More shots, rata-tat- tat!

Luke returned fire but only hit the road in front of the swerving truck, which was quickly gaining ground on the outclassed rickshaw. Luke could see one man getting ready to fire the small rocket launcher.

Luke fired again, bang, bang, bang, bang!

The last short scored a perfect hit, killing the driver and splashing blood across the truck windshield. The truck flipped and rolled six times, throwing the men and their weapons into a ditch.

"Up there! I think I see the consulate!" Raja yelled.

"Drive, drive!" Luke screamed as the last Mercedes charged around the traffic to catch up. It gained steadily, its bullet-proof glass and armor plating deflecting Luke's barrage of shots.

"Dammit, they are still coming."

The car sprouted with armed assailants. One man with a machine gun stuck his upper body out of the passenger side window and another holding a rocket propelled grenade popped out of the sunroof. Luke got off a lucky shot, killing the man with the RPG, as the remaining gunman fired away. The shots tore into the small rickshaw, puncturing the engine. Smoke filled the air. Raja turned his blinker on and pulled off the road. The shooter in the Mercedes stopped for a few seconds, apparently to reload.

"Run for it!" Luke yelled.

With $300,000 in bloody $100 bills, the bloody head of the No. 4 wanted terrorist in the world and the plans to blow up the Panamá Canal, Luke jumped from the rickshaw. He kicked his shoes off and ran like the wind. Raja followed. The assailant fired at them.

Raja smiled at Luke as they raced to the gates of the compound. A bullet whizzed past Luke, hitting Raja in the leg. Luke knelt over and with adrenaline pumping him full of superhuman strength, picked up Raja and kept running.

"Come on, Raja. We are almost there. Hold on!"

The gates were twenty-feet away. The firing behind them continued.

Two U.S. Marines stood post behind the gates.

"Hostile fire, hostile fire," one Marine yelled. They readied their weapons.

They were prepared to keep the consulate safe at all costs, and this racing pair might have been terrorists carrying out a dramatic ruse.

But who was that person in the Mercedes – was he really shooting at them, or part of an assault?

"Open the gates. I am an American! Open the fucking gates, now, open the gates, open the goddam gates!"

The Marines looked at each other, then trained their weapons onto Luke and Raja.

"Hey, Semper Fi and the Broncos won the Super Bowl in 1998."

The marines cautiously opened the gates.

The Mercedes drove away.

Luke passed out, dropping Raja and the cash bags on the ground. The plans to blow up the Canal, and the Father's head rolled out of the satchels.

The head bumped up against the shiny boot of a U.S. Marine.

C.F. Goldblatt

Chapter Thirty-One

LUKE CRACKED HIS neck while peering out the window of the olive green C1-30 turbo-prop military transport plane. Luke sat next to the window, and he was shackled to the seat. To his left was Caucuss. Caucuss sat by Luke's side during the entire 27 hour transport from India. Luke was held in the consulate detention center for two days until being handed off to Caucuss who made him a deal, "Show us where the explosives are and you will go free."

The plane circled over the Canal and the Bridge of the Americas. Luke tried to focus on where he thought the yacht had dumped the explosive canisters.

"Sir, you have a call on the red line." The petty officer told Caucuss.

"Don't go anywhere, young man," a smirking Caucuss said to Luke before getting up to take the call. Caucuss picked up the wall-mounted phone. "Caucuss here." Caucuss listened intently to the voice on the other end.

After a long pause, Luke could see Caucuss visibly getting pale in the face. The voice on the other end spoke in a slow, deep monotone, "I hear we lost our friends in the perfume factory. I also hear this man, Dodge, could spoil the whole show. What is the status? Are we still a go, and will the patsy be in place?"

Caucuss chose his words carefully, "Yes sir, I have the situation under control. The show will proceed as planned."

"Do you have the correct cell number?" the voice asked.

"64977927" Caucuss replied. "Yes sir, anything for the agency sir, anything for the Homeland."

Caucuss returned to his seat, letting a few moments pass. The corner of the blood stained blue prints that the Father had drawn up protruded from Caucusses' attaché case. Caucuss slid the blue prints out of the case, looked around, then carefully hid them under his coat jacket, and made his way to the bathroom. As the plane was about to land Caucuss hurriedly took out a grease pen obscuring the exact location of explosives, making them appear a full quarter mile from where they actually were. Caucus took his seat while glancing at his watch. The date read July 4th, 2010 - 10:30 a.m.

Luke took note of Caucus's unusual, nervous behavior. As he'd fumbled the blue prints around Caucuss dropped what looked like a cheap, local-dialing Panamanian cell phone onto the deck. Luke had quickly snatched it up and put it back inside his coat pocket.

The plane landed and taxied down the runway towards a waiting convoy of U.S. military HUM-V's. Luke was escorted down the gangplank and into the leading HUM-V.

"The prisoner is now yours. Sign this. I need you to sign for the blue prints and the prisoner." Caucuss said to the young, overly-motivated SEAL team leader as he handed him a signature form.

Luke loaded into the HUM-V, "The name is Sergeant Mack, but you can call me Mack." Mack said as he roughly removed Luke's wrist and ankle shackles.

"They tell me you know where some goodies are and that you are going to help us find them." Mack paused. "Our SEAL team… a couple of weeks ago, they sent us to chase you around the jungle. Not my favorite gig, we lost one guy, my buddy, he slipped and fell from the top of a waterfall. I am still a little pissed about that, so don't even breathe wrong or try anything funny or I will fill you full of lead, got it?"

"What day is it? I have been on that plane for two days. What time is it?"

Mack replied, "It's ten-thirty on the 4th of July."

"If you are done pissing on my boots, I think we'd better hurry." Luke said as he restrained his contempt.

"Is the President still coming for the handover ceremony?" Luke asked with concern in his voice.

"Yep."

"Does the prez know about the bomb situation?" Luke asked.

"It is D.H.S.' job to alert the president about these types of threats. It's not my job to know the *why* of things, only the *how.*"

Mack pondered his options then picked up the radio mike, "Command this is team leader, over."

"Go ahead, team leader."

"This is a gonna be a close shave, requesting that you stall the Roosevelt until we disarm the bombs."

After a long pause command replied, "Team leader, D.H.S has advised that is a negative, over."

"Roger that."

Mack escorted Luke to the rest of the Navy SEAL team of eight men. They sat waiting in an all-black 18-foot inflatable Zodiac raft with twin 175 HP Johnson outboards on the back. The eight men sat crouched in the raft holding tight to their assault rifles. They were fully clad in SCUBA diving gear, replete with black wet suites.

"Ready to roll, sir." One of the SEALS announced to Mack. Mack grabbed the blue-prints, then he and Luke stepped into the boat and shoved off. The SEAL team, who had recently humped for days in the Darién jungle looking for Luke stared daggers at him.

Mack took the helm as the Zodiac zoomed along on a plane. "Alright Dodge, now I need you to debrief us and show us where on this map we need to go and what to look for."

As they sped away, Luke could see Caucuss watching them from land. Luke watched as Caucuss got into his Lincoln Town Car and sped towards a nearby hill which is often used by Panamánian special forces as a vantage point to keep watch on the Canal gates.

Luke pointed in the direction he thought would take them to the bombs. Mack studied the blue prints.

"Dodge, what is your malfunction? These blue prints show the bombs to be over there. Don't mess with me now." Mack pointed in the opposite direction that Luke had indicated.

Mack continued, "I am authorized to use any means necessary to get you to show us what you know." Mack said while gripping his riffle.

Luke figured his memory had failed him and capitulated. "Okay, let's go with the blue prints, you are looking for a couple dozen larger barrels, do not disturb them, they are full of radioactive waste, I think. There are also several, smaller barrels loaded with SEMTEX and one has the detonator attached to it."

"Yes sir, understood sir." Mack replied to a call over the radio. "Looks like the president's ship, the USS Teddy Roosevelt will be entering the locks within fifteen minutes."

The SEAL team neared the area marked on the blue-prints. Mack shouted out his orders, "Okay, let's drop four sets of two guys- 20 meters apart."

Mack slowed the boat to five knots and called out, "Dive!" to send off each set of two divers. The divers swiftly rolled over the rubber railing and quickly disappeared into the murk. After the four teams had been dispatched, Luke and Mack sat patiently watching the minutes pass. After ten minutes with no result, Luke grew anxious and asked to see the blue prints again. This time he took a closer look and could see that the blue prints had been intentionally doctored to be misleading. "Caucuss." Luke said aloud. "Let's go. We are in the wrong spot, let's go!" Luke shouted.

"We can't just leave the other guys in the water!" Mack snapped. "In a few minutes, there won't be any of us left to worry about. I won't abandon my post," Mack replied.

"Okay then, hand me those fins, that mask, that knife and the weight belt!" Luke shouted.

Mack refused.

Luke grabbed the gear and hurriedly put it on. Then he rolled into the water.

"Halt!" Mack ordered while aiming his assault rifle at Luke.

"You pull that trigger and we are all dead." Luke snapped back.

Mack eased his finger off the trigger. Luke wasted no time in making a bee line towards the place he recalled the bombs being laid. He scoured the landscape for the three landmarks he had used to triangulate the exact positions of the bombs. One of the marks was a statue atop the small hill he had seen Caucuss heading towards. Luke took a second to focus on a car parked near the statue, *is that Caucus's car?* After five minutes of Olympic-speed swimming, Luke found the location and began to take slow and deep breaths.

Before making his first dive, Luke heard several blasts from the horn of the USS Teddy Roosevelt. The ship, a Navy Grey 400-foot long state of art battle destroyer entered the Canal locks. She was floating just a few yards from Luke's position, close enough that Luke could hear the fanfare and speeches. President Obama stood on the deck with the band playing in the background. The band silenced, the president took the podium. The Panamanian president, a white skinned, square- shaped man named Martinelli sat nearby, looking on.

"Fellow Americans and Panamanians, it is with a warm heart that today, we joyously celebrate the tenth anniversary of the handing back of the Canal. This amazing Canal connects the two great oceans of the world. It also connects two great nations, the Republic of Panama and the United States of America. For ten years, the Panama Canal Authority, amid skepticism from the U.S. and elsewhere has operated the Canal safely, cost effectively and now is nearing its goal of expanding its capacity to dramatically increase the size and number of vessels that can transit this historic waterway."

Knowing he had only seconds until the Canal gates opened, Luke took an extra deep breath and dove straight down to the bottom. He immediately found one of the larger barrels, it was covered in light green algae. *No good,* his mind screamed. *I need to get to the detonator.*

Luke broke the surface, then packed his lungs with air.

"I would like to take this opportunity to remind my fellow Americans that such engineering marvels as the Panama Canal are only achieved by free people and great nations. For this reason, it is my goal to make America free again and reverse many of our post 9-11 freedom crushing policies such as the Patriot Act and conduct a full review and, if needed, dismantle the entire Department of Homeland Security. There is no point in protecting our freedoms abroad, when we have lost it at home."

The crowd cheered loudly.

Luke did his best to catch his breath but it was no use. He caught a glimmer of light from the hilly vantage point.

It was Caucuss.

Caucuss slowly loaded his 50-caliber sniper riffle. Using a high-powered scope, he took aim at Luke. "I think your services are long longer required." Caucuss murmured as he caught sight of Luke through the scope.

The band struck up. The U.S. and the Panamánian Presidents ceremoniously cut a large ribbon and shook hands. The USS Teddy Roosevelt blasted her horn three times to signal she was about to clear the canal gates.

Caucuss lined up the cross hairs onto Luke and then squeezed the trigger. The bullet struck the water inches from Luke head. Luke took a breath and dove. This time, he found another larger barrel and one small barrel of SEMTEX but still no detonator. Luke held his breath, scouring the bottom. The urge to breathe came, and he ignored it. A few moments passed and then his vision narrowed.

He had no choice but to bolt for the surface. He broke the surface like a submarine in free ascent. As he gasped for air another bullet splashed down next to him. "Shit, this is bad!" Luke said aloud.

He desperately tried to catch his breath again. Luke knew trying to dive again would mean certain death. None-the-less by gulping breaths he forced air into his straining lungs. As he turned to dive another bullet came whizzing in, striking his left thigh. He screamed in agony. Caucuss paused to chamber another round. Through his scope he could see Luke screaming and holding his leg. There was no time, the gates slowly opened, flushing the warmer, dirtier fresh water over Luke.

Luke's animal instinct for survival kicked in. He was able to overcome his shattered nerves, shortness of breath and bleeding leg, and he had just enough life force to try one last dive. As he readied himself, time compression kicked in. He saw each passing second as if it was a full minute. Luke heard each sound in amplified, distorted, slow motion. As Luke readied to dive, another bullet splashed just an inch to his right. *The next one will be a kill shot.*

Luke rolled then tried to dive. As he dipped his mask under the water, he saw a long brown scaly back slither just a few feet under him. *What is that?* The animal disappeared for a microsecond then circled back around. This time Luke got a close-up view of rows of shiny white alligator teeth. The gator nipped at Luke, tearing off part of his left fin. The gator then did a belly roll and sunk out of sight. As the animal rolled Luke could see a large scar running from its chin to its shoulder's. *Oh, no! Not you again!* It was the same gator that had Luke had stabbed months earlier.

Luke floated on the surface, waiting for the end to come, be it from a bullet to the head or the flesh-tearing wrath of a spiteful alligator. The gator surfaced, swam slowly over to Luke. The gator put his nose just inches from Luke's face. Luke could smell the animal's warm breath as they locked eyes. There, as Luke sat waiting for his death to come, he connected with the alligator. Luke's animal instincts had become well-honed over the previous months. Sensing this, the gator no longer saw Luke as a threat nor a meal, he simply saw him as an equal. The gator eyed Luke as if he were an old college fraternity brother.

"I am sorry for stabbing you." *Zaaaap!* A bullet came whizzing through the air. The round struck the gator just above the eye, blowing its head apart and covering Luke in brain matter. *Asshole!* Luke yelled. The encounter with the gator gave Luke the time and calm he needed to catch one last breath.

Luke closed his eyes, in a feat of superhuman strength he turned and dove. His wound and slashed fin made it impossible to kick so he let himself glide to the bottom. Again, he searched for the detonator. As he scoured the bottom Luke's instinctual sense of calm kicked up a notch. Like a movie reel, Luke could see each minute of what he was doing detail by detail, frame by frame. Luke found the detonator cord and followed it to the next barrel. *Eureka!* He found the detonator box. Luke quickly took out his dive knife and began cutting the detonation cord.

The water blackened as the huge shadow of the USS Teddy Roosevelt loomed overhead. Luke cut away at the heavy rubberized cable. Blood spewed from his leg, making a big green cloud around Luke and the bombs.

As the USS Teddy Roosevelt passed by Luke's location, Caucuss took out his local Panamanian cell phone and dialed the magic number 64977927. Luke sawed away at the cable.

Come on, come on" Luke pleaded with the heavy, plastic cord.

Caucuss pressed the send key, at the same instant Luke severed the cable line. The wires sparked and fizzled but failed to set off the explosives.

"Manos arriba!" The man said to Caucuss as he covered him with a pistol. It was Gomez, the head of Canal security.

"How could you?" Gomez asked Caucuss.

"Just following orders." Caucuss replied in calm voice with a smirk on his face. Using the butt of his pistol, Gomez smacked Caucuss on the head, knocking him out cold.

As the USS Teddy Roosevelt cleared the locks, Luke struggled to make it back to the surface. Sensing blackout, he dumped his weight. A second later, his vision faded from tunnel vision to black. Luke's limp body slowly floated to the surface where it floated face down.

By now, the SEAL team had surfaced and loaded back into the Zodiac. Mack powered up the motors and headed towards Luke. "Grab him, and keep pressure on the wound." The men zipped back towards shore. One SEAL performed CPR on Luke but it was no use. When they reached land they quickly loaded Luke onto a gurney.

That day, Nici felt the need to see President Obama pass through the Canal, she thought it might remind her of why she had once loved the U.S. and the life she had shared with Luke. Nici spied President Obama standing on the ship's deck. She hoped against hope that the new president might change things for the better. Nici walked along the shore with her dog Chewy.

"Do you think Obama will change things so we can go back to the U.S. someday?" Nici asked her dog.

"Ruf, ruff!" Chewy replied.

Her gaze shifted from the President passing by on the USS Teddy Roosevelt, to a nearby commotion caused by the SEAL team. Nici stood in shock as she focused on the man the SEALs were transporting in the gurney. It was her beloved Luke. Nici went into action. "Move out of the way, I am a doctor and this is my fiancé´."

"We are sorry, ma'am, but he is not going to make it." Mack said to her with sympathy.

Nici caressed Luke's face, "My precious Luke, hold on." Then she snapped, "Put the gurney on the ground, and get an ambulance here, now!"

She began CPR, slamming her fist on his chest. "Get me a Goddam defibrillator!" she barked. Nici breathed for Luke and pounded on his chest until a medic arrived with a portable defibrillator. She grabbed the paddles and set the device on full. "Clear!"

Zaaap. She listened to his heart, nothing.

"Come back, Luke, it is not your time, sweetheart, come back to me. Clear!"

Zaaap, Luke's body convulsed. In his comatose state, Luke's nearly dead mind saw the same vision of the Puma he had seen in the jungle with the Emberá.

He had never felt so at peace. "Clear!"

Zaaap. With a closed fist Nici hit him on the chest again.

Luke coughed up blood and saltwater. He slowly opened his eyes to focus on his lovely, Dr. Nici. The only words he could manage.

"Hey babe, what's for dinner?"

With tears of joy in her eyes Nici helped Luke into the ambulance.

A look at THE LOST TREASURE OF THE DARIEN, the next book in the Luke Dodge ADVENTURE SERIES

In 1671 the cut-throat privateer Henry Morgan chopped his way across the Isthmus of Panamá, sacking the Spanish strongholds in the name of his sovereign, King Charles II of England, his country and for booty. As pirates do, Morgan stashed a golden elephant head- shaped chest deep in the Darién rain forest, planning to return one day to collect it. Four hundred years later, the mystical treasure is causing the local Emebrá Indians great misery.

After five years in exile in Panamá, Luke Dodge and Dr. Nici's battle with U.S. immigration reaches an epic climax-- but not for long. With children dying and the men near insanity, the Emberá chief beckons his old friend Luke Dodge to the rescue. To provide food to the ailing natives, Dr. Nici takes to spear fishing. She proves to be a natural hunter, taking many pargo, grouper and other exotic fish in the untouched Pacific Ocean waters near the Colombian border.

Luke's nemesis, the eco terrorist Rainbow Pristine, wreaks havoc on Luke at every turn. Both she and the Chinese special-forces will stop at nothing to prevent Luke form returning the treasure to its native land.

Explosive Crossroads

About the Author

A native son of Malibu California, at age six, C.F. speared his first fish and at 11 he signed onto the fishing vessel, *Aquarius* to learn the ways of a deckhand. After the death of his father at 12, he lied about his age and joined the offshore tuna fleet in San Diego where he worked 20 hours a day, and cut his teeth as a deckhand, then captain. At 13 he bought his first boat and did laps around Channel Islands.

C.F.'s bond with the sea has only grown more intense over time. He holds a Bachelor of Science from Humboldt State University in Fisheries and Business. As a global seafood and exotic seashell trader, he pioneered the sustainable seafood movement.

C.F. Goldblatt currently resides in Santa Barbara, CA. C.F continues to free-dive spearfish and travel the globe. He is considered a pioneer and an ocean futurist. His current endeavor focuses on making artificial reefs to enhance near shore ecosystems and improve fisheries for the benefit of locals and food security. C.F. holds a seat at the United Nation's International Seabed Authority where he is actively involved in shaping mankind's long-term relationship with the sea and the life within it.

Explosive Crossroads

CPSIA information can be obtained
at www.ICGtesting.com
Printed in the USA
FSHW022127270320
68568FS